Acclaim for Aleksandar Hemon's

NOWHERE MAN

"The kind of bold talent that doesn't come around very often. . . . Hemon again displays his prodigious gifts—nearly every sentence of this novel is infused with energy and wit."   —*Los Angeles Times*

"Hemon delivers a crazed, kaleidoscopic rendering of the waning years of Soviet rule." —*Chicago Tribune*

"The merit of *Nowhere Man* rests on far more than gimmicky, literary stunts. It's a study of the human condition, sad as it is today."
                    —*The Washington Post Book World*

"The stock immigrant tale gets turned inside out by a smart, witty Sarajevo native with an eye for absurdity."
                                   —*Newsweek*

"I wish I had written *Nowhere Man*, by Aleksandar Hemon, but I couldn't have written it, because no one can write like Hemon. He has the most unusual, poetic vision in the world. This book is moving and beautiful."   —Jonathan Safran Foer,
            author of *Everything Is Illuminated*

"Readers of *Nowhere Man* are present for the rise of an exciting new literary voice."

"Hemon paints a hilarious parodic picture of city life, but it is his language that really sings: it has the unmistakable tenor of quality, reminiscent at once of Bohumil Hrabal's *I Served the King of England* and Milan Kundera's *The Unbearable Lightness of Being.* I should not be at all surprised if Hemon wins the Nobel Prize at some point."

"Funny, profoundly moving and multilayered. . . . [Hemon] is creating a richer understanding of the immigrant experience."

"Now here's reason to get excited: a true work of art that's as vast and mysterious as life itself. Hemon, in just two books, and in just two years (if you haven't read *The Question of Bruno*, do), has quickly become essential in the way that, say, Nabokov is essential. . . . This tender, devastating book is evidence indeed that Hemon is a writer of rare artistry and depth."

"Hemon has the vision of an outsider and uses English like a new toy. . . . Highly entertaining. . . . Writing as sharp and inventive as anything you'll read all year."

Aleksandar Hemon

NOWHERE MAN

Aleksandar Hemon is the author of *The Question of Bruno*, which appeared on Best Books of 2000 lists nationwide, won several literary awards, and was published in eighteen countries. Born in Sarajevo, Hemon arrived in Chicago in 1992, began writing in English in 1995, and now his work appears regularly in *The New Yorker*, *Esquire*, *Granta*, *The Paris Review*, and *The Best American Short Stories*.

INTERNATIONAL

Books by Aleksandar Hemon

The Question of Bruno
Nowhere Man

NOWHERE MAN

THE PRONEK FANTASIES

VINTAGE INTERNATIONAL

Vintage Books

A Division of Random House, Inc.

New York

Aleksandar Hemon

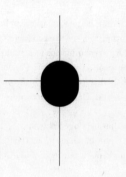

NOWHERE MAN

FIRST VINTAGE INTERNATIONAL EDITION, JANUARY 2004

The Library of Congress has cataloged the Nan A. Talese edition as follows:
Hemon, Aleksandar, 1964–
Nowhere man: the Pronek fantasies / by Aleksandar Hemon.
p. cm.
ISBN 0-385-49924-8
1. Sarajevo (Bosnia and Hercegovina)—Fiction. 2. Bosnian Americans—
Fiction. 3. Chicago (Ill.)—Fiction. 4. Immigrants—Fiction. I. Title.
PS3608.E48 N69 2002
813'.54—dc21
2002066208

Vintage ISBN 0-375-72702-7

Book design by Dana Leigh Treglia

www.vintagebooks.com

Printed in the United States of America
10 9 8 7 6 5 4 3 2 1

Ordinary facts are arranged within time, strung along its length as on a thread. There they have their antecedents and their consequences, which crowd tightly together and press hard one upon the other without any pause. This has its importance for any narrative, of which continuity and successiveness are the soul. Yet what is to be done with events that have no place of their own in time; events that have occurred too late, after the whole of time has been distributed, divided and allotted; events that have been left in the cold, unregistered, hanging in the air, errant and homeless?

—Bruno Schulz,
from *The Age of Genius*

NOWHERE MAN

1

Passover

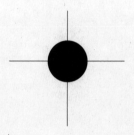

CHICAGO, APRIL 18, 1994

Had I been dreaming, I would have dreamt of being someone else, with a little creature burrowed in my body, clawing at
the walls inside my chest—a recurring nightmare. But I was
awake, listening to the mizzle in my pillow, to the furniture
furtively sagging, to the house creaking under the wind assaults.
I straightened my legs, so the blanket ebbed and my right foot
rose out of the sludge of darkness like a squat, extinguished
lighthouse. The blinds gibbered for a moment, commenting on
my performance, then settled in silence.

I closed the bathroom door and the hooked towels trembled.
There was the pungent smell of the plastic shower curtain and
disintegrating soap. The toilet bowl was agape, with a dissolving
piece of toilet paper in it throbbing like a jellyfish. The faucet
was sternly counting off droplets. I took off my underwear and
let it lie in a pile, then stepped behind the curtain and let the
water run. Wee rainbows locked in bubbles streamed into the inevitable, giddy whirl, as I fantasized about melting under the
shower and disappearing into the drain.

I went down the stairs, carrying a mound of dirty laundry, careful not to trip over the inquisitive cat. I put the laundry on top of

the washing machine, which shuddered as though delighted, and pulled the rope pending in the darkness—cobwebs sprung into the air around the bulb. I had to wait for the spin to throttle to a stop before I could put my laundry in the machine, so I followed the cat into the other room. There were boxes full of things that must have been left by the tenants—who might they have been?—who used to live in one of the apartments: wallpaper scrolls, a broken-boned umbrella, a soulless football, a bundle of shoes with crescent soles, a pictureless frame, skeins of anonymous dust. Back in the laundry room, I transferred the sodden clothes of the upstairs people to the dryer, then loaded the washing machine. In the other room, the cat was galloping around and producing noises of struggle, pursuing something I could not see.

Today was the interview day. I had called—years ago, it seemed now—and set up an interview for an ESL teaching job, strictly out of despair. I had been laid off from the Art Institute bookstore once the merry Christmas season, including the mad aftermath of the Big Sale, was over. My job there had been to unpack boxes of books, shelve the books, and then smash the boxes and throw them away. Smashing the boxes was my favorite part, the controlled, benign destruction.

Two white eggs roiled in the boiling water, like iris-less eyes. The floor was sticky, so I had to unpeel my bare soles from the floor with every step—I thought of the movies in which people walk on the ceiling, upside down. A cockroach was scuttling across the cutting board, trying to reach the safety behind the stove. I imagined the greasy warmth, the vales of dirt, the wires winding like roads. I imagined getting there, still clutching a crumb of skin, after almost being cut in half by something immense coming down on me.

I had tried other bookstores, but they didn't want me. I had tried getting a job as a waiter, elaborately lying about my previous waiting experience in the best Sarajevo restaurants, high European class all, and nonexistent on top of that. I had spent my measly savings and was in the furniture-selling phase. I sold, for the total of seventy-four dollars, a decaying futon with a rich cat-barf pattern; a hobbly table with four chairs, inexplicably scarred, as if they had walked through fields of barbed wire. I was late with my rent, and had already looked up the word *eviction* in the dictionary, hoping that the secondary, obsolete meaning ("The action of conquering a country or of obtaining something by conquest") would override my landlord's primary meaning and save my ass.

The frighteningly simple thing was that when I was inside nobody was on the porch: the green plastic chairs convened around nothing; the swing still quaked under invisible weight; the empty flowerpots faced out, like Easter Island heads. A fly buzzed against the windowpane, as though trying to cut through it with a minikin saw. In the house across the street, a bare-chested man, skinny like a camp inmate—his shoulder-bones protruding, his trunk striped with rib shadows—was coming in and out of his house feverishly, only to disappear into it in the end. I was about to lock the door when I saw the cat gnawing on a mouse's head, patiently exposing its crimson essence.

And it hadn't been just the money. When I couldn't smash the boxes, I had obsessively read the papers and watched TV (until I sold it) to see what was happening back home. What was happening was death. I had looked up that word too: "The act or fact of dying; the end of life; the final and irreversible cessation of the vital function of a plant or an animal."

The air was oily and warm, and I stood on the street inhaling. There had been a time when that scent marked the beginning of marble season: the ground would soon be soft and you didn't have to wear gloves; you could keep your hands in your pockets—waiting for your turn, revolving marbles with the tips of your fingers—until a red line appeared across your palm, marking the border between the part of your palm that was inside and the one that was outside. You would kneel and indent the soil with your knees, imprinting smudges on your trousers, progressing toward an inexorable punishment from your parents. I had a couple of marbles in my pockets, plus an El transfer card, creased and fragile.

A woman with spring freckles, towed by a giant Akita, smiled at me for no apparent reason, and I stepped off the pavement—confused by the smile, scared by the Akita—onto the ground. I let the woman pass, and then walked slowly, as if walking through deep water, because I didn't want her to think that I was following her. The Akita was sniffing everything, frantically collecting information. The woman turned around and looked at me again. The sun was behind my back, so she squinted, wrinkling the ridge of her nose. She seemed to be on the verge of saying something, but the Akita pulled her away, almost ripping her arm off. I was relieved. I preferred being a vague, pleasant memory to having to explain who I was or telling her that I had no job, and when I had one I was smashing boxes.

A teenager in a window-throbbing car drove by, pointing his finger at me, shooting. I crossed the street to look at a sheet of paper pinned to a tree in front of a building exuding dampness. The sign read in red letters:

LOST DOG

I LOST MASCULINE DOG, THIS COCTAIL SPANIEL AND HIS NAME
LUCKY BOY. HE HAS LONG, LONG EARS AND CURVE HAIR GOLD
BROWN COLOR WITH SHORT TAIL ALSO HE IS VERY FRIENDLY,
LITTLE CRAZY. IF ANYONE FOUND MY DOG PLEASE PLEASE
CONTRACT MARIA.

MARIA

Outside the El station, a man with a black bowler hat was rattling his tambourine, out of any recognizable rhythm, singing a song about the spirit in the sky in a flat, disenchanted voice. The man smiled at me, showing dark gaps between his teeth. When I was a boy, spitting between your teeth was considered a great skill, because you could achieve precision, like those snakes in *Survival* spurting poison at terrified field mice, but my teeth were too close together, and I could never do it—after every attempt there would be some spit dripping off my chin.

The station smelled of urine and petroleum. A dreadlocked woman in a yellow vest rummaged through a closet with metal doors under the stairs, then took out a shovel and looked at it with surprise—she semed to have expected something else. I ascended with the escalator onto the platform, and waited there to see the train lights. The wind was rolling an empty can toward the edge—the can would stop, trying to resist the push, then roll again, until it finally fell over the edge. A mouse scurried between the rails. I expected it to be electrocuted on the third rail: a few sparks, a shrill squeal, a stiff, dun mouse, still surprised by the suddenness of the end.

"All we ask for," said a young man, with his hands folded over his crotch, "is to give your life to Jesus Christ and follow him to the Kingdom of God." His companion, wide-shouldered, bearded, walked through the train car offering everyone a brown bag of peanuts and salvation. An old lady with a plastic wrap on her bloated gray hair grinned abruptly, as if a shot of pain went through her body at that very instant. A wizened old man, wearing a grimace of perplexed horror, and a sallow straw fedora, looked up at the peanut man. A young woman in front of me—a pointed tongue of hair touched her collar, and she smelled like cinnamon and milk—was reading the paper. DEFENSES COLLAPSE IN GORAŽDE, a headline read. I had been in Goražde only once, only because I had vomited in the car, on our way somewhere, and my parents stopped in Goražde to clean the mess up. All I remembered was being thirsty and shivering on the front seat, as my father retched in the back seat, wiping it with a cloth; and then my father leaving my cloth-wrapped vomit by the road, and hungry, desperate little animals crawling out of the bushes to devour it. The woman gave a neatly creased dollar to the peanut man, took a bag from him and ripped it open, and then started crunching the nuts. I said: "No, thank you." Granville, Loyola, Morse. The woman flipped the page, a few nutshells pitter-pattered on it. SUNNY SKIES WARM MOST OF NATION. We all disembarked from the train at Howard, leaving behind throngs of peanut shells, and a drunk in a Cubs hat, slumped in the dark corner.

———

There was something exhilarating and unsettling about going in the same direction with a mass of people. We gathered at the top of the escalator and then all descended; we went through sundry revolving bars, which patted us on the back, as if we had just come back from a dangerous mission. In the urine-scented shade of the station, buses were lined up in perfect perspective, sucking in passengers through the front doors. A weather-beaten sign on a Coke machine read NO WORKING; a torn poster on the wall behind it announced the yesteryear arrival of a circus with a half grin of a hysterical clown and an erect elephant trunk holding a wand with a bright star on its tip. I had never taught anything in my life, let alone English, but despair was my loyal ally.

I put my hands in the jacket pockets: a couple of marbles, a taper of lint, a coin, a transfer. I remember this trivial handful because I can recall looking at an old black lady: a peppered coat, a bell hat, her knuckles coiled around a cane handle, leaning slightly forward. To be able to put your hands in your pockets, I thought, was not such a bad thing, your pockets are your hands' home.

There was a bench nobody was sitting on, encrusted with blotches. I looked up, and on a steel beam high up above perched a jury of pigeons, cooing peevishly. They bloated and deflated, blinking down on us, effortlessly releasing feces. When I was a kid, I thought that snow came from God shitting on us. The Touhy bus arrived, and we lined up at the bus door. I experienced an intense sneeze of happiness, simply because I had managed not to lose my transfer.

The bus smelled of an unknown disinfecting potion, a trace of sausagey sweat, and nondescript dust dryness. The jury of pigeons fluttered up as the bus moved forward, pressing us against our seats, until we all dutifully jerked forward. I used to have a friend—he was killed by an accelerating piece of shrapnel—who liked to think that there was a quiet part of the universe where a body could have a steady velocity, going in the same direction, at the same speed, never stopping or entering a gravitational field. This bus, for instance, would have moved with smooth, pleasant velocity, down Touhy, not stopping at the lights, on to Lincolnwood, Park Ridge, Elk Grove Village, Schaumburg, Hanover Park, and onward through Iowa and whatever there was beyond Iowa, all the way to California, and then over the Pacific, gliding across the endless water until we reached Shanghai—we would have all got to know one another on this ship, we would have gone all the way together.

The bus stopped abruptly at Western, the driver honking violently, then glancing at us in the rearview mirror. A man crossed the street in front of the bus, carrying a rolled-up carpet, which was breaking on his shoulder, its ends touching the ground. The man was sagging under the burden, his neck bent, his knees stooping, as if he were carrying a weighty cross.

We moved on, passed Inner Light Hair Sanctuary, AutoZone PartsWorld, Wultan Monuments, Land of Submarines; crossed California, gliding by Barnaby & Scribner Family Dining, Mt. Sinai Medical Center, Eastern Style Pizza—I got off the bus across the street from a Chinese restaurant. New World, it was called, and it was empty, only a sign in the window saying FOR LEASE.

I had a few more minutes before the interview, and I was not ready to go in and get a job (How could I teach anyone anything?), so I lingered in front of the photo shop next to New World. A sign in the window—thick black letters—read:

OLD PHOTOS COPIED

ANY SIZE

COLOR

OR

BLACK AND WHITE.

There was a photo of black-and-white miners, their eyes twinkling behind a mask of gray dust. They held their pickaxes solemnly, their helmets pressing down their faces. In another photo, three kids in knickers and jackets with sleeves that could not reach their wrists stood a step away from one another, with the same tenebrous eyes, shorn hair, and large ears spreading out like little wings.

There was a Before photo and an After photo: the Before photo showed a man with a long curly beard slowly swallowing his face and dark wrinkles above his murky eyes. He sat with his hands coiled in his lap. A younger man stood on his left, his right hand cautiously touching the old man's shoulder. The upper right-hand corner of the photo was missing, including half of the young man's yarmulke. Both men were cut by a jagged white line (the old man across his chest, the young man across his waist), with a trail of white blots spreading toward the old man's beard—a crease and its offspring, created in somebody's pocket. The After photo had no blots, had no crease, and the yarmulke was restored. Their faces were whiter, and the young man's hand firmly grasped the old man's shoulder—wherever they were now, they were in it together. If only I could afford to succumb to this depleting sorrow, to stop walking with my chin up, and just collapse, like a smashed box, things would be much simpler. There was a photo of the Lake-in-the-Hills Mall at night, all glaring neon blue, neon yellow, and neon pink.

I needed the job. I calculated: if I got a thousand dollars a month, I could pay the March rent, and a part of the April rent right off, and then buy a mattress for fifty dollars or so. I had butterflies in my stomach, ripping off one another's wings, biting viciously through one another's abdomens. The lawn in front of Ort Institute had spring sores. Over the bushes a fleet of gnats hovered, still dizzy from a long slumber, deciding what to do: settle for the lumpengreenness of the bushes, or fly into a windshield and end it all with a splatter.

The receptionist was a slender woman, thickly made up, as if she had never unmade herself up, had just kept adding layers and layers. "Take seat," she said, pouted and narrowed her eyes, as if suspicious of me. I sat on an ochre sofa, and as I landed a nickel leapt up at me from the other end of the sofa, so I pocketed it. The receptionist talked over the phone, her lips so close to the mouthpiece that she smudged it with lipstick, glancing at me all along, as if she were describing me: he was tall and chunky, a cubical head, not very well dressed, spoke with an Eastern European accent, a scar stretching across his throat. Across the hall, there was a menorah on a pedestal, at the foot of which there was an inscription in Hebrew. From somewhere beyond the menorah, I could hear a discordant choir chanting, I could hear rigid consonants and willowy vowels:

> I have never read *Moby-Dick*.
> I have never seen the Grand Canyon

I have never been in New York.

I have never been rich.

The walls were pale brown, and the carpets were dispirited brown, and the woman who walked toward me was leaning forward, moving fast. She briskly halted, stretching an invisible leash to the end. "Hi!" she said. "I am Robin." She spoke in a belabored warbly way, eager to be liked, but sensing that the chances were slim. I introduced myself, and then got off the sofa quickly, so I could catch up with her. We passed an announcement board with leaflets in Russian and handwritten notes. There were doors suggesting dark basements, and there were chaotic footprints, as if somebody had danced drunk in muddy boots. Robin flew down the hall and flung open a door, then stood waiting for me to enter it. Her eyes were one size too big for her face, which was embroidered with gullies filled to the brim with powder. In a flash, I recognized how ludicrous my hope was, how comfortably everything was beyond the reach of my will. "Come on in, and take a seat," she said. "I am going to get Marcus."

I did not know who Marcus was, but I walked into the room; it smelled of sharpened pencils and paper glue and Robin's perfume and burnt coffee and chalk. On a round table there was a nightmarish chain of cup rings and a coffee cup (the possible culprit) next to an abandoned dictionary.

There was a pile of newspapers on the table, the front page facing me: DEFENSES COLLAPSE IN GORAZDE. When I was thirteen I had spent the summer at a seaside resort for Tito's pioneers and fallen in love with a girl from Goražde. Her name was Emina, and she taught me to kiss using my tongue, and she let me touch her breasts—she was the first girl I had ever touched who wore a bra. U.S. SEIZES BOAT CARRYING 111 IMMIGRANTS, a headline read. My palms were sweating, my fingertips moist, and the paper smudged up my whorls, making them visible. I had once read a pulp novel in which there was a genius criminal, the notorious King of Midnight, who had altered his fingertips, but the master detective recognized him by his distinctive voice. The ceiling fan revolved on the coffee surface, slightly curved. Someone named Ronald "Ron Rogers" Michalak had died—he was the beloved husband of the late Patricia. Sunny skies warmed most of the nation. The Bulls bowed, but did not look back. Chicago Jews celebrated Passover.

A woman opened the door and stepped in, still holding the door with her left hand, as if ready to escape. "Is Robin around?" she asked. The sleeves of her blue shirt were rolled up and I could see the sinews on her forearms tighten, fighting off the weight of the door.

"No," I said. "She went to find Marcus. I am waiting for her too."

"I'll just come back later," she said, and turned around, and I recognized the back of her head: the edge of her blue collar, and a lean neck with a feathery vine growing toward the mainland of her hair and the gentle twirl on her pate—she had been on the train too, sitting in front of me. I could see the wings of her earrings on the insides of her earlobes, and stray hairs touching the tips of her ears as she slipped out. MASSACRES RAGE ON, a headline read. BODIES PILE UP IN RWANDA.

Robin seemed to have oversized glass marbles instead of eye-balls, like a doll—she was either not blinking or she was blinking when I was blinking. Her eyelashes bent abruptly upward, like little scythes. Marcus was puckering his upper lip so his mustache hair could touch his abundant nostril hair, as if forcing them to couple. He looked at me cautiously, his hands comfortably placed on his belly ledge.

"Do you have any previous teaching experience?" Robin asked.

"No," I said. "But I have huge learning experience."

"These people can be demanding," she said. An ambulance passed down the street chirruping hysterically.

"This job," Marcus said, with a scrupulously nasal voice, "requires patience. Petulance just would not do it."

Robin glanced at him, frowned and blinked, but then restored her grimace of befuddled doll. I had no idea what "petulance" meant, and the dictionary was beyond my reach.

"What is your point of origin?" Marcus asked.

"Sarajevo, Bosnia," I said.

"Oh, man," Robin said. "That is so neat."

"I spent years studying other cultures," Marcus said. He stood up and walked toward me; he had a squash-shaped body, with the small, narrow feet of a ballet dancer. He leaned toward me and whispered: "I used to work for the government."

"Really," I said. Robin's perplexion was flaming now—her cheeks ruddy, burning through the blanket of makeup.

"Yes. In the NSA, the DLI, the Slavic languages section, translating all kinds—*all kinds*—of information," Marcus said. "I can peruse seventeen languages."

"Wow!" Robin said.

"*Dobar dan!*" Marcus said.

"*Dobar dan!*" I replied.

"*Da li je ovo zoološki vrt?*"

"Holy moly!" Robin said. "What does that mean?"

"Good day. Good day," I translated. "Is this the zoo?"

Someone knocked and peeked through the door and said: "Teacher, I can talk to you?"

"Not now, Mihalka," Robin said. "Wait outside."

"It is a must," Mihalka said.

I turned around and looked at him: his head was ascetically shaved, his scull scarred, and his face punched in by an immense force, as if he had been a boxer. A mountain ridge of wrinkles rose across his forehead. He reminded me of my uncle, who lived in Canada now, working as an exterminator.

"Just wait outside, Mihalka," Robin said.

"Some of them possess scintillating minds, and some have rather perplexing personalities," Marcus said.

"I am sorry," I said. "I do not understand everything that you say."

"He is from Czechoslovakia," Robin said. "You are from Czechoslovakia too, right?"

"He is from Yugoslavia," Marcus said. "It's a wartorn country."

"I am from Bosnia," I said.

"You know," Marcus said, "I was on a *mission* in Bosnia once. I met some brave men and beautiful women there."

"When was that?" Robin asked, and rubbed her temple. The skin on it wrinkled and unwrinkled under her finger, the pain still untouched. It must have been taking a lot of strength to maintain the expression of permanent bafflement.

"Long time ago," Marcus said. "I fell in love with a majestic, passionate woman, but circumstances too-fatuous-to-detail took me elsewhere."

Mihalka's head popped in again without knocking and Robin's face changed into a grimace of mild annoyance.

"Teacher," Mihalka said. "I must tell you."

Robin got up, rolled her eyes to the tilt, and went out. Marcus surveilled my face, trying to get into my eyes, then nodded, having found the expected evidence.

"You know a lot about hardship, don't you?" he said.

"I do not know," I said, uncomfortably. "Which hardship?"

"You look like someone who knows a lot." He sighed, as if recalling a host of pleasant memories, and turned toward the window.

Robin walked back in, shaking her head and rolling her eyes, as if she had just heard the strangest confession.

"Why don't we visit a few classrooms," Marcus said, "so you can see what takes place in them."

"All right," I said.

"I do not understand these people," Robin said, still shaking her head. "I simply do not."

We walked up the stairs, awkwardly careful not to be too far from or too close to one another. The back pocket of Marcus's pants gaped open as he tiptoed delicately upward, and a bundle of envelopes was about to fall out. I ascended in the wake of Robin's sugary perfume and the wet-bandage smell of her armpits. We stopped in front of one of the classroom doors, Robin conspiratorially whispering to me:

"This is level two, pretty basic. You might be teaching a lower level, so this could be interesting to you."

"Do not be vexed by the student body," Marcus said. "They are a little sedate occasionally."

"Okay," I said. Robin opened the door, and we walked in.

"Hi, guys!" the teacher said, the moment she saw us. "I am Jennifer."

She had a dear-blue sweater and a lacy collar, a narrow waist and a wide skirt. She had pink lips, a pair of glasses that magnified her eyes, and a willow-tree crown of hair. There was a map of the world on the wall behind her—North America was at its center and the oceans of the world were the same hue as Jennifer's sweater.

"Do not be surprised," Marcus said, slowly, to the class. "We are just visiting different classes, exposing him"—he pointed at me—"to the trials and tribulations of language acquisition."

As Marcus was speaking, the people in the class tightened, as if the classroom had contracted: the older women in the first row, the veteran mothers, sporting gigantic amber brooches on their bosoms, gripped their pencils; the men behind them, with tuber noses and the yellowish faces of chain-smokers, sunk in their chairs; a young man in the corner with a long, unkempt beard bent over his notebook. I could see a herd of distorted pyramids in the margins.

"All rightie," Jennifer said. "We don't mind guests, do we?"

She beamed at the class, expecting them to beam back, but they didn't.

"Do we?" she said with a tinge of threat in her voice.

"Yes, we do," the class chanted back.

"You mean: No, we don't," Jennifer said.

"No, we don't," the first row, only, responded.

"Okie dokie," she said, went to the chalk board, erased "Simple Present Tense," and wrote "Passover." We hovered near the door, ready to escape. Marcus knotted up his arms on his chest, while Robin blinked incessantly.

"What is Passover?" Jennifer asked, and with an optimistic face panned over the class. They stared at her, not moving, congealed in collective silence.

"What is Passover? Sergei?"

Sergei—a man in his forties, with a collection of warts sprouting randomly all over his face, with the greenest eyes I had ever seen—scowled at Jennifer.

"What is Passover, Sergei?"

Sergei tightened his lips, and straightened up in his chair, clearly determined not to say a word.

"What is Passover?"

"Jewish vacation," said a woman in the first row, in a voice like whistling steam.

"A Jewish holiday. Great!" Jennifer said. "And what do Jewish people do for Passover?"

A chair screeched in the back. The veteran mothers flipped through their books languidly. The young man in the back looked out the window. The raindrops began crawling down the pane.

"What do Jewish people do for Passover?" Jennifer asked again, not giving up on her smile, but glancing at Marcus warily.

They said nothing.

"How many of you are Jewish?" she asked, and stepped away from the chalkboard and toward them.

"Don't be frightened," Marcus said.

Two first-row women raised their hands, and then another half a dozen.

"Okay," Jennifer said. "Sofya, can you tell us?"

Sofya took her glasses off—her eyes were blue and she had a crescent scar under her left eye.

"Jewish people run from Egypt," she said, reluctantly, as if it were a well-kept secret.

"But what do they do today?" Jennifer asked.

The silence filled up every corner of the classroom. We could hear the staccato rain against the windows and the swooshing of trees, the anger and the sorrow.

"We must depart," Marcus announced, without waiting for an answer, as Sofya's words stopped at the edge of her lips.

"*Dosvidanya!*" Sergei said.

So we departed, and as we did I could hear Jennifer saying to her class: "Oh, guys, you can do better than that."

"This is level seven," Marcus said. "A rather demanding body of knowledge."

He opened the door without knocking and we burst into a small room, startling the teacher and four students. Robin slowly closed the door behind me. On the board, "Siamese twins" was written, along with "abdomen," "ache," "dysfunction," "solitude."

"You may proceed," Marcus said. The teacher was the woman from the train, and I realized how pretty she was. She feebly smiled at us and said: "We are reading an article about Ronnie and Donnie, the Siamese twins." She had a pointed chin; fair, boyish hair; dark eyes with two delicate eyebrow horizons. She gave us photocopies of the article. Ronnie and Donnie were facing the camera, their abdomens attached, their faces identical: large glasses, big jutted jaws, torturous smiles. They had four legs, and only one torso.

"Ugh, gross!" Robin said, and ardently widened her nostrils.

"Pretty bad," Marcus said.

"I must say," the man whom I recognized as Mihalka said, "that it is not perfectly pleasant when I watch them."

"They are monsters," said a woman in a dark, stern suit. She had long, immaculately combed white hair that tenuously touched her shoulders.

"Monsters," repeated the young man sitting next to her. It was obvious that he was her son: the same stout apple cheeks; the same oval nostrils, the same pierogi-shaped ears; the same intense frown, as if the cheeks and the forehead conspired to squeeze the eyes out.

"They are humans," Mihalka said, then lifted his index finger, annunciating an important statement. "When I had been a little child, I had had a friend who had had a big head."

He made a vast circle around his head with his index finger, suggesting the immense circumference.

"Every child had told him about his big head and had kicked him with a big stick on his head. I had been very sad," Mihalka said, nodding, as if to show the painful recoil of the big head.

"We are learning Past Perfect," the teacher said to us, and smiled benevolently—I readily smiled back. She had chalk smudges all over her denimed thighs. The white-haired woman and her son exchanged glances.

"I must know Past Perfect," Mihalka said, and shrugged resignedly, as if Past Perfect were death and he were ready for it.

"The Nazis," the fourth man said, "killed all people like that."

He had a square, large head, and his face was familiar, with the grimaces of someone from former Yugoslavia: generous facial movements and oscillating eyebrows. He shaped and then sliced obscure objects in front of him with his hands, as if angry at the molecules of air.

"They cooked them and tooked their bones and put them in museum," he said. "They wanted German people to watch monsters."

"Ugh, gross," Robin said, and shook her head, with her tongue out.

"Yes," the teacher said pensively, with her index finger touching her chin. Her wrist was dainty, with two slightly asymmetrical knobs. I imagined stroking that wrist, then her forearm, then her shoulder, and, finally, her neck. She continued: "They would show the skeletons of midgets and Siamese twins in public exhibitions, in order to convince the German people they were superior."

The fourth man was watching the storm, jerking his left knee.

"There had been one scientist who had gathered human heads, and he had wrote one book for Himmler and his soldiers must have read it to think Jews had been monsters," Mihalka said.

"I think you use Past Perfect too many times," the woman with the son scoffed.

"Excuse me," Mihalka said. "But I must know Past Perfect."

The fourth man smiled wistfully at Mihalka, and I suddenly recognized the smile: the raising of the left side of the upper lip; the exposing of teeth, which had evenly wide, spitting-conducive gaps between them, the toy-dog nodding; the narrowing of the eyes. I knew that man, but had no memory of him. I stared at him intently, waiting for more familiar signals.

"Okay," the teacher said. "Let's read on. Paul, why don't you read the paragraph beginning with: It is true—they often have..."

"It is true," Mihalka began, "they often have—the same—dreams. They also feel the same pain, which is not surprising—*surprising*—since they share a few internal—*internal*—organs.

The pain, they like to say, is usually—*evenly*—disturbuted—*distributed*, or sometimes even—*doubled*."

The fourth man propped his chin on his left hand. His Adam's apple flexed a little, like a Ping-Pong ball. He stroked his chin with the back of his hand, occasionally looking out the window. His ears were small, like a child's.

"Thank you, Paul," the teacher said. "Do we understand this?"

"Doubled means two times. Yes?" the son said.

"Yes," his mother said.

"Okay. Joseph, why don't you go on?" the teacher said.

The fourth man began reading in a very low voice, as if confessing:

"Ronnie and Donnie give a new meaning to the word insep—*inseparable*. 'A lot of people think that the worst thing is the lack of—privacy,' Ronnie says, 'but they don't understand what is it like—what *it is* like—to share not only your life, but your body as well, with someone that you love. Donnie is me, and I am Donnie.' "

A boy kneeling on the soft ground over a constellation of marbles, brushing away pebbles and twigs and litter between the two marbles a foot apart: one of those two marbles was small with three orange fins inside the glass globe; the other one was solid marble white. He picked up the orange marble, got his knees off the ground, and squatted. He wrapped his index finger around the marble, put his thumbnail behind it. The fist contracted, ready to launch the marble. He aimed at the white marble, closing his left eye, squinting with his right one, then released it. His marble flew low over the dirt, and then hit the white one—ping!—and the boy smiled. The white marble was mine and I lost it, and the boy was Jozef Pronek, the man reading about Ronnie and Donnie. I remembered him, there he was, out of nowhere. I was bedazzled by the clarity of the memory.

" 'What people often don't realize,' Ronnie says, 'is that if one of us dies, the other one is going to die too,' " Pronek read.

He had lived in the building across the street from mine, which had displaced a set of decrepit houses with overgrown gardens. My friends and I used to roam the gardens, as if they were unexplored continents. We would eat cabbage as if it were exotic fruit; we would burn cabbage snails in sacrificial pyres; we would protect our territory from intruders, other kids. We found a stray, scabby dog and imagined it to be our guard dog and we patrolled the gardens. So when they built a fence around the gardens and started digging them up, the world went askew. They built an ugly high-rise, which we hated along with its tenants. So we would throw stones into the windows of the building and set their garbage on fire. We would corner a kid from the building and beat him up viciously. Pronek lived in the building and when we cornered him, he would never put up a fight—his nose would bleed, and he would look at us with scorching fury, and then he would just walk away. Eventually, the war against the building withered away, and we ended up playing with those kids. They were not our enemies any longer, but they were not our friends either. They were still newcomers, some of them spoke with strange non-Sarajevan accents, and we were the natives. We let them settle, but they were still in our land, and we never failed to let them know that.

And there he was, reading in heavily accented English, not looking up.

"When they were children, they were known for being good at climbing trees, where they would—hid—hide from other kids and watch them play. 'It was strange,' Will Senson, a childhood friend, says. 'You would look up and there would be four eyes—*star*—staring at you from above.' "

"Thank you, Joseph!" the teacher said.

Pronek looked up straight at me. I didn't know if he could recognize me—I had changed a lot, having gone through a long and debilitating illness—but he was staring at me. I looked away, my heart thundering inside. How did he get here? Was he in Sarajevo under siege? Or was he besieging it? I hadn't talked to him in years, if ever. He leaned back in his chair, but my gaze was avoiding his. What should I say to him? What was his story? What was his life like?

"This is morbid," Robin whispered to Marcus.

"Saturnine indeed," Marcus said, and got up to leave, so I obediently stood up. As I was leaving the classroom, I glanced one more time at Pronek and he looked straight back at me, perhaps—and perhaps not—recognizing me. He still seemed angry.

We went back to the office. I said: "I would really like to work here."

"We could use you here," Robin said.

"We will call you by the end of the week," Marcus said.

Outside, dark umbrellas were weighing down on people. The wind side of tree trunks was soaked; the lee-side branches shivered in anticipation of cold rain, wagging their twiggy ends at me as if saying, no, no, I wouldn't do that. But I did, I walked through the rain—it was cold. I passed a dingy building: A cat was perched in the window of an apartment, watching me somberly, in complete control.

And I remembered cornering a mouse—this had happened a long time ago—in the hall of my building, after it had made the mistake of leaving its tunnels. I tried to grab it by its tail, as it trembled in fearful rage. With the tips of my fingers I managed to grasp its tail—a rubbery tentacle—and lift it off the ground. I remembered Pronek being there, watching me, hating me for what I was doing. The mouse twitched in my hand, desperate, and I giggled, enjoying my power—there must have been some girls around too—until the mouse somehow swung itself upward and bit my palm, two little needles piercing my skin. Pronek was watching me with a smirk, as if he knew all along what would happen. I screamed and let the mouse go, and it scurried away, happy to be alive. I was gripping my right hand, trying to prevent the pain from spreading.

"You find my dog," a dark-skinned woman asked me. She accosted me in front of my building, as if she'd been waiting for me. "I losed my dog."

"No, I am sorry," I said.

"You sure? Little dog."

"I am sure."

She went on down the street, looking between and under the cars and into the narrow spaces between buildings, yelling, "Lucky Boy!" all along. I could hear the storm rumbling away.

I walked into my apartment, the floors creaked me a welcome, and I suddenly felt a tide of warm giddiness overwhelming me, dewing my neck. I sat down on the floor, where the futon used to be, in my jacket, with a frightening premonition that most of the things in this world would go on existing whether I lived or died. There was a hole in the world, and I fit right into it; if I perished, the hole would just close, like a scar healing. I should have told Pronek who I was, I needed him to know. "Lucky Boy!" I heard the woman shouting. "Where are you? Where you go?"

2

Yesterday

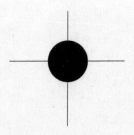

SARAJEVO, SEPTEMBER 10, 1967–

JANUARY 24, 1992

Jozef Pronek was born in the Sarajevo maternity hospital, on September 10, 1967, after thirty-seven hours of excruciating labor, the culmination of which was his mother's oath, as Jozef's little head was stuck between her legs halfway into the world, that she would strangle him with her own hands if he didn't come out *immediately*. His mother regretted her threat the moment she saw his crumpled face, dominated by a screaming mouth, like an Expressionist painting. In her delirium she found it extraordinarily beautiful.

It was that very same Expressionist face that was exhibited to Jozef's father, who was outside in the sunny hospital park littered with drunken fathers. Pronek Sr. labored to stand straight, propped up by his friend Duško, with whom he had celebrated his son's arrival into this woeful world. In a moment of peculiar inspiration, seeing his wrinkled, furious face, Father compared him to the notorious Tshombe, the man who killed Patrice Lumumba. Duško, on the other hand, found the nascent Jozef to resemble Mahatma Gandhi, perhaps because of a sheet of gauze wrapped across his minikin chest. On little Jozef's part, all he can remember (he still implausibly claims) from that day—the first in an as yet unconcluded sequence of days that constitute his life—was a frightening deluge of blazing light coming at him through the window pane, as if the first thing he ever saw were a nuclear explosion.

Jozef's infancy was typically uneventful: sucking, sleeping, shitting, diaper-changing, sleeping, sucking, burping, and so on. Out of the molten lava of his early experiences, a few awkward rocks formed: during an afternoon stroll along the Miljacka River a chestnut in its spiky armor fell directly into his lap; a neighbor's dog thrust his head into the shade of the perambulator and licked Jozef's face; during a diaper change, he peed in a perfect arc on an electric heater, discontinuing the stream just in time not to get electrocuted, the piss evaporating like an unfinished dream; a mouse, indigenous to the damp basement apartment his parents were renting, crawled into his crib and onto his stomach, whereupon Jozef put his hand around it and grasped the furry, warm body, throbbing with life and fear.

As for Jozef's toddlerhood, it was rather more eventful: his drunken uncle Dragan (who would, many years later, driving to the seaside through the Neretva canyon, give a left-turn signal and steer his car into the abyss) dangled him over the balcony fence: gravity stretched out his crooked little legs and strained his arms to the verge of shoulder dislocation. I must mention his first independent walking expedition, whereby Jozef escaped his mother's attention, entered the elevator, and then toddled over to Hotel Bristol, armed with nothing but a pacifier. There he encountered a busload of Chinese table-tennis players, all competitors in the Table Tennis World Championship—one of them juggled Ping-Pong balls, mesmerizing Jozef and impeding his advance until the distraught arrival of his mother. I should also submit a picture of Jozef with the hairdo of a provincial basketball coach, tottering toward the camera with a hand extended, ever eager to go beyond the boundaries of his domain.

Perhaps it was Jozef's adventurous spirit proving to be a little too much for his parents that made them import Grandma Natalyka from the countryside. Grandma Natalyka arrived late one night in a dark dress, equipped with boxy suitcases. She kissed his parents without submitting to an urge to smile, then looked at Jozef with a serious face, as if assessing the amount of work necessary to mold this chunk of raw humanity into a decent person. Hence Jozef's childhood is marked by Grandma Natalyka's doting presence: she provided milky meals in the morning; she administered afternoon walks and supervised playground activities. She protected him from unmerited (and merited) pushes and punches. This might have prevented Jozef from developing lasting playground friendships—upon Grandma Natalyka's merciless fillip or bloodcurdling shout, other kids, backed by much feebler forces (adolescent distant cousins; baby-sitters reading romances; simply nobody), kept their distance. There he is: digging a meaningless hole in the sandbox with a plastic shovel misshapen by his anger, while everybody else is gathered on the other end of the sandbox, filling up one another's buckets with sand. And there is Grandma Natalyka, looming on the horizon like a battleship, furiously knitting another warm sweater for little Jozef.

She strictly enforced afternoon naps, mitigating her strictness by scratching Jozef's head until he fell asleep. After the nap, Jozef would have to endure a rehearsal of her knitted collections—he stood still for many long minutes, fully dressed in a wool sweater (stretching his arms out, as if he were sending a semaphore message, the sleeve-ends hanging over his fingers), wearing a pair of mittens and a hat with a cluster of silly pom-poms. He would desperately await his parents' return from work, and then revel in their attention: he would employ his father's gigantic foot as a hobbyhorse, while his father watched the news cross-legged; he would listen to his mother singing Bosnian songs while ironing, occasionally reaching piercing heights, which would make his father turn up the TV. Grandma Natalyka would retreat into her room and do the who-knows-what of elderly women.

She returned at bedtime to deliver stories. He was squeezed between a cold wall and her warm body, his head in her armpit bay exuding the scent of cinnamon and sauerkraut brine. She narrated a cycle of stories featuring a gallery of animals that all lived in the far-off land of her childhood. There was a brave ewe, who attacked trespassers and thieves and passersby. There was a dog who thought of the kids as sheep until he got so old that he had to be killed with an ax blow to the head. There was a swarm of bees that her grandfather made hang from his pate like hair to the kids' delight. There was even a dolphin that came in one day with a carny. It was supposed to jump through hoops, but instead lay sunk and puffing at the bottom of a hole full of cold, muddy water the kids (paid in candy currency) brought in buckets from the local well. Before landing on the soft cushion of sleep, he speculated about the dolphin's fate: he imagined a savior buying it from the carny; he imagined the dolphin running away with the help of other carny animals; he imagined a numinous boy with resurrective powers. But the salvation never came in time—the dolphin suffocated, despite all the imaginative effort he put into it. Often Jozef would slip into a dream that did not care about the dolphin but carried along according to its own cruel, selfish logic—Grandma Natalyka or his parents were dying, he could do nothing to stop it, and he would wake up weeping. Grandma would be asleep, the steady hum of her snoring increasing. He would watch her dream-frown, feeling the rumble of her slumber, the slight vibrations of her upper lip and nostrils as she exhaled.

I can safely say that Jozef's conscious life fully began the day he looked at the sleeping Grandma Natalyka and her face was much too tranquil: no snoring, no nose-hair shudder. Her body warmth slowly vanished, as Jozef lay facing the wall, trying to convince himself that if he went to sleep and woke up a little later, she would be back in the kitchen, banging the pots. But he couldn't fall asleep, constantly tickled by the thought of death sharing the bed with him. He looked at her again, and her eyes were only half closed; he could see the glassy corneas. It seemed that she was looking at him through the slits from somewhere far away, and he could not think of any reason why she wouldn't come back. Everything in the room was perfectly still, as if it all went away with Grandma and only left its shapes behind.

Thus death entered Pronek's life. He watched his mother sob and his father cry, and a procession of black-clad people, towing unnaturally quiet children through their apartment, as if through a train station. He felt guilty for not being able to produce a respectable amount of tears. In a moment of inspiration, which was to provide a sentimental delight to his family for years to come, Pronek cut an onion in half and applied the halves to his eyes, producing more tears than necessary and a couple of hours of complete blindness.

Pronek's early boyhood was spent shedding the stigma of cuteness signified by the pom-poms and frills, by his round cheeks and girlish curls. Wearing a Grandma-produced sweater, Pronek crawled under steam trains lounging in the train station near his home and pulled plugs that made the steam go *shshhshhs* and produce fluffy clouds. He fought as a foot soldier in a street war against the kids from the Tito building (it had a huge Tito picture on its top), under the command of the boy who called himself Zagor Te Nay, after a comic book character. Jozef talked his friends into eating some wild fruit that looked like grapes, but were possibly poisonous and tasted bitter and disgusting, thereby experiencing early the bliss of leadership. He won the game that consisted of collecting points for lifting miniskirts of the young women walking down the street. He stuck nails into electric outlets and threw rocks on streetcars. No one would have thought of Pronek as a cute six-year-old when he spat at his father and told him to fuck off, after Pronek Sr. demanded from him an apology for calling his mother a bleating sheep. Pronek Sr. sentenced Pronek to twenty-five lashes, the execution scheduled for the time between the evening cartoons and the news. It was furthermore judged that school, beginning that fall, would still allow enough time for mischief, and Pronek was enrolled in English and accordion lessons the next day.

In the tiny workshop of his mind, Pronek can assemble a model of the English classroom in the Pioneer Center Blagoje Parović. The room is dark green, because of the heavy green curtains filtering the sunlight beating at the windows. There is a map of England, with London like a wound in its side, ruptured blood vessels stretching toward Scotland and Liverpool. There is a poster with two cartoon men (their heads square, their eyes dots, their noses sharp angles) shaking hands, and saying: "How do you do? My name is ————." The green coating makes the teacher look like a corpse, with her sagging cheek apples and thin, tight lips. (Mirza, who is to become his best friend, is reading comic books under the desk. Pronek can see Mandrake hypnotizing two goons with guns: they stand petrified with glassy eyes.) The teacher raises her hand with its mauve claws and they all start singing: "Catch a falling star and put it in your pocket, save it for a rainy day."

The English classes were bearable in comparison with the accordion classes. The accordion torment was conducted by a music teacher with a thick, brushy mustache, who clearly hated his students. They sat with the heavy accordions in their laps, stretching the beasts across their narrow chests, repeating the simple melodies ("Little Gypsy Girl Steps into the Water") over and over again, melodies that Pronek carried home in his head, resulting in dreams with Grandma Natalyka playing the accordion up to her ankles in icy water.

The first day in school sums up well Pronek's early educational experiences: droves of girls with nicely combed hair shimmering under sunlight; the pleasant contrast between their navy blue school uniforms and virginally white stockings; mobs of boys, tripping each other, causing sprained wrists and severe elbow injuries; a spitting contest, won by one Amir, who could spit between his teeth, like a snake; Mirza reading comic books under the desk (*Prince Valiant*); a gentle boy, with longish, dark hair, sniveling in the front row, while his mother poked her head into the classroom, speaking to him sotto voce. The teacher, an auntly woman who spoke with stern inflections and wrote with the fountain-pen point upside down, touched the boy's head with her gnarled hand, but it helped little—he kept bawling, a little puddle of tears forming on the desk in front of him.

The first day they learned that Nature was everything that surrounded them; that Tito was president; that the most important thing in our society was preserving brotherhood and unity; and that our planet was in the Solar System, which was in the Milky Way, which was in the Universe, which was everywhere, much like Nature. The knowledge imparted was significant only in its eminent uselessness: when his parents asked him what he had learned that day in school he said: "Nothing"—the word that he was to use throughout his schooling to describe his progress.

The only thing that distinguished Pronek in school was that he never, ever volunteered to do anything: no question was worthy of a voluntary answer; no task was challenging enough for him to step out of his daydreaming. In parent-teacher conferences, the teacher told Pronek's parents that he had *potential*, delivering her verdict with a grimace of mild disgust, as if *potential* were an odorous skin condition.

Through the fifth grade they learned more about Nature, though Society entered the picture in the fourth grade (Pronek liked Society more than Nature); they read books about freedom-loving forest animals ("The Squirrel's Little House") and lonesome dwarves ("The Dwarf from a Forsaken Land"). Nor was their physical development neglected: they climbed ropes, and rolled medicine balls in circles like disoriented dung beetles. On state holidays, they celebrated Tito's birthday and other important dates from the proud history of socialist struggle and self-management. The school choir sang appropriate songs about miners striking and dying for freedom, about the revolution akin to a steely locomotive.

Pronek liked singing, but he preferred the songs they learned in the English classes at the Pioneer Center: "My Bonnie Lies over the Ocean"; "Yellow Submarine"; "Everybody Loves Somebody (Sometimes)." He would sing at the top of his lungs at home, to the dismay of his parents, too tired to tolerate Pronek's roaming up and down the scales. Besides, they did not understand English, which was why they were suspicious regarding

the real content of those foreign songs: drugs? prostitution? masturbation? Those songs were so much unlike the songs the elder
Proneks liked to sing: the quiet Bosnian songs, sung in the spirit
of calm realization that life would pass like spring bloom and
that there was nothing but infinite darkness in the end. They
demanded to know what in the world was Jozef singing about.
At first he refused to divulge the real content of the songs, but
then started to make it up, enjoying his power over his ignorant
parents. Thus "Yellow Submarine" was about a balloon that
wanted to be free; "My Bonnie Lies over the Ocean" was about a
little squirrel that was run over by a big, bad truck, but was then
resurrected and lived in Grandma's pantry; and "Everybody
Loves Somebody (Sometimes)" was about a burglar who stole
from rich old people and gave to poor kids. "Nice," said the parents, as the idea of social justice appealed to them. Still, his
father, a police inspector, maintained his suspicion and decided
to find and enlist a colleague who could speak English enough to
decode the lyrics—a failed attempt as none of his colleagues
spoke any foreign languages.

It was in the summer after the fifth grade that a small reconnaissance unit of pubertal hormones—the avant-garde of a
great army—entered the unconquered Pronek territory. He was
spending a couple of seaside-vacation weeks with his parents in
Gradac. He absorbed sun on the beach, swam in the deep waters,
hoping to encounter some dolphins. He had noticed before that
there were girls who didn't have to wear a swimsuit top and that
there were girls who did, but for the first time that summer he
realized that there was a fundamental difference between them,
so much so that he got a slap on the back of his head for staring
at a girl in a pink swimsuit, her nipples swollen.

In the evenings, when pines gave off bounteous resin smells, when the breeze off the cooling sea brought forth tickling saltiness, when warm bodies exuded coconut-milky sun-lotion scent, there was a dance for kids at the hotel. The first evening, Pronek spotted a long-legged girl with her hair bleached by the sun, clearly playing for the top-wearers. She was dancing with her father, a burly man in a white undershirt, his belly bulging forward, Pronek circled around her like a hawk, until she noticed him and smiled at him, whereupon he circled some more, as hormone reinforcements kept arriving at the front. The second evening, the circles narrowed. He stopped in front of her, his head still spinning, and asked her to dance. His attitude aimed to suggest that he wanted to dance only because there was absolutely nothing else to do. They clumsily danced, like infatuated zombies, avoiding bodily contact, yet craving it. By the end of the first week, they were spending time on the beach together. Her name was Suzana, and she was from Belgrade. At the beach they had to perform a complicated glance dance, eschewing looking at each other's interesting areas. Midway through the second week, they could not hold themselves back: their lips stiffly touched, their teeth clacking. They were sitting right at the water line, tiny waves crawling between their toes, Pronek's arm over her shoulder, like a dead fish. The sun was setting, providing a tacky orange spill that often appears on postcards and can still bring tears to Pronek's eyes. By the end of the second week, as his departure was looming on the glum horizon, Pronek licked her ear, as his hand was resting on her belly button, paralyzed in the nether area between the two fantastic possibilities. He, then, proposed, determined to spend the rest of his life with her. She needed to ask her father, an army colonel with a frighteningly hairy chest. He forbade her to see Pronek ever again, an order she bravely defied: they met for the last time in the bushes behind the hotel. They squatted, whispering the vows of love. With her head on his shoulder, her tears trickling into his armpit, Pronek susurrously sang "My Bonnie Lies over the Ocean," trying hard not to keel over onto a used condom someone left behind, his throat tight with sorrow.

By the time he got back home in Sarajevo, the Pronek territory had been fully conquered. Mirza informed him in an audibly deeper voice that he was considering shaving his legs, as they were far too hairy. Shortly after the new school year started, Pronek received a letter from Suzana, barely mentioning their eternal love and containing a picture of her "friend," a lanky pimplehead in a Sex Pistols T-shirt with the fine name of Tadija.

The hard part in writing a narrative of someone's life is choosing from the abundance of details and microevents, all of them equally significant, or equally insignificant. If one elects to include only the important events: the births, the deaths, the loves, the humiliations, the uprisings, the ends and the beginnings, one denies the real substance of life: the ephemera, the nethermoments, much too small to be recorded (the train pulling into the station where there is nobody; a spider sliding down an invisible rope and landing on the floor just in time to be stepped on; a pigeon looking straight into your eyes; a tender hiccup of the person standing in front of you in line for bread; an unintelligible word muttered by a one-night stand, sleeping naked and nameless next to you). But you cannot simply list all the moments when the world tickles your senses, only to seep away between your fingers and eyelashes, leaving you alone to tell the story of your life to an audience interested only in the fireworks of universal experiences, the roller coaster rides of sympathy and judgment.

Thus I am forced to describe the significant events occurring after Pronek's first love disaster: he locked himself up in his room and refused to come out for three days, his mother leaving food in front of the door, only to find it untouched; he announced his decision to abolish his accordion studies; he got drunk with Mirza on the cheap stuff (with labels brandishing drunken sailors and knights with javelins) from his father's booze chest; he got caught masturbating at his desk, instead of studying Nature and Society; he demanded in no uncertain terms that he be granted funds for acquiring a guitar, which was initially declined mainly because of his brash manner, but then approved with the hope that he would stop being such an ass; he woke up in the middle of the night overwhelmed with sourceless anger, then roamed the apartment, hoping to startle his parents out of their tranquil dreams.

Nevertheless, let us zoom in on an insignificant moment: he walked down Štrosmajerova and stopped in front of the music store and saw a Beatles songbook. Let us face the store window with him. Let us be aware that an old man with a crooked hand that trembled on his walking stick stood next to him. Let us turn toward the cathedral and see the street rising to meet its stairs. Let us hear the cathedral's bells. Let us believe that Ringo winked at him from the songbook cover. If we have done all this, there is the final step: let us foresee the future in which Pronek is surrounded with girls who all shake their heads following the magic rhythm of his guitar, their tresses quivering—let us be rewarded with a pleasant tingle of an intense epiphany.

From thereon in, Pronek embarked on a secret project of getting the songbook—weeks of pilfering his mother's wallet for change, or searching through his father's pockets, finding an occasional banknote, and sometimes a condom, all the while managing to keep his operation covert.

The day he acquired the songbook belongs to the category of significant events: I need not describe all the adolescent emotional excess, but I do need to mention that he rushed to his friend Mirza's, protecting his acquisition as if it were a sacred manuscript. They feverishly flipped through it—Pronek tried to sing a song or two, the logic of music clear to him (despite misreading a few notes) like a bright winter day, when you can see the snowy mountain peaks around Sarajevo and feel that life has no limits.

In Mirza's parents' living room—a picture on the wall of a rosy-cheeked boy with a teardrop twinkling below his innocent eye, an array of crystal glasses in the cupboard tinkling as Pronek and Mirza moved around the room—it was decided that they would have a band that would play the songs from the Beatles songbook. Pronek was to be John, Mirza was to be Paul, and they needed a George and a Ringo. Then they began searching for the name—The Beatles, obviously, was already taken—so they came up with *Gospoda* (translating as Gentlemen); KGB (would not do well in the West); FBI (short for Fucking Boys International, would not do well in the East); Los Bosancheros. Finally, they settled for the simple translation of The Beatles—*Bube*. By the end of the week, they already had designed their future album covers (the two of them, plus George and Ringo, sinking in a boat; an aerial picture of Sarajevo, with four stars sparkling in four different parts of town: Čengić Vila, Baš Čaršija, Koševo, Bistrik).

As soon as Mirza got his guitar, they found George: their classmate Branko, who took violin classes, and was shy and sensitive and could read music. Pronek and Mirza recruited Faik, their English classmate, who was an owner of a tambourine with little rattly cymbals and who, more importantly, looked like Ringo: meaty nose, droopy mouth, and rogue demeanor. *Bube* rehearsed mainly in Mirza's living room, to the audience of the tear-boy and rejoicing jingling glasses, playing "She Loves You (Yeah Yeah Yeah)," "Girl," "Nowhere Man," "Help!"

They had their first performance in their music class, the audience exchanging glances and giggling. The disgusted music teacher, a decrepit man with hair in his ears, considered it all jungle music. Yet, you could tell they were seen differently after the gig—*Bube* had done something none of their classmates dared do, a few catastrophic blunders due to sweaty palms notwithstanding.

After the success of their first show—which triumphantly ended with tepid applause—they were ready to play at a school dance, where eighth-grade girls would be in the audience, in abundance, deep enough into puberty to create a shapely landscape. The show was scheduled for May 4, 1980. But May 4, of course, was the day Comrade Tito died: the news showed wailing soccer players and hysterical mothers and people standing frozen on the street as if their batteries had abruptly drained. When *Bube* arrived in the school gym where the show was to take place, there was already a Tito picture under the basket, framed by a morose black ribbon. They stood with their guitars and their radios, meant to be the amplifiers, watching the school janitor—a stocky, mean man—taping I POSLIJE TITA TITO, letter by letter, on the wall. Pronek was afraid that they might be conspicuous in their eagerness to perform, so they furtively left the gym and stood in an empty entrance hall, mad at Tito and his selfish mortality. Recollecting, in whispers, this moment several days later, they all agreed they should have produced some tears, and they unpatriotically hadn't.

Bube never played at Pronek and Mirza's school, to the relief of the principal, who was uncomfortable with their English songs, clearly inappropriate at the time of the great loss. But *Bube* got over their loss, distracted by the completion of their elementary education. They received their school diplomas in a subdued ceremony (the country still mourning its leader's untimely demise) that nonetheless provided an opportunity to have a last glance at all the girls budding in their pioneer uniforms.

They spent the summer of 1980 practicing more Beatles songs. Faults, however, already started occurring. Ringo tossed his tambourine on the floor and declared that he was bored playing only the Beatles songs—he had received a Clash album from his cousin in Munich and wore Vibrators and Buzzcocks buttons on his (deliberately) torn shirt. He started hitting his tambourine much harder than necessary (which was echoed by the furious neighbors, sometimes producing interesting syncopation) and snickered derisively as Pronek sang "Yesterday" with what seemed to be a genuine feeling. The final blow came when Pronek brought in his own song. Heavily blushing, his vocal chords constricted to a squeal he attempted to conceal as sensual whisper, gently strumming his mistuned guitar, Pronek sang: "If you know her name, tell her I love her... If you know her name, tell her I'll never forget her..." Midway through the song, devoted to Pronek's as yet unmet eternal love, Ringo started gagging. Pronek stopped, blood rushing to his ears, with a momentary vision of breaking his guitar against Ringo's fucking face. This is stupid, Ringo said. First, why did it have to be in English—it was not their language. Second, who is this *you*? And if he didn't know her name, did he know her? And did *you* know her? Is there anybody who knows her name? Ringo un-leashed a deluge of scholastic and rhetorical questions, as the rest of them witnessed Pronek's eternal love disintegrate into plain nonsense. *Bube* never recovered. Ringo changed his nick-name to Sid and became the drummer for a punk band named *Depresija*. Shortly after Ringo's departure, George informed them that his brief existence in this world as George came to an end, because his violin teacher ordered him to drop the guitar as it was ruining his touch.

Pronek himself had a period of severe self-doubt after John Lennon was killed. On a December night, he spent a few hours staring out the window at the snow swirling under a light pole. He imagined himself mortally wounded, hastening toward death in a speeding ambulance, trying to say something appro-priate for such a grave moment: "Take care of my world." Or: "There must be something behind this wall." He imagined a song that would include those words, and started shuffling lines and rhymes, but it occurred to him that if his was a life in a par-allel netheruniverse, if he and *Bube* echoed the life of John and the Beatles, then he might die soon too. The dark night and the lonely light posts with snowflakes sparkling under their sorrow-ful gaze, it all scared him in its endless sadness. He escaped his room and joined his parents, watching *Sherlock Holmes*. He sat in silence, while they wondered, half panicking, what it was that made him spend time with them voluntarily.

Pronek and Mirza mourned John Lennon and the band for a couple of weeks, then discovered that Mirza's parents hid a stack of magazines with naked women in the couch. They spent a few weeks studying their anatomy and reading readers' letters, which all involved randy random encounters in the darkness of movie theaters or on desolate beaches haunted by arousable German housewives. No wonder then that Pronek spent the summer vacation pressing his desire against the hot sand, acquiring sunburns on his back, as foreign women strolled on their way to fornication through the field of his blurry vision.

It might strike the reader that the life of this hero is not particularly exceptional, for many a boy indulged in fantasies in which the readiness of unknown women to make passionate, yet educational, love to a gangly youngster was directly proportionate to the impossibility of such a scenario ever occurring. What young man or woman did not vacillate between the conviction that no one in their right mind would touch *this* body and the insight into one's own implausible, youthful beauty? Is there anybody who doesn't remember the first shy moments of caressing someone else, the moments when all the idiotic pornographic fantasies perish in the face of a person who has a voice and a smell and a particular imperfection—say, a birthmark shaped as a crescent moon—visible only as your lips slide down her neck, as you feel the growl of pleasure in her body? The reader must remember, before judging the commonness of such recollections, that they gain in value when that person is dead (as is the owner of the crescent moon, killed by a shell in 1993). Your memories become fantasies if they are not shared, and your life in all its triviality becomes a legend.

Years later, displaced in Chicago, Pronek often wondered whether there really had been a Karen, who arrived in a Trabant from East Germany and lived in a first-floor apartment, whether her long and silky pigtails fluttered, like birds on a leash, around her head as she jumped rope; or if he really had seen a dead man, bobbing facedown in the shallow Miljacka, a chunk of flesh missing from his neck; or if he had ever seen his father's single tear, rolling from under his sunglasses, exactly replicating the tear of the boy in Mirza's parents' living room, his father telling him the story about his high-school girlfriend who fell off her bike and died of a brain hemorrhage; or if he really had ever cut off buttons from old shirts, and assembled them on the floor so as to replicate the constellations he found in the atlas of the sky.

But let us turn off the time machine and not rush toward the inescapable future. Let us wipe the misty windshield of memory and look at him standing dazed in front of the beehive-like building of *Prva gimnazija*. In one of those tedious, serious conversations about his life, forced upon him by his mother and father, Pronek had professed his desire to be a music teacher, a toy idea thrown to his worried parents while he was attending to his real plans, which mainly consisted of not being separated from Mirza. Future music teachers (and Mirza) were going to *Prva gimnazija*, which claimed to have a *cultural* slant, and this aura of *culture* attracted sophisticated, urban girls, all wearing skimpy skirts and demeanors of experienced boredom. In no time at all did his guitar playing and his repertoire of Beatles songs come in handy—the cultural girls all spoke English and had crushes on foreign rock stars. Soon the Pronek-Mirza tandem was a staple at every party—the girls to boys ratio happily five to one—where they played "Yesterday" and "Hey, You've Got to Hide Your Love Away" and "Michelle" to an audience of teary-eyed, soft-skinned schoolmates. They expanded their repertoire to include domestic songs (*Sevdalinke* and corny hits from the elementary days), appropriate for the later hours of more thorough inebriation, songs that could be played only by gently strumming the strings, as someone's warm temple was pressing against the tired arm. At even later hours, they covered for each other—one of them would be steadily producing the romantic, candlelight atmosphere, while the other poured sweet poison into a beautiful ear, murmuring that tonight, "Yesterday" was just for her.

They could not have cared less about the cultural body of knowledge they were supposed to absorb. Mirza and Pronek were expelled from a literature class in which the teacher—a young, enthused man, who surely had stacks of poetry hidden away under his bed—tried to make them see that life was a fish in *The Old Man and the Sea*. They were thrown out of the philosophy class because they started sniggering, after the teacher told them about the philosopher who had a stunning revelation and exclaimed: "What is *is!*" They learned more songs for the late party hours, going deeper into the feeling that Bosnians call *sevdah*—a feeling of pleasant soul pain, when you are at peace with your woeful life, which allows you to enjoy *this very moment* with abandon.

And there were moments. Sarajevo in the eighties was a beautiful place to be young—I know because I was young then. I remember linden trees blooming as if they were never to bloom again, producing a smell I can feel in my nostrils now. The boys were handsome, the girls beautiful, the sports teams successful, the bands good, the streets felt as soft as a Persian carpet, and the Winter Olympics made everyone feel that we were at the center of the world. I remember the smell of apartment-building basements where I was making out with my date, the eye of the light switch glaring at us from the darkness. Then the light would go on—a neighbor coming down the stairs—and we would pull apart. I also remember that a thug nicknamed Nikson sold me a brick and smacked me around in front of my girlfriend. I remember that my apartment was broken into and that there were two footprints on my parents' bed. I remember the hateful moments in crowded, smoky bars, when I could not stand to look again at the faces I had known since birth. I remember the guy in the hospital bed next to mine whose thighs and ass were all cut up after a toilet bowl fell apart under him. But I choose not to think of those as important, my memories irrevocably coated in linden syrup.

Let's go back to my friends.

Pronek and Mirza went to Jahorina mountain for winter break, and spent weeks skiing and hanging out, shacking up in a friend's family cabin or someone's hotel room, all because of their entertaining skills. Here is the winter pleasure inventory: blue skies, white snow, suntanned faces, crisp air, speed, slopes, fireplaces, warm rooms, and hearing the scrunching of footsteps on a cold night, the moon like a silver coin. It was in a Jahorina cabin, after a particularly inspired performance of a Beatles set, into which "If You Know Her Name" was stealthily included, topped with a *sevdah* set, plus—when the party climax was reached—a few pseudo-Gypsy songs, producing a few yelps of pseudo-abandon . . . it was (let me start all over again) in a Jahorina cabin that Pronek climbed to an upstairs room with one Aida. She was willing to let him explore "the jungle below the equator." Pronek, however, got completely lost in the jungle: he kept banging his knees against the sides of the bed, and his head against the wall. He had great difficulty pulling off Aida's tight jeans, managing to bring them down to her ankles, whereupon he crawled in between her legs. With his underwear stranded at the Antarctica of his feet (the room was unheated, save for their cumbersome passion) he attempted to penetrate her panties, convinced that he was up against a sturdy hymen. It was an unmitigated fiasco—she started laughing uncontrollably, when Pronek, in the middle of it all, said: "Let me just love you."

It took them longer to disentangle than it took them to en-tangle. That night, Pronek confided in Mirza, who was expect-ing stories akin to the readers' letters in his parents' magazine. Pronek told him that he could never understand how making love could be pleasurable. He offered (rhetorically speaking) as evidence the bumps on his head, scratches on his knees, and bruises on his penis.

A few days later, Pronek went with Aida for a mountain walk under a starry sky. They held hands, despite the thick wool mit-tens, and ended up in her room, where Pronek played a few songs—purely pro forma—while Aida mindfully wore a skirt, which kept sliding up her thighs. In a four-minute flurry of pas-sion, Pronek was deflowered, at the blessed age of fifteen and a half, while Aida was flowered, so to speak, with his gratitude: he mindfully asked her if she had enjoyed it, and she, her kind soul glimmering in her green eyes, she said she did.

It is hard to say whether Pronek and Mirza's decision to start a band, again, was related to Pronek's entrée into sexual adult-hood, but it followed soon thereafter.

They needed electric guitars—their long-untunable acoustic guitars reminded them unpleasantly of their innocent preado-lescent days. They spent the summer of 1983 moving around sacks of cement for measly money, mainly in order to convince their parents they were serious about getting the guitars. Too tired to play or think, they drank beer after work, still gray with cement dust, well aware they were collecting legitimate life ex-perience—toiling for a dream, even if only for a few weeks—that was not unlike a real rock-star life experience. The Beatles, after all, worked on the Liverpool docks, they would excitedly (and wrongly) recall. They imagined a future in which they played on huge stages, a firmament of stage lights above them, and the drummer twirling his sticks. They traveled around the world—London, Amsterdam, Chicago—on a bus with a fridge. They had millions of dollars: Pronek bought a house in Liverpool, where the Beatles (minus John) lived, and Mirza owned a horse farm and a riding range.

By the fall of 1983, they had electric guitars (Harmonia, the cheap East German make). They started producing songs, drinking pitchers of raspberry concentrate diluted in water, as if it were the wine of divine inspiration. Pronek wrote the lyrics, in English (the bus with a fridge beckoning him), that would have, he hoped, universal appeal, while conveying love for the one that was meant for him (but the one that didn't exist—he did not call Aida, and avoided her on the street). *The one* was present in the songs metonymically, mainly through her eyes, though sometimes her face would appear as well. Although those lyrics have been lost (in fact, they were probably burned by his parents in a little cast-iron stove during the siege), we still have the titles: "Her Eyes Are Like Stars"; "I Could Drown in Her Eyes"; "Her Face"; "Her Eyes Are Watching You"; "Did You See Her Eyes?" The paradigm for his songs was provided by "Yesterday," and they resembled one another so much that Pronek often hallucinated he had a style. Yet, he was frequently tormented by the doubt that invades the heart of many an artist: that his art, excavated from the deepest recesses of his soul, was just plain shit. On some days, he would be so ashamed that he would cancel the practice. He could not bear thinking of his own songs—his talentlessness stretched before him like the Sahara before a tired traveler on a stinky camel. On other days, practicing stage moves in front of the mirror, he would admire his craftsmanship, even detecting the ineffable presence of his true self in some of his songs, particularly "Her Eyes Are Watching You."

Once, desperate for recognition and hoping to justify the financing of the electric guitar, Pronek made the cardinal mistake of performing for his parents. He played the complete Eyes song cycle, midway through which Pronek Sr., comfortable in the armchair, started snoring, which at first sounded like supportive humming—a delusion shattered by a loud oink. Mother Pronek's face assumed an expression of encouraging interest, her hands in her lap grasping each other, as if preventing an uncontrollable applause, her eyes darting sideways. The final dagger in his artistic heart was her genial applause, waking up Papa Pronek, who leapt from his chair and swiftly assumed a karate fighting stance—a memory of his days in the police school, deeply inscribed in his body, still recurring in his dreams.

Be that as it may, Pronek and Mirza still needed a rhythm section and a name.

But the plans were put on hold when Pronek unexpectedly fell in love. Her name was Sabina—she beamed at him out of the crowd in front of the café-bar called *Nostalgija*. She gripped her drink with a sunny slice of lemon floating in it, ostensibly talking to a couple of tall potential boyfriends. When her glance first hit him, her eyes huge and strong, blood drove out of his head to the suburbs of his body and he stood paralyzed. The night after the original visual encounter, Pronek recalled in his bed the moment they were connected, respectfully keeping his hands out of the groin area.

Sabina was his schoolmate—he had known she existed and had found her cute, but her gaze suddenly transformed her into an obsession of Pronek's. He kept going back to *Nostalgija*, lingering in front of it for warm weeks in September 1983, hoping she would show up. And she did, wearing a light summer dress, her hair ponytailed, her lips carmined and easy to monitor: they touched the brim and squeezed the lemon slice. Pronek could not help feeling stupid, his skin constantly goose-bumped, all his antennas pointed toward her. Sometimes she wore tight white shirts and denim pants and the space around her body curved. He tried to exorcise her before going to sleep by playing the guitar. "Yesterday," he sang, "all my troubles seemed so far away." She was ruining his life, he didn't go out with Mirza anymore, had only fitful phone conversations with him, giving him fallacious reports about the rhythm section search.

Almost every day he would decide to go to *Nostalgija* no more, and showed up early, before anyone arrived. He would find a position from which he could see her coming up the narrow street, sipping his gin and tonic as if he were sixty (rather than sixteen) years old, his tongue dancing around the lemon. And then she would arrive and the same glance-waltzing would go on, the same torture, his body throbbing with anxiety. Her ankles were delicate, she had the long, elegant fingers of a piano player, she leaned forward when she laughed, pulled back when she asked a question, and her nipples were extremely sensitive to temperature fluctuations.

Finally, he confessed to Mirza what his affliction was. Mirza, it turned out, knew her well—their parents were friends. It was decided that they would go to *Nostalgija* that night and Mirza would meet her, as if accidentally, and introduce Pronek to her. Pronek spent the night sweating, taking a few showers in the middle of the night, to the bafflement of his father (his mother was fast asleep), who got up to remind him that the electricity used by the water heater was not free of charge. While tossing in bed, as if on a barbecue grill, Pronek confronted the ugliness of his body; he envisioned his face with plantations of pimples stretching toward the horizon of his hairline. He met the pink dawn convinced that anyone who would have such low love standards as to get involved with him must be desperate and not worthy of his attention.

Many years later, in Rolling Meadows, Illinois, while canvassing for Greenpeace, Pronek would for a few instants stand in front of a woman who had Sabina's eyes. The woman would slam the door in his face, and he would spend the evening remembering that first night, which had commenced with him facing a cruel mirror, drained of hope so thoroughly that he didn't care anymore. For the rest of the evening he would canvass in a daze that guaranteed many befuddled door-openers and many slammed doors. He would call Mirza in Sarajevo and ask him if he knew where Sabina was. She had lost both of her legs in the breadline shelling, Mirza would say. He saw her on TV, lying in the middle of the mayhem, her husband pressing his torn shirt against her blood-spurting stumps. But he heard she was in Germany now, with her husband and daughter.

Back at *Nostalgija,* Pronek stands with his hands hanging awkwardly at his sides—too sweaty to be pocketed, too weighty to be moved around in expressive gestures. Mirza is introducing him to Sabina, flanked by two squeaky friends, who keep asking questions he cannot comprehend. The conversation is burdened with unwieldy silences, incomprehensible jokes, and bulky laughs. The only thing Pronek is aware of is her scent—the anchor that keeps him from being blown away by this storm of nonsense—her lemon-and-milk scent coming from the hidden meadows of her skin. He inhales it like a mountain-climber reaching the summit, the world sprawling all around.

He walked her home, up the steep streets of Džidžikovac. They reached her building panting and leaned against the wall, next to beaten-up, pillaged mailboxes, saying nothing. A car drove by and lit a couple clinched on a bench in the park, and they both looked away. Pronek knew that he had to ask her out, since he had gotten this far, but could produce no words. Finally, without warning, he grasped her hand and kissed the valley between her middle and index fingers, her ring touching the corner of his mouth. She said: "It took you awhile." He said: "It always takes me awhile." With those words uttered, they were officially dating, and were to meet tomorrow night in front of *Nostalgija*, whereupon they would go to a quiet place to touch each other.

Then came the days of sharp falling in love; of eagerly agreeing with whatever the other had to say; of cautious kisses in the dark halls of her building, Pronek's palms gliding along her back under her shirt; of pushing through the crowd in front of *Nostalgija* as a unit. Then months of groping on benches in dark parks, occasionally interrupted by a drunk who fondly remembered his first gropings on the same bench, years ago, and then shared with them the fear of the Medea waiting for him at home. They waited for her parents to go away for the weekend, then ventured into the first penetration in their bed, followed by frantic washing of the bedsheets. They went to parties and danced in clubs, managing to explore each other's mouths and necks while spinning and jumping. They had romantic nights: candles, wine, sexy songs leading to soft caresses and equal attention to many areas of the body, culminating in lovemaking that made them dizzy and happy to be alive.

Pronek would always remember the moment of seeing Sabina on TV, marching in the opening ceremony of the Sarajevo Olympics, in a snow-white suit, ahead of the Chinese national team, tall and lank and elegant. He could always recall the warmth and tranquillity he felt at that moment, which he would understand as an epiphany of love, a moment that was to become unrepeatable once his world had collapsed.

Then a couple of years of relationshipping. He condescendingly tried to explain to her why Patti Smith was shit. She felt uncomfortable around Mirza, who, she claimed, was checking her out. They spent time with each other's parents, trying to seem respectful as the parents talked nonsense and made tasteless marriage jokes. They camped at the seaside in the summer, frequently fighting over who was to wash the dishes. She told him that he didn't understand women, after he tried to explain that he only liked to look at other women, but they didn't really interest him. He had intermittent bouts of fury, whereby he would destroy things around him—once he snapped in half all the poles his mother used to support her plants and flowers, and Sabina cried, seeing all the flowers bowing down, as if their spines were broken. And a sense sneaked upon them, a sense that love was not enough to keep them together—they sat on a bench on the Vilsonovo and watched deflated soccer balls roiling in a Miljacka whirl. They were eighteen, and felt very old.

Thus they broke up: tears; meaningless late night phone calls; a few letters in the handwriting of love and helplessness; a series of Pronek's late night guitar-playing sessions, interrupted by his sleepy parents, demanding the cessation of the wailing. Mirza told him that whatever didn't kill him made him stronger, and gave him a 45 with the song entitled "I'd Rather Go Blind Than See You Walk Away from Me." It was mortifyingly sad, and Pronek played it over and over again, sinking into the blue depths of pain. Somewhere along the way, he finished high school, and went to the prom night, where the carousing drunken teenagers squealing with joy irked him terribly. He left early, and wandered the streets, ending up on a bench by the Miljacka, watching the same soccer balls still revolving, like planets in turmoil.

The following summer was long and torturous: he spent a few weeks in Makarska with his parents, whose idea of vacation was lounging on a pebbly beach (many a pebble tar-coated) and then playing Ping-Pong, his father winning every single game hands down. They went for family walks in the evenings, Pronek walking a few paces behind them, so as to appear sovereign, licking ice cream, which always had the same taste regardless of the alleged flavor. Worst of all were the bonding attempts on the part of his father, who would take him out for a beer. "The men will have beer tonight!" he would announce to Mother, and then made him drink raspberry juice. Father Pronek would tell his son endless, pointless stories about their Ukrainian ancestors, about his childhood growing up barefoot and poor. It was important that he understood, Father said, that this family rose from poverty and now can drink beer and raspberry juice just because they felt like it and not because they were thirsty. Now they could have vacations in Makarska— "Look around you!" Father demanded. Pronek did and saw a cheap touristy town, with armies of lobster-red bodies marching, hauling the bodies of screaming children; and here and there an attractive body clinging to a hairy forearm, well beyond his reach, painfully implying Sabina's absence. Sometimes, Father would tell him his police stories, a story about the prison guard who killed nine people because he saw them covered with gnats; about the mother who killed her son with a knife in the back because he came back late that night; about a mailman who attacked his neighbor with a chainsaw, but stumbled and sliced off his own foot.

Pronek spent sleepless nights sharing the room with his parents, listening to the tussling under the sheets. Without his guitar, stuck in the room at the age of eighteen with his own horny parents, Pronek reached the edge of tears, and then stopped there, forcing himself to think about a year in the army, only a couple of months away.

He fantasized about the tough army life, about doing thousands of pushups, crawling under barbed wire, astonishing his commanding officer at the shooting range with his precise eye. He imagined coming back from the army strong—his shoulders wide, his face hardened and hairy, with a scar across his cheek (barbed wire). Having entered the pleasant space between fantasy and dream, Pronek went on reconnaissance missions, sneaking up on an unsuspecting enemy guard, ready to break his neck or cram a blade into his kidney. He put out an enemy sniper on top of a tall building, Pronek's bullet hitting him between the eyes. Pronek spent months in the trenches with Mirza, sharing the food, waiting for the enemy to attack, and once the enemy poured into the trenches and overcame them, he detonated a hand grenade and died for freedom. When he slipped into the realm of pure dream, there were mushrooms on the horizon and enemy soldiers naked and aroused, and he would be stuck in a cave full of mice and frogs. Once his father put his gun to his temple and said: "Should I kill you now or after the cartoons?" Pronek sprang back into the reality of a hot Adriatic night, cicadas producing a steely, twangy sound, as if sawing the trees outside. His father peacefully snored, and Pronek could see his mother's feet peeking from under the cover, her corns moonlit.

Pronek's father had some army connections and he wanted to

use them to arrange for Pronek to serve in the military police. Pronek, however, hoped to serve his country in an army orchestra, somewhere close to Sarajevo, but was too attached to his fantasies to say no to the masculinity a military-police boot camp would provide. Strange are the ways of the military, however: Pronek ended up in an infantry unit, in a Macedonian town called Štip, which reeked of coconut-flavored chewing gum, as a candy factory was the only thing beside the army garrison.

As if bent on punishing Pronek for his fantasies, the army's idea of what becoming a man meant was the exact opposite of Pronek's: perpetual humiliation was its main tool. First the conscripts went through a warehouse, where the soldiers distributing clothes threw pieces of uniform at them, guessing the size or simply indulging their whims. Pronek received a shirt too small, a cap too big, pants that could accommodate a small man beside him, and underwear that had no rubber band. Then his head was shaved and he was sent into the showers with two hundred other soldiers, one of whom decided to urinate on Pronek's thigh, thereby baptizing him. The water coming from the showers was cold, and Pronek spent too much time soaping himself. The water was discontinued before he could rinse.

Let us look at Pronek now, coming out of the latrines, a brand-new soldier of the Yugoslav People's Army: the cap pressing down his ears, making him look jug-eared; his pants ballooning around his thighs; his underwear sliding down to his knees, impeding his step. Carrying his civilian clothes in a stinky white bag, he totters toward the promised land of manhood with his eyes teary from the soap dripping off his forehead.

Pronek rolled in mud, ran up hills, ran down hills, ran through a forest with a gas mask, slamming into trees, marched across Macedonian plains, and guarded ominous magazines, learning to sleep on his feet. He was less than mediocre at the shooting range, because he closed his eyes when pressing the trigger. He stole his comrades' clean socks and looked at pictures of their girlfriends, all presumably fucking someone else now. Pronek showed them Sabina's picture—beautiful, on a sailboat, in a swimsuit—which he regretted when they started making lewd jokes.

He silently endured shrieking corporals and the howling platoon commander, Captain Milošević, who liked to alarm them in the middle of the night and have them stand at attention for hours. He tried to stay awake through the political-education classes as Captain Milošević explained why socialism was the fate of America. You could never be alone: in the bathroom, in the dorms, in the canteen, at night, in the morning, in your dreams, there were young men—skinny, stinky, ever eager to talk about women and fear furtive homosexuals, ever hungry and ready to get drunk, ever sharing the same repertoire of jokes, uniformly revolving around farting. Sometimes, at the swearing-in of new soldiers, or at a celebration of a Party-congress anniversary, there would be an orchestra and Pronek would wistfully watch the guitar player absentmindedly strumming his strings, performing a song about the people's joyful spirit.

Pronek lied to his parents, presenting his army experience as one of bonding with other young men from all across Yugoslavia, strengthening the brotherhood and unity that kept the country strong and united. Sometimes he embellished his letters with appreciation of the simple soldierly life, or expressed pride that the good people of Yugoslavia, his parents included, were peacefully sleeping because Pronek himself was dwelling over their freedom. His dwelling was more due to the frantic nocturnal masturbation of Spasoje, a shepherd who had spent the past ten years alone with sheep in the mountains of southern Serbia and liked to bang his feet against the bunk-bed bars in the throes of self-passion.

Pronek told the real story to Mirza, who already knew it, having scrubbed ship hulls in the navy and gone through the same spectrum of debasement. Both of them came to the conclusion that only an idiot can enjoy the army, and they felt guilty for not being patriotic enough, for not being tougher, for despising their comrades content with the pleasures of masturbation and bad cigarettes. Aware that the army censors might be reading their complaints, they conveyed their unpatriotic misery in the code of Sarajevo slang—which I regret not being able to translate well enough to render its impenetrability.

After three months of basic infantry training, Pronek was nowhere near the pledged masculinity. Indeed, he took a step back when he was transferred to the kitchen. It was a cozy duty, precisely because it was nearly absolutely mindless: he washed skyscrapers of oven pans and dishes; he peeled galaxies of potatoes. Pronek worked, ate, and slept, while time crept. He got a potato-peeling companion, a Bosnian from Banja Luka named Ahmed. Ahmed was a cook, but had been demoted after repeatedly talking back to his superiors, all of whom, according to Ahmed, were first-rate motherfuckers. He was a huge hairy man who talked in an abrupt, peevish manner, as if insulted by the other person's unflinching existence. The first time they peeled the potatoes together, Ahmed kept scowling at Pronek's dumb ways, criticizing the unnecessary thickness of the peel, and kept showing him the right knife angle. It shortly turned out that Ahmed knew Pronek's cousin in Banja Luka, that he believed that *sevdah* was the Bosnian version of blues, and told him he should listen to John Lee Hooker and Zaim Imamović and he would see. They came up with their own *sevdah*-blues songs, describing the potato peeling and the horrors of the army and faraway women. Ahmed liked to read—he was to study literature after the army—and would tell Pronek abbreviated, even if often convoluted, versions of the novels he had read. He liked hard-boiled detective novels and Dostoyevsky. He gave Pronek *The Idiot* to read, and Pronek found it mind-numbingly tedious and never finished it, but said that he liked its *philosophy*. After Ahmed went back home a month earlier, Pronek slept sixteen to eighteen hours a day, getting up only to eat and supervise the potato peeling of the kitchen novices, whose hands were covered with cuts and incisions, the buckets in front of them full of bloody water.

After coming back from the army, Pronek refused to answer any of his parents' questions and provide them with any reason to be proud of his newly acquired manhood. Then he started his studies of General Literature at the Faculty of Philosophy. He chose General Literature chiefly because he had heard from Ahmed th. you didn't have to work much, just read a lot, and that you could bullshit extensively. Within a month of commencing his studies, he stopped attending the classes. It was hard for him to get up in the morning and go to a class knowing that he would have to listen to the self-important suit-and-tie professors delivering their lectures on Ancient Greeks or the lives of Serbian saints. He could not bear to look at the comely, coy young women, ready for a lifetime in a library; scruffy young men, with goatees, and rotten teeth, for whom the line between being drunk and being inspired was forever blurred. Pronek did not hate them or despise them. Looking at them resulted in sorrow clawing at his heart—

couldn't they see how untrue and pointless it all was: the future librarians making copious notes; the poets scribbling their latest confession to themselves in a dog-eared notebook; the professor reading in a droning voice about the saint suffering on top of a mountain?

Thus Pronek skipped early morning classes and spent the morning in bed, staring at the ceiling—a dot here and there, mosquitoes murdered years ago—feeling as if a heavy black cat were sitting on his chest, growling in his face, ready to gouge his eyes out if he just moved. He would try to think up a reason to fight the cat and get up, but couldn't think of any.

It was on one of those mornings that Pronek entered his poetry-writing period. The first lines of poetry he ever wrote in his native language translate as: "What's that thing growing out of me/Like a tumor on a sunny day?" The poem was about nothing in particular, apart from his ambition to get the ceiling-staring feeling out. He entitled the poem "Love and Tumors." The second poem was tougher: he sat facing the empty, blazingly white sheet of paper, and tried hard to think of something he needed to say. Before he wrote the first line, he had the title: "The Deep Sleep." And so it went—he got out of bed to write poems. They never rhymed, had no stanzas, and made no sense. Soon he started believing that what he wrote was not poetry, but something else, something deeper and more ineffable; something that expressed his feeling of life: a taut heart, tears hiding from his eyes, the liberating hopelessness. Those poems were blues, Mirza ascertained, no doubt about it, and Pronek had an epiphany: he saw himself old and black, sitting on a ramshackle porch with a rambling guitar, delivering narratives of his woes and metaphysical peregrinations. And he was blind too—the only thing he could see was the darkness of his soul.

Quickly did "Love and Tumors" become a blues song. So did "The Deep Sleep" and "I Am Hiding Tears from My Eyes" and "Do Not Close Your Eyes." Pronek spent days, while his parents toiled for his sustenance, in his room singing, howling (like Howlin' Wolf), and screaming (like Screaming Jay Hawkins), sometimes getting things out from such depths that their neighbor, a streetcar operator who worked night shifts, banged his fists furiously against the wall and offered to strangle him with his bare hands.

Thus was Blind Jozef Pronek and Dead Souls born of pain and confusion. Mirza, naturally, was the first Dead Soul. They played in the overcrowded Dental Students Club, called predictably *Zub* (the Tooth) and the Medical Students Club, called, a little less predictably, *Kuk* (the Hip), to an audience of drunken students, horny and uninterested. Pronek tap-tap-tapped his foot, like Blind Lemon Jefferson did with his cane, Mirza played his short, heartfelt solos, inaudible over the speakers, drowned in the noise of students eager to forget bleeding gums, jars full of fetuses, and spongy hearts. But sometimes, everything would be just right and the smoke from people's nostrils floated toward them and formed a cloudy aura, like fog coming from the Delta swamps. Pronek would see a pair of eyes watching him just above the surface of the crowd, as if trying to see through to his sinful soul. I could have been the owner of a pair of eyes, as I went to *Kuk* and *Zub*, but I do not recall listening to a blues band in those places—I could have been simply too drunk to notice. Toward the end of the song, he would skillfully close his eyes, suggesting that he had just plunged into his own depths. He felt the tickling of gazes moving across his face and neck like long-legged, lithe spiders.

Soon enough, Mirza and Pronek recruited a bass player,

named Zoka, and Sila the Drummer, a punk who worked in the Maternity Hospital as maintenance and liked to drink like a fish at *Kuk*. Sila demanded an explanation of Pronek's lyrics—he didn't want to play what he couldn't understand. Pronek didn't quite know what the songs were about, except that they were about his feelings. Under Sila's ferociously inquiring gaze, Pronek had to spin out an elaborate exegesis, comparing himself implicitly to John Lee Hooker and Dostoyevsky, which did not help clarify the lyrics at all. Finally, Pronek used soccer references to explain that "Love and Tumors" was about the game you knew you were losing but you still wanted to score, while "Do Not Close Your Eyes" was about being aware what position you were playing on the soccer field of the universe. They played more gigs, even having a couple of shows in Zenica and Mostar, where they almost got beaten up because an idler in bermuda shorts demanded "normal music" and Sila rhetorically fucked his mother. There were no stars in Sarajevo, as everybody knew everybody, and nobody ever forgot the days when you rolled in mud or played marbles, and the local thugs would set you straight if you were too cocky. But there were young women smiling at Pronek and Mirza and even at Sila on the main street. A rotten-teeth poet from General Literature told him that *they* expected a lot from him. Mirza's cousin's boyfriend, who worked for a student paper, asked Pronek if he wanted to write music reviews. "Little money," he said, "but you'll have a voice." "I already have a voice," Pronek said, but consented.

And a couple of years after coming out of the army on a Tuesday morning, Pronek woke up happy, leapt out of bed, and left his room singing to himself "Something Stupid," the Sinatra song. He cordially wished a good morning to his flabbergasted parents—indeed, he had coffee with them and showed some interest in their welfare. His mother suffered from arthritic pain, and his father had been demoted to desk duty—new people were coming, he said, their ethnicity their only qualification. Then Pronek went to the offices of *Valter*, the student paper, to submit a scathing review of the new *Bijelo dugme* album, which he described as "the lowest form of Balkan peasanthood hidden under the gingerbread veneer of hard rock stolen from the stadiums of America." He kept repeating it to himself, as if it were a poem.

The trouble with happiness was that it was not a good foundation for blues—Pronek wanted to cover "Something Stupid," but the song could not be taken for blues, not even in Bosnia, as remote from the Mississippi as a country can be. Sila refused to play "Something Stupid," demanding that their songs be heavier. He wanted more steel, he said—he was into The Cult. He even brought in his own songs, determinedly not in English, with titles that translated as "Dig Your Grave, Disco Brother," and "I'll Cut the Throat of Love."

The issue was unresolved when Mirza and Pronek went to the seaside in the summer of 1990. They spent it entertaining throngs of dark-skinned, blond young women from Hungary and the Czech Republic, getting laid frequently and indulging in a fantasy that life would never end. When they came back to Sarajevo on a rainy August day and said good-bye to each other they had a profound sense that something was over. And it was: Blind Jozef Pronek would not practice for months, as Zoka was preparing for a medical exam and Sila discovered heroin and was shooting up in the bushes by the Miljacka. Pronek wrote more reviews, only occasionally playing old Beatles songs with Mirza, and even went back to studying General Literature—he enjoyed reading *The Divine Comedy*. He spent more time mountain hiking with his father, who had been forced to retire. His father told him stories: about the unresolved murder of a soccer referee, found in the Miljacka, with his asshole cut out; about his great-granduncle who left Ukraine and went to Chicago, where he was a hotel detective, while his brother went to Bosnia; about old Ukrainian songs his mother sang, which he could still remember to a word. They stood looking at Sarajevo at the bottom of the cauldron of mountains: streets curving like furrows on a great palm; people flowing in the streets like ant columns; the buildings reflecting the setting sun, as if in flames. It was incredible, his father said, how one could clearly remember the things that took place so many years ago and could not remember what happened just yesterday.

After a six-month hiatus, Pronek got his band together in the winter of 1991 and they had a sloppy rehearsal—the songs sounded weak and hollow, completely devoid of feeling. A couple of days later, Pronek and Mirza went to the rehearsal space—the basement in Zoka's deaf grandmother's house—and discovered that all their equipment had been stolen. Many months later, they would find out that it was Sila who had stolen it and sold it for heroin, after he was caught pilfering money in the Maternity Hospital from the purses of women in labor.

The year 1991 flew by Pronek, as if he were watching a passing train, the lit window strip rushing by in the night, and he barely able to discern the faces of people going in an unknown direction. In March 1991, he dreamt that he was shooting up heroin, and the blessed calm that came upon him in his dream was so pleasant that he woke up fearing he had become a junkie without ever even trying junk. In May, he often found himself wandering parks and the Vilsonovo, nagged by a titillating possibility of picking up women sitting alone on benches—he ogled them with crazed glances that made the women get up and pick up their pace. In June the trouble in Croatia started—the news arrived of skirmishes between Croatian volunteers and the army and roaming murder-units coming from Serbia, conveyed with images of corpses with gouged-out eyes and cut-off noses.

In July, Pronek was invited to visit the American Cultural Center and talk to its director. The young director spoke woeful Serbo-Croatian and Pronek, tempted a few times to correct him, had a hard time following him. The director said that Pronek's writing had attracted favorable notice and asked him about his "life and work." He sped through his life in a few brief, uneventful sentences. It appeared to him as perfectly fraudulent, and he feared that the American would accuse him of lying, pulling out documents and photographs that proved differently: he had never had a band; he had never studied English; he had never been in the army—*and here we have a photo of you playing the accordion at your cousin's wedding!* The interview, it seemed to Pronek, was a catastrophe. The same month, his father told him that a man he knew in the Association of Bosnian Ukrainians was looking for someone who wanted to go to a summer school in Kiev, to learn more about their heritage. Pronek had no interest in his heritage, as he had suffered through his father's histories, but he thought that leaving Sarajevo and the war in Croatia for a month would help his mental health. He went to Ukraine.

But that is a different story, and I have never been in Ukraine—someone else will have to talk about that part of his life. He met a woman he would one day visit in Chicago, thus reaching the place where he would live unhappily ever after and where I would recognize him in a classroom. I know he was in Kiev when the putsch happened, when the Soviet Union collapsed, which caused his parents some worry—both the collapse and his presence there. He came back older, perhaps even wiser, having witnessed a historic event, having fallen in love. He joked that he had gone to the USSR to fix a few things, and now, he said, was ready to fix Yugoslavia.

Upon his return, Sarajevo was under a heavy cloud. Mirza, a law student at a lawless time, was working on moving to Canada, because, he said, he could not think here anymore—it was as if his brain were invaded by the Serbs and Croats, slashing each other's throats. Pronek frequented clubs and bars, as he couldn't stand being at home and listening to his parents talking about dying soon. He watched people dancing half asleep and picking up whoever was left on the dance floor. Pronek did it himself—at dawn he would be groping in the main park with a woman whose name he didn't quite catch and whose beer breath he inhaled, trying not to gag. In the morning, he hated himself, but, he thought, who didn't. He stopped writing poetry, or playing his guitar, just wrote idiotic reviews nobody read ("The guitar solos are a rich boy's idea of a slave's pain, and they sound like amplified masturbation"). A guy he knew offered him heroin one night and Pronek accepted, but then reneged when he saw the guy vomiting, having rubbed the junk into his gums—he had lost his syringe, he said.

He went hiking with his father more often. It was fall already, and they didn't go far because it was cold and wet and they had heard rumors of army patrols shooting at people who drifted close to their positions. Father Pronek, in fact, saw army units digging trenches in the mountains near Sarajevo, but he thought they were doing that to protect the city. The last time Pronek went with his father, in October, they looked at Sarajevo, muffled by the dusk. They heard a hum, a gigantic hum, like the Big Bang echo. It was the sum of all the life noises Sarajevo produced, his father said: the clattering of dishwashers and buses; the music from bars and radios; the bawling of spoiled children; doors slamming; engines running; people fucking—and he nudged his son. They looked up and there were disinterested stars in the sky. Some of those stars didn't exist any longer, they had become black holes, Pronek said. Black holes, Father said, and nudged him again.

In November, he got a call from the American Cultural Center and the director's secretary said (the director had left, because Sarajevo was becoming unsafe) they were inviting him to visit the USA and learn more about it, as he was a young journalist likely to promote the values of freedom. "When can I go?" Pronek asked immediately, though he was not sure what his relation to freedom was.

So, here we are at the Sarajevo airport, January 1992. Pronek's father drops him off without entering the airport, because there is no parking. Pronek watches the jalopy car pulling away, his father slouching over the steering wheel as if shot in the back. He can see his hairy neck and his eyes in the rearview mirror, tired and old. Pronek feels abrupt sorrow, dragging his suitcase with its blocked hind wheels leaving two trails behind, like the heels of a corpse. He waits for his plane in the airport restaurant, sipping vinegary coffee. He watches a family cluster: bags, suitcases, children, surrounded by men smoking and women wiping their eyes.

Then he is on his plane, buckling up, looking warily at the mountains encircling the airport. The seat next to him is empty. The plane goes up, his stomach goes down, and he is careful not to show that he is afraid to die. He looks down and can see a line of dots trickling out of the airport building toward another plane.

One of those dots is my head, with a hairless medallion in its center, following Pronek like a shadow, moving toward my plane and my destiny. I look up and see the plane disappearing into the clouds. Pronek takes the last look at the city sprawling in the valley, as if kissing a dead person, the fog creeping along between buildings. He is oblivious to me, as a wall is oblivious to a shadow dancing on it.

The plane penetrates the clouds and Pronek can see nothing. By the time the plane exits the dark wool of clouds and enters the bright starless sky, he already cannot remember what happened yesterday. The sun is blazing through the window, so Pronek pulls down the shade.

3

Fatherland

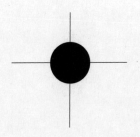

KIEV, AUGUST 1991

Meantime we will express our darker purposes. Chicago, London, Amsterdam, Vienna, Warsaw, whence I took a cheap train to Ukraine. I boarded my train, found the couchette waiting for me, enveloped in thick veils of smoke and an obscure cologne called Antarctica: I watched the man in the bed across splashing a few palmfuls out of a gelid-blue bottle before the train left the station. He unbuttoned his shirt, as if stripping for me, slowly divulging his sooty tapestry only to stop an inch above his navel. The discomfort I felt then I am inclined to see now as a sense of momentousness—doubtless a rearview interpretation. The man lit a cigarette, eagerly opened a booklet with a chesty damsel in sexy distress on the cover, with a title that I— the uncertain, occasional speaker of an obsolescent Ukrainian dialect—decoded as *The King of Midnight*. —see p.14

The King of Midnight offered me a sip now and then from a smudgy bottle. Having quickly slurped his way to the bottom, he threw himself on his bed with such force that an earthquake suddenly took place in my dream: the earth cracked open, swallowing swarms of citizens; roads whiplashed, throwing cars around like matchboxes; buildings collapsed flat. As the train crawled through Poland, I crept through a series of nightmares—all sequels to the earthquake one and involving a Wal-

Mart and the Sears Tower, plus mice, midgets, brooms, and other Freudian gewgaws. The final one was staged on the Soviet border: a mob of shabbily uniformed men with humongous flat hats waited in a shower of sallow, gnat-infested light; they stepped into the shadows and then onto the train. They alternately looked into the King of Midnight's passport and into his woozy face, as if comparing them until they matched. They flipped through my American passport, determinedly not impressed with the plentiful freedoms it implied, let alone the rich collection of visas collected on my existentialist peregrinations. They still let me in, albeit with a humbling frown, conveying that they could stop me, indeed vanish me, had they only wished to. But they wished other, more profitable things, so they practically threw my passport at me. I went to have breakfast in the dining car.

The dining car is a generous description of a few tables adorned with tablecloths that looked like a canvas of the local Jackson Pollockovich. A painfully bored attendant was reading the papers, his body telling—*begging*—the tired traveler to go away and never come back. Two men were sitting at one of the tables, their foreheads occasionally touching above the full ashtray in the table's geographic center. They argued over something, downing a glass of vodka (which, for a moment or two, I hoped was water) between florid bursts of rhetorical affection. From what I could understand, the focal point of their argument was one Evgenij, whose distinguishing feature was that he was simultaneously a filthy bastard and the kindest man alive. You could never know with Evgenij, who would stick a knife between your eyes, but who would also give you the undershirt off his back if you asked him: they agreed and kissed and downed a glass of vodka, and then another one. It struck me then—and I still have an ocean-shaped bruise where it struck me—that there was no reason whatever to talk about me, that I was extraneous to almost all of the conversation taking place in this world at any given time. And I envied Evgenij, the kindest living son of a bitch.

I went back into the couchette. I fell asleep again and woke up only after the train entered Kiev with a poignant decrescendo. The King of Midnight sat up with a grunt, clawed at his chest for a minute, then hawked and mindfully spat into one of the empty bottles.

Humid evening heat; the streets covered with a dark, oily placenta. A man named Igor was waiting for me, holding a sign with my name on it. He was blond, blue-eyed, sinewy as a marathon runner, cautiously clever—painted with many colors, as they say. I present that as a fact, while it was barely a somnolent impression at the time. I got off the train, stepping on top of a steam cloud (though the train was not a steam train—what we have here is a remake of Karenina getting off the train to be welcomed by Karenin and his banal big ears), walking slowly toward the station building as the arriving women kissed the waiting men. I got into Igor's car, which reeked of vomit and pine. A man named Vladek silently sat in the back seat, inhabiting a magnanimous smile. We glided through the streets of Kiev, entering light from darkness, darkness from light. I could not speak, as I was tired and dazed. I managed to understand whatever Igor was saying in his guttural Ukrainian, but what he was saying I do not remember. I do remember occasionally looking back at Vladek, to check if he still existed, and he grinning with the demented enthusiasm of full-fledged existence, flexing his eyebrows and winking at me, as if we had already become fellow conspirators in an obscure plot.

Everything in the building was exceptionally orderly, hall carpets stretching straight, walls white like Christmas snow. Igor told me that the place was a Party school, normally, but that they were permitted to use it for the summer.

He opened the door of a room, I walked in reluctantly, Vladek dropped my suitcases, and winked the final wink. My roommate-to-be was frisking a pillow, bare-chested, wearing only shorts with an anchor pattern. "I am Jozef," he said, and offered his hand, still warm from patting the pillow. "Jozef Pronek." Allow me to introduce myself: I am Victor Plavchuk. Nominally I came here for the sake of connecting with my roots, but really was looking for something to do until I figured out what to do. Now allow me to invoke Jozef's slouched shoulders, his square chin, and his eyes: almond, dark, and a mile deep. This is how I remember it now—the excitement is ex post facto—but it was much different then: thus is his cheek a map of days outworn. We stared at each other for an embarrassed moment, waiting for Igor to say something and pull us out of the mud of silence. Then there is a confusing blank: what we did or said after Igor left, I do not remember.

When I woke up the next morning, Jozef was still in bed, hence I pretended to sleep, so as to eschew the awkwardness of waking in a room with a stranger. I heard him straightening up in his bed, scratching (his chest? his thighs?) with such unfaltering vigor that I suspected masturbation for a moment. Then he rummaged through his stuff, closing the door, then leaving—his steps echoing in the hallway. I got up with a heavy steel ball in my belly—the regular morning meaninglessness of everything, when all the uses of this world seem weary, stale, flat, and unprofitable. I unpacked my stuff, hung up my shirts next to my roommate's. The color of his shirts was predominantly Eastern European bleak, and the sneakers at the bottom of the closet were well worn, so I was self-conscious putting my attire next to his: my sandals, my sneakers, my shoes, and a lavish collection of khakis and colorful shorts in need of ironing. For an instant, I could not remember why I had them all: the arbitrariness of those choices appeared abruptly transparent, and all the other choices I had ever made seemed absurd. I liked (and still do) the smell of his clothes—the musty smell of a lived life.

When my roommate walked back in, I was sitting on the bed with my head in my hands, looking at my toenails in dire need of truncation.

"Good morning," he said earnestly, which forced me into replying.

"How are you?" he asked. I was pretty tired.

"You want one coffee?" he asked. "Bosnian." Sure, I said.

"You Americans always say sure," he said. I didn't see the point of arguing, so I said sure, and he chortled.

My name was Victor. "I know," he said. He put a little pot with a long handle on the table between our beds. He dipped what seemed to be two razors attached to a wire, with a button between them, in the pot, then plugged the bare ends of the wire into a socket. I calmly realized that he was risking his life, along with my mental welfare, by doing that.

"I know this from army." You were in the army? Whose army?

"Yugoslav. We must go. It was many years ago, when I was eighteen." How old are you now?

"Twenty-four," he said.

He had a rotund nose, which seemed swollen, and thick meaty lips, which he kept open. He had the darkest eyes I have ever seen, like two perfect marbles. We sipped coffee, too bitter and biting—I furtively abandoned it. The birds just outside the window warbled, and someone in the room above ours was apparently tap-dancing. He was from Sarajevo, Yugoslavia. He used to have a band and write for papers. His father was Ukrainian, just like mine, though his was born in Bosnia. He came to Ukraine to see his grandfather's fatherland, but he also wanted to be away for a little while from "crazy things" in Yugoslavia. He had this idea they (who were they?) put things in your head and that you have to make it empty. I had stomach cramps and needed to go to the bathroom.

"We must go and eat breakfast," he said. "I wait for you."

Sure.

It was while spending time in Eastern Europe that I learned to appreciate unremarkable things, and the cafeteria I entered, following Jozef, occasionally bumping into him (our steps had not yet synchronized), was spectacularly unremarkable. The light in it was gray; a window wall looked out at a parking lot, which had no cars other than a gigantic black Volga, like a beached walrus. On one of the walls there were men leaning forward with fiery eyes and mountainous muscles bulging under their work uniforms. The women in folk uniforms facing them off hugged tall stalks of wheat that used to be golden and now were merely washed-yellow. There was a long line of people sliding their screeching trays down a rail, toward the food. Some of them were foreigners, recognizable in their clean, crumpled clothes, glancing around, trying to figure out where they might be. We took our trays and they were sticky, still wet in the corners, reeking of socialist grease.

I piled different sorts of blebby pierogi and a cup of limpid tea on my tray. The young woman in front of us, with arms that were bones coated with skin—Jozef introduced her as Vivian—put on her tray one pierogi, which looked like a severed, ashen ear. I lost my appetite instantly. I sat across from Jozef, and he munched his pierogi, while I sipped the absolutely tasteless tea.

"What are you doing?" he asked me, looking straight into my eyes.

"I am drinking my tea," I said, suddenly perplexed as to what it was that I really might be doing.

"No, in your life."

"Oh," I said. "In my life." My life. Ripeness is all, and I ain't got it. "I am writing a Ph.D. thesis."

"I see. What are you studying?" Let it be made clear, I did not want to have that conversation. I did not want it to be known that I was not doing what I claimed I was doing.

"Shakespeare," I said.

"What about Shakespeare?" He was an unrelenting bastard, looking straight at me all along. Look away, you knave, look at the men with fiery eyes, look at Vivian nibbling her pierogi, preparing herself for a bout of bulimia. "What is called your thesis?"

I must have blushed. I sat there facing a Jozef from a crumbling country, up to my neck in fucking Kiev. I said: "Queer Lear." I was about to say: "The Collapse and Transformation of Performative Masculinity in King Lear," but Jozef said:

"My little horse he thinks it is queer, that there is no house near."

"Not quite queer in that sense," I said. It occurred to me that what I was doing was *inapplicable*, that I could spend days explaining it to Jozef to no avail, under the forlorn mural, the world's fresh ornament. I used the opportunity to change the subject. "You like Robert Frost?"

"I was reading him on faculty," he said. "I am also studying litrch—litrchoo—I am studying books."

It was as he was fumbling the word *literature* that I befriended him. It was painful for me too to utter that word, and I grinned in warm understanding, wanting to hug him like a stack of wheat. Even now, when I teach, when I am forced to utter the world "literature," I have a strange sensation—my nipples tickle, my eyes well up with tears.

There was a time, I freely confess, when I thought it noble not to know where one was heading. I thought that being lost meant being in mid-chapters of one's own Bildungsroman, but then I became very lonesome climbing up the steep, craggy cliff of self-knowledge. I kept reading and thinking, and thinking and reading, and drinking, in order to figure out what life was all about, and whose fault it all was, before I even started living. Then I went to graduate school. I learned that desire was important, in a class populated by lonely, insecure searchers who sought people like themselves in literature written centuries ago. (The teacher's claim to academic fame was entitled "Karaoke and (Re) Presentation.") My father once asked me what I desired in life, and I was happy he used the word *desired*, for by that time I considered myself an expert on the matter. My father was the kind of man who fixed old chairs and obsolete magneto-phones, thereby restoring the original order—no search, just restoration. Anyway, I followed the path of desire, but it led me nowhere, and I roamed and wandered, and became a typical American young existential tourist—Jack Kerouac was my travel agent. And for reasons I could not fully understand at that time, I had a terrifying feeling that sitting in front of Jozef, answering questions he had no right to ask, I had reached the terminus.

"You want to eat that?" Jozef asked, and pointed at the re-mains of my sorry breakfast.

"No," I said.

"Can I eat that?"

"Sure."

He grabbed a pierogi and devoured it.

"Always is sure," he said.

"Sure," I said, and laughed, with a gurgle of pleasure, for we had already acquired an inside joke. He stood up with the tray and said: "See you later, alligator." I resisted an urge to follow him, studying instead the differently shaped grease blotches on the table, and their relation to the straight lines that ran across the table—the configuration all made sense then, as if it had been a coded message. I looked at Vivian. "Hi," she said, in a whispery voice, and nodded as if to confirm that she really meant it.

Vivian was a graduate student too, but in Slavic languages—she spoke five of them, including Ukrainian. She was in school in Madison. She told me there were other Americans here, and pointed vaguely toward the undiminished food line. There was Will, who was a tennis player, he was from Somewhere, California. And there was Andrea, who was from Chicago. And there were Mike and Basil, who never had breakfast. Vivian would punctuate the end of every sentence with a nod, and an occasional tucking of her hair behind her ear, on which a fence of rings stretched across her earlobe. I could not see her eyes, because she kept looking down at her plate. She had a shirt with a sunflower pattern, with a wide, open collar, which exposed her chicken chest and the slight curves of her breasts. She told me that this place was *okay,* that she spent a lot of time in the library here, that we were all going to take a train to Lvov tomorrow, early in the morning, and stay in Lvov for a couple of days. I complained about not being informed about it, allowing for some good old-fashioned solidarity of Americans in a hostile foreign country, then took off, having made up my mind to spend the rest of the day sleeping. Good night, lady, good night, sweet lady, good night, good night.

We all got up at the crack of dawn—Jozef had shaken me out of my weighty slumber—picked nocturnal crud out of our eyes, then crawled into a bus stinking of harsh cigarettes and machine oil. The bus took us to the train station, down the same desolate streets that I had roamed yesterday, which created a profound sense of moving in circles, even if there was a wobbly morning worker here and there. A statue of Lenin or a socialist hero ambushed us from behind every corner, invariably leaning forward, implying a future. I wanted to point out those things to Jozef, who was a few seats away from me, too far for conversation, close enough to be aware of me.

The train station was swarming with citizens dragging their overstuffed bags and underfed children, anticipating torturous departures. There is a history in all men's lives, figuring the natures of the times deceased. Pensive and ponderous I was indeed, squeezed in the middle of an alien rabble—a fog of garlicky sweat and exhaustion wafting about us. "Look on us, we are like salt going out of hand," Jozef said. I envisioned identical grains of salt, slipping out of God's furrowy palm. It was humbling, to say the least.

The train was much too salty: the Soviet masses everywhere, wearing the expression of routine despair: women with bulky bundles huddled on the floor; stertorous men prostrate up on the luggage racks; the sweat, the yeast, the ubiquitous onionness; the fading maps of the Soviet lands on the walls; the discolored photos of distant lakes; the clattering and clanking and cranking; the complete, absolute absence of the very possibility of comfort. I thought that if another revolution were ever to break out in the USSR, it would start on a train or some other public transportation vehicle—the spark would come from two sweaty asses rubbing. I survived the prerevolutionary grappling only because I followed Jozef, who cheerfully moved through the crowd, the sea of bodies splitting open before him. We found some standing space in the compartment populated solely by our schoolmates—the only ones I recognized were Vivian and Vladek.

There was Father Petro—whom Jozef called Father Petrol—a young, spindly, pimply Canadian priest, who kept touching his left tit as he spoke. I could easily see a future in which Father Petrol's parish, somewhere deep in the Canadian Western provinces, was in a community-tearing upheaval, after Father Petrol had been caught innocently fondling a gentle boy. There was Tolya, a teenager from Toronto or some such place. She used every chance to press her melons against Jozef, who endured the assaults with a bemused, avuncular expression. Vladek, the man with a "Komsomol face" (Jozef)—wide-open eyes, freckles, and an impish lock on his forehead—kept hugging Tolya, trying to pull her away from Pronek, sharing his bottomless vodka flask with her and anyone interested, including myself. Priggish and prudish though I may have appeared, I had a few hefty gulps that scorched my throat and earned me approval from the mob and a smile from Jozef. There was Andrea, the Chicago woman, with whom I avoided eye contact, for I did not want to detect any common acquaintances, and she played along. Like all tourists, we wanted to believe that we were alone among the natives. Jozef kept glancing at her, and his upper lip teetered on the verge of a seductive smile. There was Vivian, sitting in the corner, refusing drinks, and, incredibly, trying to read, which she eventually abandoned for talking to Father Petrol about—as far as I could discern—martyrs and saints. In the next compartment—I peeked in, hoping against hope that there would be seating—there was Will, with two other guys who looked American in their flannel shirts and an assortment of traveler's gadgets: backpacks rife with pockets, pouches pendant on their necks, digital wristwatches with an excess of useful little screens.

Needless to say, windows could not be opened, and within a couple of hours moisture painted pretty sparkling pictures on the panes; the walls were sticky; my skin was itchy and I kept gasping for air. The train was speeding through a misty forest, through an army of parallel trees visually echoing the tranceful clatter. Then the train slowed to a stop in the middle of a ravine. In total silence, the trees around the ravine loomed over a couple of brawny does grazing.

"It is beautiful," Jozef said.

"Yeah," I said.

"How can you kill them? I don't understand?" Jozef said.

"I don't either," I said.

The does looked up at us as if aware we were talking about them. Jozef said nothing, but raised his hand slowly and waved at them. One of them made a little step forward, as if trying to see us better—I swear to God the does knew we were watching them, they did see him waving at them. It seemed like a natural, ordinary gesture, just a simple motion of the hand. I did not dare do it, because I realized Vivian was looking at me, and I was embarrassed. The train moved on, the clatter accelerated, and the does turned their butts toward us and galloped away. Jozef and I stood wordless for an hour or so, our backs pressed against the damp coldness of the pane. I often recall that moment (the moist morning mist, the collective clamminess; the mirth of Jozef's body, etc.), and I am forced to own up to the fact that I had never had—and then lost it again—what Jozef had: the ability to respond and speak to the world. Then it was Lvov, and we disembarked from the train together, stepping into a nipping, eager air. We inhaled deeply, simultaneously, as if holding hands. What country, friends, was this?

It was in Lvov that Will the Tennis Player fully entered my field of vision. He stood in front of the glum Lvov train station, with his arms akimbo, giving assured directions to the random som-nolent sojourner. He had piercing blue eyes, sinewy tennis arms—his right asymmetrically thicker than his left—and the squat, sturdy body of a Ukrainian peasant, no doubt the sludge from his ancestors' genetic pool. Quickly did I succumb to his wise leadership—he led me and Vivian and Vladek and Tolya and the others toward a bus identical to the one that transported us in Kiev. I took a window seat, and looked out, when Jozef slumped his body next to me. In front of us, Vladek was telling a lame joke in lamentable English to Vivian, who managed to produce a gracious giggle.

I woke up in front of a morose building, with my cheek pressed against the promontory bone of Jozef's shoulder. Will informed us—he always seemed to know where we were and why—that was the student dorm that would provide lodging while we were in Lvov. The students coming in and out retracted their heads between their shoulders, their chins poking their chests, their mood clearly surly. I could tell that the showers in the dorm did not work.

Jozef and I shared a room, which was, to put it mildly, ascetic: bare walls (although my memory keeps stretching on its toes to hang up a Lenin picture); steel-frame beds with thin, sunken mattresses; a wobbly chair and a wobblier desk, which sported two symmetrical nails on the insides of its rear legs, a student-torture contraption.

Will burst into our room, asked us—me, in fact, for Jozef ignored him—if everything was all right. It was, I said. Will announced that he was trying to find out if we could have better accommodations, and stormed away.

"Who is this?" Jozef said. "I don't like him."

"He's okay," I said. "He just wants to help."

"Maybe," Jozef said, and then just as abruptly walked out. I did not want to be abandoned in this dreadful place, but I could not just follow him. So I was alone, sitting on a bed that reacted with a screech to the minutest muscle contraction, staring at an empty wall that called for a Lenin. I pressed my hands with my knees, until they were numb, distilled almost to jelly with the act of fear.

I thought of the day when my father took me to a baseball

game, after years of my pleading and weeks of my mother's lobbying. He loathed baseball—hitting a ball with a stick for no discernible reason, producing mind-numbing, indulgent boredom, that was how he saw it. He had informed me that there would be no hot dogs or soda for me, but I was still giddy with excitement. We sat in the Wrigley Field bleachers, and I had my baseball mitt (a present from my mom), which had spent long months closeted. I was convinced that I would catch a ball, that it was my day, when everything would come perfectly together. My father refused to stand up for the national anthem, because he was still Ukrainian, as if "The Star-Spangled Banner" wounded his Ukrainianness. He made me stand up, he wanted me to appreciate America, for I was born here. During the game, he was bored out of his mind, and he kept looking anxiously at his watch. It did not happen, I caught nothing. We left in the sixth inning, and I hated my father for being a fucking foreigner: displaced, cheap, and always angry.

Whereupon Jozef walked in with a handsome bottle of vodka, unscrewed the cap, and said: "You want drink?"

"Hell, yeah," I said, and took a throat-parching gulp.

"Do you like baseball, Jozef?" I asked him.

"It's stupid," he said. "You kick ball with stick, it is nothing."

"Yeah, I know." I told him the sad story of the eternal misunderstanding between my father and baseball. Jozef listened to me not with the mandatory we-have-all-been-there interest, but with a detached, patient involvement, leaning slightly, and kindly, toward me. Now I realize that it could have been because he was trying to decode my English words, which still does not diminish my belief that he understood me better than anybody, precisely because he could go beyond my vapid words. He told me how his dad used to punish him: he would sentence him to twenty-five belt lashes for a transgression (going through the pockets of his father's suits, or stealing) and determine the time of the execution—normally, Jozef said, after the evening cartoons. He spoke in his broken English, with articles missing, with subject, verb, and object hopelessly scrambled—yet I understood him perfectly, clearly visualizing the sequence of punishment. There was no screaming or yelling, no random disorderly violence—so much unlike my father, who would rip off kitchen cabinet doors and slam them against the walls. After the cartoons, they would go into the bedroom, and the lashing would take place, red butt cheeks and all—I am loath to confess that I envied him for having had those moments.

"Fathers," Jozef said. "They are strange."

Then we talked about our mothers, and their domestic sufferings. Jozef remembered how he had always hoped that his mother would come into the bedroom and stop the lashing, but she never did. I told him how my mother would throw things out of the kitchen cabinets onto the floor, smash the plates, fling pot lids at my father like Frisbees, and they would bounce off him. We talked about women, our first loves—a topic that required some embellishing and enlarging on my part. We talked about our childhoods, the friends that we had had and were now gone—except Jozef's were not gone, they were all in Sarajevo. The silly adventures in school: snorting Kool-Aid in order to sneeze in the biology class (Jozef), smoking pot in the tenth grade, and then being high and afraid to climb down the rope in the PE class (me). The trite acts of rebellion which seemed revolutionary in our adolescence: saying "Fuck you, bitch!" to a nun (me); throwing a wet sponge at a Tito picture (Jozef). We compared Chicago and Sarajevo, how lovingly ugly they were, and how unlovingly parochial. Our mouths went dry, vodka diluted our blood and rushed to our heads. I was so drunk and excited at dawn that I wanted to hug him, but did not want him to think that I was strange. When we finally went to bed at dawn, I lay with my eyes open, watching the sunlight crawl across the wall above Jozef's bed, discovering stains shaped like Pacific islands, my heart throttling in my chest. I could still hear Jozef whispering, telling me the funny story about the loss of his virginity. His breath kept tickling my earlobes, even as he was tossing in bed, and the soft nurse would not come and stroke my curls.

Oh, Lvov, with your old downtrodden monuments of comfortably bourgeois times; your Mittel-European ornaments on the facades, barely visible through the thick filth of progress; your squares with nameless statues of obscure poets and heroes! Did I fail to mention I had never been in Ukraine before? All I knew I heard from my father, who had left a long time ago. Jozef and I wandered the streets of the old town and were sickened by the geometrical landscapes of the new town—to him all of it had familiar Eastern European shapes; to me it all seemed like a dream dreamt by another dream. Somewhere there—but where I knew not—was the Lvov my father had grown up in and had since left, and, bad son that I was, I had little interest in seeking it out.

Jozef needed to have coffee in the morning, so he was on a quest: we found an Armenian coffee shop, where we drank the muddy liquid, not unlike Jozef's Bosnian coffee. I am an herbal-tea man, so having had coffee that you could spread on a slice of bread, I was jittery and warbly, could not stop talking. Everything had to be told, and fast. I talked about my father, about his being born in Lvov. I talked about all the things he had never told me, things I found out eavesdropping on my mother's furious rants when they fought. I told him that my father had been a member of a secret Ukrainian organization—very secret indeed. They prepared for a war of liberation, and hated Russians, Poles, and Jews. And then in World War II, he was an eighteen-year-old fighter with Bandera partisans, fighting Bolsheviks and avoiding fighting Germans. Bandera himself was imprisoned by the Germans and then was shot by the KGB after the war and ... "I know," Jozef said. Anyway, my father and his fellow fighters hid in the woods around Lvov, here and there robbing a truck of supplies, paying a high price in lives. They drank water from poisoned wells, ate cattle corpses found in villages burnt by the Germans or the Bolsheviks, then died of animal diseases, boils exploding all over their faces. Man's life was as cheap as beast's. The few surviving fighters slipped into the disorder and carnage of the German defeat, and ended up happily imprisoned in the Allies' POW camps. My father had been a student of music—he was a baritone—so he sang in those camps: old Ukrainian ballads, Italian arias, and prewar Paris chansons that had somehow reached Lvov. He went to England, lived in Liverpool, worked on the docks, then he was off to Canada, where he ran the memberless Ukrainian-Canadian Opera Society and sang at weddings and funerals—mainly funerals. Then he went to Chicago, where he conceived my miserable self.

My father rendered his pre-American days in disconnected details: how during wartime they all shared cigarettes when they had them, and smoked lint from their pockets when they didn't; how he was the handsomest, most sonorous singer in Lvov; how the POWs wept when he sang "Ukraine Hasn't Died Yet"; how he and his best friend embraced in the snow, warming each other up with their breaths, until his best friend's breathing ceased; how he had sung opera only once, in Kitchener, Canada, in the role of Wotan, terribly miscast in a local production of *Die Walküre*. Sometimes, at home, he would break out into the Magic Fire Song, which always scared the crap out of me.

Boy, was I on a roll, I kept babbling—it is very possible that Jozef did not understand most of my prolix monologue. As a matter of fact, out of the blue sky, so I was a little irked, he said:

"You know, Bandera, when he was young, he wanted to be strong, to not feel pain. So he put his finger in door and then close door so he can see how long can he feel pain. He has did that every day."

What could I say? I said: "That's crazy."

Anyway, after the demise of the Opera Society, my father drove a truck—my mother told me once that one of the things he had transported was foreigners across the border. He drove his truck to the US and he met my mother in Chicago. My mother was a South Side Irish girl, nineteen at the time. He knocked her up, possibly deliberately, in order to get American citizenship (my mother screamed out that secret in the middle of one of their more destructive fights). In any case, he married her, maybe for his sense of manly duty, maybe for the passport—I did doubt it had been love, for love was hard to come across in my father's words and deeds. He was, I attested, an unaccommodated man.

"It's like American novel," Jozef said.

"Yeah," I said.

But that could be because my older brother, born a few months after they had got married, was killed in Vietnam ("Vietnam—big war," Jozef said). I remembered him as this remote uniformed presence, someone who had thrown a baseball at me not trying to hit me in the nose. Here on my desk (Please, take a look!) I have a picture of him in his uniform, smiling, with a baseball mitt, yawning like a carnivorous plant, on his left hand. My brother was blown to pieces by a land mine. Years later, we received a visit from his army buddy, who was now peddling booze money in exchange for the true story, and who in pathologically gory detail described my brother's death: spilled guts still throbbing in the dirt, ungodly howling, a Charlie sniper shooting off his knees, etc. My mom blamed my dad for her son's death, she blamed all his fallacious army stories, all that sleeping-in-the-woods bullshit that deluded my brother into thinking that the army built a man's character—it kills the body, she wailed, screw the character, my son's body is gone. My father thought that every man needed character—that a life that produced pain built your character the way that door built Bandera's. So my brother's absence, the paint of his death on the walls of our home, *that* had built my character. My father, nunckle motherfucker, never talked about it, just went to the Chicago Avenue church, sang in the choir, his jaw eternally clenched. My brother was killed a week before he was to be discharged. He was twenty-three, his name was Roman.

"Very interesting," Jozef said. "Roman means novel in my language."

"Oh, fuck you," I said, and that was the first time I got mad at him. But it didn't last long: we sat on the bus next to each other again, in silence, and I was just about to tell him I was sorry, when I realized he was asleep, the wanton boy, his head on my shoulder, his saliva dribbling on my sleeve out of the corner of his mouth, my hand levitating above his nape, a touch away from his gentle neck.

Returning to Kiev a couple of days later was like coming home: the smell of socialist grease and vinegar was as familiar as my mother's kitchen; in the humble room, a pair of silk socks I had taken off upon my arrival waited crumpled under my bed. Jozef dropped his bag, leapt out of his shoes, and threw himself on the bed, its steel edge leaving a scar on the wall. I did the same thing, but a little more cautiously. We stretched on our respective beds, staring at the ceiling, in silence, as unspecified words were choking me—I wanted to talk, because silence seemed to be undoing our friendship.

"This is microphone," Jozef said, and pointed at the fire alarm on the ceiling with frightening certainty. "Maybe also camera."

It made sense, of course, we were in the Soviet Union, in a Party school dorm—if there had been only one camera in Kiev, it would have been here. I started recalling all the things I might have done under the fire-alarm gaze: shaking my naked booty; singing aloud while dancing in my underwear; lying on Jozef's bed, sniffing his pillow; investigating his suitcase and touching his things. I imagined the man who was watching me: a bored, mustached man, with a stainful tie; his armpits crusty with perspiration; playing chess with his ulcer-tormented comrade; not paying attention to the flickering screens, until they sense the motion of a funky American on one of them. Then they would ho-ho-ho and ha-ha-ha, and they would call the fatherly officer, who would come in, impeccable and humorless. He would not care that I put on Jozef's shirts, still in the groove. He would loathe my weakness—as my father had when he caught me masturbating once—and order them to keep the camera on and bring him the tape every day.

The camera annoyed me terribly, for your sense of sovereign self, of the completeness of your body, entirely depends on the illusion that no one can see inside you, that the only people you ever allowed to enter you would be the people you loved and knew well.

Jozef, on the other hand, was waving at the camera and saying: "Hello, comrades. My name is Jozef Pronek and I am spy."

"Don't say that," I said. "Just don't."

"And this is my friend Victor, also spy. He is American and he works for CIA."

"Don't say that."

"Please come and arrest him. He was bad. I tell you everything what I know about him."

"Stop it," I yelled. "Stop it."

So he did—yet another awkward silence—but then he got up and left the room, leaving me alone with the buzzing camera over my head.

The camera incident notwithstanding, the days upon our return from Lvov were wholesome. We would wake up, my beloved roommate and I, into a blissfully sunny morning. The memory of the view from our room contains an implausible sheet of snow, covering the parking lot below and the tips of the trees on its edge, straight as pencils (beyond which, I learned, was Babi Yar), solely because the summer sunlight was so bounteous that it washed everything white. Jozef was one of those people who are happy in the morning: he started his day humming a song that was a sound track for his dreams (I recognized "Something Stupid" and "Nowhere Man," for example); then he sauntered in his underwear, gabbing steadily. It was in the morning that he told me about his numerous girlfriends; about his crush on Andrea (which, he freely admitted, provoked serious erections); about his band (Blind Jozef Pronek and Dead Souls) and his best friend, the rhythm guitar in the band; about his ancestors (a granduncle shot by Stalin; another who worked for the Austrian railroad; another an orchestra conductor in Czechoslovakia, a long time ago); about his family (parents, aunts, uncles, hard to follow).

I remember my brother doing pushups bare-chested on the floor next to my bed. His panting, yelping, and chest-slapping woke me up. Sometimes, I woke up scared, and my brother comforted me, stroking my hair, smiling. Then he did stomach crunches—it seemed to me that he was going through hurtful convulsions, but nothing could harm my brother's morning joy. I am exactly the opposite: I had long ago—but wherefore I know not—lost all my mirth. Hence I passively absorbed Jozef's cheerfulness, never quite responding, often wanting him to shut up, for I realized that he would talk to an armoire with the same morning enthusiasm. I wanted to be alone, but you couldn't be alone with Jozef—he brought buckets of cold world into your life and poured it over your head and you gasped for air.

We would head toward breakfast, down the stairs in synchronized steps, his hand on my shoulder, lodged gently on my collarbone. Seldom would we be alone at the table—all of a sudden he had an army of friends—which forced me into reticence or, worse, into nonsensical utterances, all sounding like pretentious misquotations: "Everybody knows someone dead"; "Words are grown so false that I am loath to prove reason with them." Jozef would indulge in dalliance and glance-exchange with Andrea ("You had nice dreams?"), which would always make me recall his erection; he would tease Father Petrol ("You dreamed pretty women?"), which would make Father Petrol's pimples sinfully purple; he would greet the Polish teenage twin brothers, who had been following Father Petrol like a double dose of temptation ("You switched names last night?"); he would provoke

Vladek, asking him what kind of information he provided to the KGB ("Tell them I am spy"); he would make a crass remark to Vivian, whom he didn't seem to like because she was a vegetarian ("I have sausage for you"); he would even address Will, reading the *International Herald Tribune* he brought with him ("What are news?"); and he would embarrass Tolya and me, suggesting that we could "make love" after breakfast. We all revolved around the axis of Jozef's morning mirth, and the revolution could make you nauseated.

After breakfast, we were expected to go to classes and expand our knowledge of Ukrainian history and culture. I usually skipped the Ukrainian language classes, but I went to the Ukrainian history class, much with the same interest that would make me gawp at a train wreck, but also because Jozef was in the class. We would sit high in the amphitheater, almost at eye level with the solemn pictures of Marx, Engels, and Lenin, looking down at Vivian's emaciated back as she took notes, looking at Will's persistently raised hand, and at a puny Toronto professor who had written a thousand-page book on Ukrainian history. I made intermittent notes, chiefly out of graduate school habit, while Jozef frantically drew herds of butterflies and demented rectangles. I was raised with my father's version of Ukrainian history in which frequent and regular defeats were in fact triumphs of martyrdom; in which feeble intellectuals and hesitant politicians misled the common man and betrayed the hero; in which pogroms were merely self-defense; in which Ukrainians preserved Orthodox Christianity from Poles and Communists. "Empty story, yes?" Jozef said. He liked the empty story about the Cossacks throwing mud at their elected chief as part of the inauguration ritual. He thought that everybody should do it, and add some shit to the mud too. Once, as the Ukrainian SS division was being wiped out by the Red Army in its first and only battle, our knees touched, and a little furry animal of troubling pleasure moved for the first time in my belly, but I quickly smothered it with the soft pillow of denial.

In the evenings, we would go out, stroll by the Dnepro, while the greatest fleet of mosquitoes ever assembled attacked us, wave upon wave, some of them resembling small storks—it was hard not to think of Chernobyl, and evolution taking a different turn in these parts. We would embark upon a quest for beer, up and down Andriivski Uzhvis, usually ending up in an Armenian restaurant, frequented by all the other foreigners in Kiev. Once the entire school crowd went to the restaurant and ordered a whole piglet—Jozef's royal idea. He delightfully gnawed on the bones, greasing up and licking his fingers, daring everyone to try the brain, and no one dared except Andrea. (Vivian paled at the far end of the table.) I retch at the very thought of eating pig's brain, but they put the decadent morsels into each other's mouths with delight. Strange is the taste of desire.

We would go back to the dorm and drink in someone's room, cheerfully exchanging funny anecdotes, talking over each other, though I cannot remember what about. Jozef would disappear to make out with Andrea, and I would be stuck with a ranting-in-Russian Vladek, whose idea of fun was to drink vodka out of a vase; with Father Petrol, who would pontificate (mainly to the twins) about the spirituality of beekeeping; with Vivian, who was somehow always sitting next to me, trying to commence a quiet conversation about bad food or the water shortage in the dorm. I would depart only when I was sure that Jozef was not in our room with Andrea, quietly humping in the darkness, while a moonbeam sneaked into the room and tickled his bare dolphin-like back.

––––––––

One day, all the Americans in the school were summoned to Igor's office. I cannot say that the possibility of a summary execution of the imperialist enemy did not cross my mind, but I went nonetheless. There were six of us: there was Will, with his flaxen hair, half-open mouth, and undergrowth of blond hair on his tight forearms—he in fact came with a tennis racket in his hand. There was Mike, whom I hadn't ever talked to, from Schenectady, with a large Slavic head and an itch in his crotch, to which he responded by constantly touching his penile area ("You play tennis?" he asked Will). There was Vivian the Vegetarian, with her translucent skin and knobby joints. There was Andrea, with her rangy Chicago prettiness, freckles and all ("You're from Chicago too?" I asked her. "Yup," she said, and that's all the conversation we had). There was Basil from Baltimore, with thin-rimmed spectacles, positioned at a studied equidistance from anyone, and a stack of money neatly held together by a silver clip—he was a banker ("I am a banker," he said). And there was me, a graduate student, mired in the middle of a project called "Queer Lear."

Thus, in streaming bad English, spoke Igor: the American president George Bush was coming to Kiev for a goodwill visit. The people of Ukraine wished to welcome and accommodate the American president, because the people of Ukraine had a lot of respect for the American president, and they wanted to develop friendship with the American people, and so on in a portentous voice. He said we were needed, since we could speak Ukrainian and English, to be on hand as interpreters. "Sure," Will said instantly. "I'll be proud to serve my country," Basil said. "Bush is a prick," Andrea said. "No way I'm gonna do it." Then Vivian and Mike agreed, and it was up to me. The way I remember it, which is most certainly inaccurate, is that they all turned toward me, in slow motion, tilted their heads slightly—it took me a few long moments to decide. I am one of those people who is always a little embarrassed to stand up and turn toward the flag at a baseball game, though I always do it, my father's invisible hand pushing me. And I never thought that my brother's death was quite worth it. But it was different now: there were these people in a foreign country and I knew them—we were a "we." I was tired of confusing, unrelenting perceptions and feelings. I wanted to go to a familiar place. I said: "Okay," and avoided Andrea's gaze.

A bus was supposed to pick us up Thursday. We would be accompanied by a person from the consulate. Igor thanked us very much and told us how important it was that our school could be part of the historic visit. Igor had no shoes on, just snow-white socks, except for a red blot on his left foot, suggesting that his big toe was painfully bleeding.

But there was throats to be cut and work to be done: we boarded a humble bus, with smudges on the window panes probably predating Brezhnev. And in that decrepit ark we sailed together with other unnamed Americans, collected around Kiev, who all sat in the front seats. We were heading to the airport, we were told by a red-haired young woman in a neon-blue suit. She was from the consulate, her name was Roberta, and she said she was delighted to see us, but then she instantly forgot us, firmly focused on the Kiev streets ridden with potholes and her goals—say, a position in the Moscow embassy and an affair with a good-looking CIA man. I liked the way she raked her fluffy hair with her carmine claws.

I sat next to Vivian, attracted by her scent of coconut sweat and her radiant skin—she gripped the handlebar on the seat in front of us and I could see her velvet veins bulging. I could also hear her breathing, her tresses' ends dithering from her breath. Her bare legs brandished a bruise here and there, amid goose bumps. It terrified me to see how fragile she was. I believe that Vivian was aware of my gaze, for she looked straight ahead, only occasionally smiling, exposing her gums reluctantly.

But then Will threw his tennis body onto the seat in front of us, and said: "Roberta said we might get to see the president."

"Wow," Vivian said.

We arrived at the airport, at a back lot, with no one around, except a square-shouldered man in a dark suit, a cubical jaw, dark sunglasses, a gadget in his ear, his hands lethal weapons— exactly how I had imagined a presidential bodyguard. I get a kick out of meeting someone who is a cliché embodied. It produces a pleasant feeling of a world completed, of everything arranging itself without any of my involvement, yet not veering out of control. And a diminished Vivian was reflected in his sunglasses. He ushered us into a waiting room, told us to wait in a voice that sounded synthesized, and then vanished.

There we sat waiting.

We were killing time, choking every little minute with the muscly hands of mortifying ennui. There was absolutely nothing in the room: no pictures on the walls, no magazines, no paper or pencils, no crass inscriptions on the chairs, not even dead flies in the light bowls. I exchanged irrelevant information with Vivian: our favorite Dunkin' Donut (same: Boston Kreme); our favorite TV show (*Hogan's Heroes*); our favorite Beatles song ("Yesterday," "Nowhere Man"); our favorite salad dressing (she had none, I couldn't think of any). We agreed on almost everything, and that cheered Vivian up. But I must confess—and if you are out there somewhere, Vivian, reading this woeful narrative, find it in your heart to forgive me—I lied about everything, agreeing with her only because that was much easier than professing the flimsy beliefs I had never firmly held, and it was nice to see her smiling.

We turned to silence, and time simmered until it evaporated. They took us back to the school, but they told us that the president would speak at Babi Yar that evening and that we might be needed again. 'Tis the time's plague, when madmen lead the blind.

The Babi Yar ravine was full of people, swarming against the green background of trees. They grew out of pits that once upon a time had been filled up with human flesh, which had on me a disturbing effect of feeling unjustly alive. President Bush walked on stage, in the long dumb strides of a man whose path had always been secure—around him a suite of tough motherfuckers bulging with concealed weapons and willingness to give their lives for the president. We were close to the stage, over which the monument loomed—I could not make out what it was: a cramped lump cast in black bronze. We—Will, Mike, Basil, and Vivian, and I—watched him appear before the Ukrainian crowd that followed his every move, like a dog watching a mouse, with detached amazement: it was now in front of them that he became real. His bland, beady eyes scanned the crowd for a loyal face—a habit from back home, where voters grew like weeds. He looked at his watch, said something to a man carrying a clipboard, all efficient and chunky. The man nodded, so the president approached the microphone. The microphone screeched, then the president's voice cracked in the speakers. He touched the microphone head with his lips, receiving a jolt from it. He tried to adjust the unwieldy microphone, as if choking a snake, speaking all along. His voice then came from a tape recorder deep down inside him, plugged into the electric current of his soul. Nobody was translating.

"Abraham Lincoln once said: We cannot escape history . . ." he said somberly, still wrangling the microphone. Under the stage, there were men in uniforms, squatting, leaning on their rifles. Their heads brushed against the wooden beams. They had striped sailor-shirts under the uniform, which meant they were from the KGB. They smoked and seemed absolutely oblivious to what was happening right above them.

"Today we stand at Babi Yar and wrestle with awful truth." He pronounced Yar as Year. The men under the stage were laughing about something, one of them shaking his head in some kind of disbelief.

"And we make solemn vows," the president went on, his voice getting deeper, the microphone making a *wheeee* sound. I spotted Jozef in the crowd, his face beaming out of the crowd's grayness, standing close to the stage, with his hands in his pockets, Andrea next to him.

"We vow this sort of murder will never happen again."

The KGB men under the stage simultaneously dropped their cigarettes and stepped on the butts, still squatting, as if they were dancing *hopak*.

"We vow never to let forces of bigotry and hatred assert themselves without opposition."

I realized that President Bush reminded me of one Myron, who would eat earthworms for a quarter when we were kids: he would put a couple of earthworms between two pieces of bread and bite through. You could sometimes see their ends wiggling between the slices, while he chewed their heads. With his quarters he would buy some booze—Colt 45 or Cobra or something.

"And we vow that whenever our devotion to principle wanes [the microphone suddenly went silent] when good men and women refuse to defend virtue [silence] each child shot [*wheeee*, silence, *wheeee*] none of me will ever forget. None of us will ever forget."

The setting sun peeked through the treetops and blinded Bush, who squinted for a moment, a fiery patch on his face. Jozef whispered something into Andrea's ear and she started giggling, with her hand on her mouth. The people standing behind the president on the stage were uneasy. The men under the stage were on their backs now, looking up at the stage ceiling, their AK-47s laid next to them. Vivian silently moved next to me—the coconut aroma perished from her sweat. The chunky guy with the clipboard shook up the microphone, as if it all were a matter of its stubbornness, and then gave up.

"May God bless you all [.....*wheeeeeumph*.......] the memories of Babi Yar."

And then Bush came off the stage and after a sequence of microevents that I cannot recall—you must imagine my shock—Jozef was standing in front of Bush, behind the moat of the bodyguards' menacing presence, his face extraordinarily beautiful, as if an angelic beam of light were cast on his face. Jozef was looking at him with a grin combined with a frown—which I can recognize in retrospect as his recognition that the moment was marvelously absurd. Bush must've seen something else, perhaps his divine face, perhaps someone who would make his presidential self look better on a photo (and the cameras were snapping), someone who looked Slavic and exotic, yet intelligible—the whole evil empire contracted in one photogenic brow of woe. So he asked Jozef, looking at the fat man, expecting him to interpret:

"What is your name, young fellow?"

"Jozef Pronek," Jozef answered, while the fat man was mouthing a translation of the question, spit burping in the corners of his lips.

"This place is holy ground. May God bless your country, son."

"It is not my country," Jozef said.

"Yes, it is," Bush said, and patted Jozef on his shoulder. "You bet your life it is. It is as yours as you make it."

"But I am from Bosnia . . ."

"It's all one big family, your country is. If there is misunderstanding, you oughtta work it out." Bush nodded, heartily agreeing with himself. Jozef stood still, his body taut and his smile lingering on his face, bedazzled by the uncanniness.

I knew then that I was in love with Jozef. I wanted Bush to embrace him, to press his cheek against Jozef, to appreciate him, maybe kiss him. I wanted to be Bush at that moment and face Jozef armed with desire. But Bush took off, his body exuding his content with his ability to connect with everyone. Would I were a rock—I stood there trembling with throbs of want, watching Jozef, with the sun behind his back. I replay this scene like a tape, rewinding it, slowing it down, trying to pin down the moment when our comradeship slipped into desire—the transition is evanescent, like the moment when the sun's rays change their angle, the light becomes a hairbreadth softer, and the world slides with nary a blink from summer into fall.

"Isn't that your roommate?" Will asked.

"Yes," I said. "Yes."

Jozef saw me then, waved at me, and shrugged, as if it all were an accident, rather than destiny. Oh, smite flat the thick rotundity of the world so we may never be apart.

———

Naturally, I stayed away from Jozef thereafter. That same night, I succumbed to Vivian's persistent, quiet presence, invited her to my room—as Jozef was off carousing somewhere—where we made out in my bed. She pressed her lips against mine and sucked them, I let my hands wander across her ribs and breasts, and tried to push my tongue into her mouth. It was a cumbersome protocoitus: I kept banging my knees against the steel edges of the bed, she—my slim Ophelia—kept slipping between the bed and the wall. In the end, we never managed to get to the penetration point, though there was some heavy, nervous petting. Need I say that I was distracted by Jozef's absent presence, that I could smell his clothes, and that, as I was trying to approach the lovemaking process from a different angle, my leg slipped off the bed and I stepped on his shoe? The part that I enjoyed, however, was the talk after our hapless semi-intercourse had been abandoned, under the pretense of everything being too soon. We were facing each other, inhaling each other's breath, whispering about the times when we were kids, when joys were simple and bountiful. She told me, her hand softly on my hip, how she had been so little as a kid that she could hang on a kitchen cabinet door and swing herself, back and forth. I remembered how my brother would swing me between his legs, then swing me somehow above his head and put me on his back. I did not want to fuck Vivian, I just wanted to hold her and talk to her. Even as she talked, I kept imagining Jozef in his bed, in his shorts, absentmindedly curling the hair around his nipples. Ah, get thee to a nunnery!

I spent a lot of time with Vivian henceforth: we were, for all intents and purposes, having a relationship. We would go to classes together, and sit next to each other—Jozef way above, behind my back, beyond my gaze. We would ask each other: "What do you wanna do tonight?" and respond: "I don't know, what do you wanna do?" It was always the same thing; we would go for a walk, then to the Armenian restaurant, then to Vivian's room— her roommate, one Jennifer from Winnipeg, was sleeping with Vladek somewhere else—where we made out a little, inching toward the ever remote penetration (Vivian was not ready yet, still afraid of the pain, though she was not, she said, a virgin), then exchange our memories. We had progressed to high adolescence, when I had taken up drugs, and she had taken up vegetables. Sometimes, she would decide to stay in her room and read about Ukrainian history, or translate some lousy Ukrainian poem, and I would play tennis with Will. He would easily crush me, generously suggesting exercises that would improve my regrettable footwork. Or we would play doubles: Will and me versus Mike and Basil. Will demanded an elaborate high-five after every win, though I never had anything to do with it. Then we would play poker, drinking infernal vodka. Will seemed to know everything about the current baseball season and we discussed it enveloped in the air of elite expertise, conscious that nobody in that damn country knew or cared about it. They also liked to talk about women: they wanted to know about Vivian's fucking habits (I could tell them little), while they seemed to possess information about Andrea (Mike claimed she liked to suck uncircumcised dick) and Jennifer of Winnipeg (she paid Vladek per fuck) and Father Petrol (who was caught jacking off in the bathroom). I was disgusted, of course, but on the other hand, their idiotic discourse was familiar and comfortable—it was my summer camp all over again.

I would go back to my room, feeling guilty, as if I had betrayed not only Vivian, but Jozef as well. He would sometimes be awake when I came in drunk, and we would engage in small talk. He told me about his little adventures in Kiev: in the post office, a man had whispered to him about the Stalin days, when people used to disappear, but you could buy sausage in stores; he had had some kvass and it was so horrible that he was happy he had tried it, because he could now tell everyone about it; Andrea had bought a Red Army officer's hat from a guy, who was also selling night-vision goggles—he was thinking about getting the goggles tomorrow. It was all laughter and amiability, but I felt as if we had broken up and were only friends now, desire banished from our land, even if it had never settled there.

Wide awake, I would stare at the ceiling camera, wishing I could get my paws on those tapes and watch Jozef waking up in the morning, his skin soft, with crease imprints, the fossils of slumber, on his bare shoulders; or see him making out with Andrea. I would close my eyes, and my mind would wander with my hand across his chest, down his abdomen. I would stop it on the underwear border, forcing myself to think about Vivian— you have to understand that I had never been attracted to a man before. It frightened me, and it was hard sometimes to discern between fear and arousal: the darkness throbbed around me, in harmony with my heart.

Occasionally, I would feel a compulsion to confess to Vivian: to tell her that being with her was only out of need for something safe and familiar; to tell her that I could not stop—and God knew I tried—thinking about my foreign roommate, even as she touched me and breathed into my face. But instead of confessing, I lectured her about my thesis and the homosocial relations in *King Lear;* and how the collapse of Lear's society was rendered by the emasculation in it; and how Lear's being alone with Cordelia before she dies was when he went beyond his masculinity, entering a different identity. I babbled and babbled, understanding along the way that I understood very little. Incredibly, she found it interesting: she swore in faith 'twas passing strange, 'twas wondrous pitiful. But what she actually said, I shall not recall before the next lifetime.

Jozef, naturally, suspected nothing: he cheerfully walked around half naked, was convinced that our new distance was due to our respective new girlfriends. I assumed this fake voice of male solidarity—the voice, I suspected, often heard in army barracks and trenches before nightly masturbation sessions—as we shared petty treasures, trinkets glittering only to easily arousable men: a vivid description of Vivian's nipples; a joke about Andrea's orgasmic yelps; the standard fantasies about having more than one woman in bed, and so on.

I remember the time when my father had been fired from his work as a security guard, spending a lot of time at home, mainly drinking, telling disconnected Bandera-times stories, and ripping cabinet doors off. But occasionally, he would be in a somber mood, slouching on the sofa in the dark living room, blinds rolled down, watching a daytime talk show with the sound off. I was sixteen or so, prone to avoiding my father's proximity as much as I could, but he seemed so helpless and aching at the time that I would just join him and watch TV in complete silence. I could never muster the audacity to prompt him to talk, and he never wanted to talk. We could hear Mother trudging through the apartment, but she was as shut off as the talk show. Once, as some shoddy porn stars were being interviewed, my father said, slowly, as if he had been thinking about it for a while, that he had some porn tapes and that we could watch them together sometime. I retched—I swear to God—it was so unthinkable to me. So I said: "No, are you fucking crazy?" and stormed out of the room. Yet, despite the nausea I still feel, that seemed to be the last time my father had wanted to give me any-thing and I had declined it. Men have died—worms have eaten them—but not for love.

The days after Babi Yar were days of torment. I spent a lot of time with people who ultimately made me feel frightfully lonely. More and more often, I roamed the streets of Kiev alone, collecting random particles of someone else's life: a throng of wizened carnations, sold by a decrepit *baba;* a woman tottering under the weight of bag clusters in her hands; a naked man-nequin in the dust-infested window of an empty store; a boy waiting with his father in front of a kvass kiosk, pale, a chenille of greenish snot stretching over his lips to his chin; the gnarly bars on the post office windows, eaten by rust; the ashtray brim-ming with cigarettes, lipstick moons on their ochre filters, in front of a post office teller named Oksana, who provided me with a phone line to Chicago.

My mother picked up the phone. I could hear the echo of my voice, and she was confused by the delay, so our words kept run-ning into one another:

"Mom, how are . . ."

"Victor, how . . ."

". . . you?"

". . . are you?"

"I'm good, . . ."

"Are you . . ."

". . . Mom."

". . . okay?"

"How . . ."

"Is everything . . ."

". . . is Dad?"

". . . okay?"

"Everything . . ."

"He . . ."

". . . is okay."

". . . is okay."

"Great."

"He is only . . ."

"Is he . . ."

". . . a little weak."

". . . okay?"

"Hello?"

"Okay?"

He was sick, I understood in spite of the echoes. High blood pressure, my mother said. He wasn't eating, couldn't digest food, my mother didn't say why, and I knew he wouldn't see the doctor, claiming he was fine, meaning he was tough. But I didn't want it clarified, I wanted to pretend that it was all so distant, many echoes away, because I could not deal with it. I finished the conversation with love that was to be shared by my mother with my father, an unlikely event. This was mid-August 1991.

I went down the stairs, still hung over, vaguely afraid of breaking my ankle and tumbling down the stairs only to have my neck snapped. As I was sinking into the hall, I saw Natalyka, the cleaning woman who would often walk into our room and admonish us for the mess; I saw Natalyka sitting despondently, watching TV, her head on the blubber-padded shoulder of another cleaning woman. Her log-thick legs were crossed at her swollen ankles. She kept her hands in the pockets of her formerly blue jacket, as if despair were a marble in her pocket. No one had ever watched TV in the hall, let alone this early—it was breakfast time. There was a crowd of people, whose faces had wandered through my hazy stay in this building, whose faces were now richly made up with dread and desolation.

August 21, 1991, will always have Natalyka's sorrowful face.

I sidled up behind the crowd and peeked at the TV, the way I join onlookers calmly watching an accident aftermath. A Brezhnev clone with a bass voice read a proclamation, sitting uncomfortably in the midst of a horrendous purple-velvet set, his tie breaking over his belly. It took me awhile to shake off my daze and parse what he was saying. The people around me shuffled their feet as if rattling their shackles. They murmured and sighed: somebody, I understood, took over the power, declared martial law, because of anarchy and disorder.

"Gorbachev is out," Will said, suddenly standing next to me. "There's been a coup."

"Oh, fuck!" I said.

"Exactly," Will said.

I must mention this: abruptly and against my will, as it were, I was close to Will—abruptly, he was someone I could trust. But I felt a cramping urge to locate Jozef and break the news to him, to produce wonder in his heart and excite him. So I flew upstairs, not caring about my ankles or my neck, followed by an echo of Natalyka's tormented gasp. I burst into the room without knocking, and Jozef was naked. I could not help noticing— and I was too excited to try—a hair vine crawling up from his sooty crotch to his navel, and curls spiraling around his nipples.

"There's been a coup!" I nearly hollered.

"What?"

"There's been a coup!" I hollered.

"What is coup?" It was rather annoying, his ignorant calm, his boxers sliding up his alabaster thighs.

"A coup, a violent takeover of power."

"Take over from where?"

"You know, a fucking revolution." What was wrong with him? He couldn't understand the basic information, let alone assuage my fears. What was I doing here?

"Revolution?" Jozef said, his eyebrows raised, the sun of comprehension rising from behind the dark mountain of his dimness. "Where is revolution? Who is organizing revolution?"

"God damn it, a putsch. Gorbachev's out." That was going to be my last attempt. He had no chest hair, and his navel had a birthmark satellite, shaped as a mouse.

"Putsch," he finally understood. "Maybe they want to arrest us."

Now, I have to confess that I hadn't thought of that—why would anyone want to arrest me?

"Trouble, trouble," he said.

I needed to talk to Will, so I left Jozef behind to wallow in his fake wisdom, muttering something in his weird language, and I ran downstairs. Down in the hall, there was no one but Natalyka, sitting in the same place, but no shoulder to support her, her hands dead in her lap, like hairless bloated hamsters, her round little body aweary of this great world. She was watching the Red Army choir, handsome men endowed with mandibular strength, thundering a victorious song.

I ran to the cafeteria, where there was a hopeful line of second-helpers, led by the indomitable Vladek, as if nothing had happened, but there was no Will. I ran to his room, leaping across stairs, rapidly running out of breath, and I found him there, with his ear pressed against his transistor radio.

"What's the news?" I asked in a series of pants that must have suggested frenzy.

"Haven't found any news yet," Will said. "I'm trying to find the Voice of America."

I had never been in Will's room—his clothes were neatly stacked in the closet, and he had tubular boxes full of fluorescent-green tennis balls positioned unrandomly around his room like little watchtowers. He had a family picture on the nightstand: there were five of them, Will in the center, flanked by his sisters, Mom and Dad standing behind them. They were sublimely beautiful, blond and suburbanly, all resembling one another as if they were a variation on the same person, a family procreated by fission rather than fucking.

"What are we going to do, Will?"

"Well, they can't arrest *us*. And even if they arrest us, they will exchange us. We don't leave anyone behind."

"I never thought of it that way."

"I mean if the American embassy knows we are here, they are going to get someone to get us. They might send a bunch of marines or something. We take care of our people, right?"

"Do they know we are here?" I imagined a herd of robust marines storming into the building, the sergeant bellowing: "Move! Move!" shooting to pieces whoever unwisely stood in their way, crawling along the walls, exchanging mysterious finger signs, patriotic paint smudged all over their endearingly familiar faces.

"I don't know," Will said. "I hope they do. I want to go home."

"But what are we going to do until they come?"

"We're gonna stay put. Get your stuff ready in case we have to leave soon. I'm gonna talk to other people. We oughtta have a meeting."

I ran back to my room, but Jozef was not there. All that running: maybe I didn't run at all, but now as I remember it, it all seem speeded up, with plenty of huffing and puffing and urgency. And I was tired and the running (if indeed there was any) seemed pointless. The bed beckoned me and I stretched on it, pulling the blanket over my head. Here is a confession: When the future is uncertain, when there are many events in the womb of time about to be delivered, I take a nap. I roll down the shades and creep under a blanket and cover my head, and I try to imagine a safe, warm place—a tip from my therapist. Usually, it is my tent. We are on a camping trip in Wisconsin, somewhere near a shimmering lake. The sides of the tent are throbbing slightly. I can hear the crickets on the fragrant pines, and I can hear my mother humming an Irish song. The shadows of the pine's branches are quivering above my head, and I can hear the splashing of the struggling fish my dad is pulling out of the lake.

A cold hand on my forehead woke me up, and before I could see her face darkened and haloed by the background light, I recognized her smell: sweet sweat and coconut.

"Are you sleeping?"

"What do you think?"

"Have you heard?"

"Yup."

"How can you sleep?"

"How can you not sleep?"

"Can I come into bed with you?"

"Sure."

Vivian took off her sandals and her hairpins and weightlessly landed her body next to mine. She had on the flowery dress, which slid up to her thighs, and I could feel them against mine. She kissed my neck, and I curled her hair behind her ear. She put her hand on my stomach and then it edged toward my underwear.

Never mind the details: there was penetration, there was pain, and she was a virgin; there was guilt and avoiding each other's eyes afterward, yet there were touches that implied the required postcoital closeness; there was sweat mixing. And there was embarrassment with the rich assortment of bodily imperfections: a solitary red pimple gestating on my chest; her asymmetrical, cross-eyed breasts; my nose hair; the charcoal-dust hair on the fringe of her cheek. We exchanged sussurous, empty words, not quite lies, but certainly not truthful, while my body tensed and tightened, eager to get out of her hold. I imagined describing the whole haphazard event to Will, Mike, and Basil and the salvos of laughter I would get, knowing all along that I could not do it. And I kept fretting that Jozef might come in, trying to think of things I could say to dispel the accusatory, questioning gaze, and the only thing I could think of—eminently useless—was: "We're just friends." God help me. It was much easier to succumb to sleep than to expect Jozef, and succumb I did, again.

Then the door of our room went down with a horrible crash and a bunch of KGB men with painted faces burst in, ripped us out of our beds, threw us on the floor. One of them stepped on my neck, pressing it with his boot viciously. The pain was intense, my neck stiffening up, but it was pleasurable and when they handcuffed us together, Jozef and me, I found myself wanting a second helping of that pain. They pushed us down the stairs and I twisted my ankle, but Jozef kept me from falling and breaking my neck. Then they ushered us with their rifle butts into a Black—very black—Maria. And when we entered it, I could not see anything, and I did not know whether it was because we were blindfolded or because the darkness was so thick that I could not see Jozef's face, even if our breaths embraced together. But I could feel his bleeding wrist fidgeting on the other end of the handcuffs that tied us. Then we escaped from the Black Marenyka, when they stopped to pick up more arrestees—I recognized Mike and Vivian and wondered where Will might be—Jozef head-butted a guard and barged forward. We heard shouts and shots and the gallop of boots, but we were hidden by the darkness. I just followed Jozef and we ran and ran, but it was as if we were skidding along the surface of a placid sea. I simply let myself go, gliding over water, and then we hid in the forests of Ukraine. We dug a hole in the ground, and woke up sheathed with frost. We bit off chicken heads and drank the blood straight out of the necks. We hopped on a train, where Jozef strangled a policeman, while my hand-cuffed hand shook like a rattle in front of the dying policeman's crooked eyes. We crossed borders and more borders, some of them were hedges, with watchtowers and sharpshooters strewn all over, waving at us, letting us through, so they could shoot us in the back. And they shot and I could feel their bullets going through me. Then we slept on a train car floor, like hobos, there was no one there, but as we slept, it filled with furniture and people sitting in armchairs and on sofas, and Jozef and I were sitting next to each other, and somehow our hips were handcuffed, and where the handcuff bit into my flesh there was a hole and I was leaking out, buckets of bile.

It was Will who walked in on us. It was morning again, we slept with our backs turned to each other, Vivian's full frontal nudity facing the door.

"Jesus," Will said, and Vivian covered herself. Jozef still was not in the room. Will brandished a tennis racket, as if it were a sword. He leaned over us—we could see our distorted little heads in his glasses—and said: "Meeting. In my room. In fifteen minutes."

I may be this, and I may be that, but when I am told there is a meeting, I get up and attend the meeting.

"I need to go to my room," Vivian said, pale and in need of a carrot or something.

"Okay."

The meeting, ah, the meeting: Vivian and I, sitting on Will's bed next to each other. Mike and Basil on the other bed, and Will amidst us—his family benevolently beaming at all of us. Andrea was not there, probably stretching in her bed next to Jozef. Will told us what he knew: there had been a coup; Gorbachev was in the Crimea, under house arrest; hard-line Communists and generals took over; there were arrests everywhere, people disappearing; street fighting in Leningrad, tanks on the streets, bloodshed; large army contingent movements from western Ukraine and Belorussia toward Kiev. He had received a call at Igor's office from his father, who for some reason was in Munich. Will told us everything was good at home, and I may be misremembering a collective sigh of relief.

"We gotta get the hell out of here," Basil said.

"We gotta wait," Will said, "until we know what is going on. I think we are okay here."

He ordered us not to leave the school and to let him know at any given time where we were. Throughout this performance, he had a somber frown and kept pushing up his glasses, mindfully allotting his glances in equal numbers to all of us. He instructed Vivian to inform Andrea about our meeting and its conclusions, and he told Mike and Basil that he needed to talk to them after the meeting—I seemed to be out of the loop, though I didn't know what they were looping for.

Jozef was back in our room, radiant on his bed, not able to suppress his grin, his hand roaming under his shirt, as if marking the kiss traces, the tongue trails.

"It looks like you had some fun last night," I said.

"Love is beautiful thing," he said, pronouncing *thing* as *ting*.

"It is indeed," I said, for a moment entertaining the thought of telling him about my *ting*.

"They demonstrate on Khreschatek," he said. "Many people, all night. Police is everywhere. I go now, again. You want to go?"

"Oh, I don't know. I have to talk to Will."

"Why?"

"Well, because we had a meeting this morning."

"Which meeting?"

"Meeting, you know. We organized ourselves. We have to know where every one of us is, in case of trouble."

He put his left foot on his right knee, the sole facing me, and then went on picking on corns, peeling off dead skin, sliver by sliver, his toes watching it like five retarded hick brothers.

"You are like child. You must tell your parents where are you."

"No, man. It's just common sense."

"When you don't tell parents, you are bad boy. Bad boy," he said, scowling at his heel.

"That's stupid," I groused. "I don't have to prove anything to you, you know."

"I know. I go now."

"Who the hell do you think you are?" I said, and threw a pillow at the other pillow on my bed.

"I go now," Jozef said. "You don't want to go?"

I followed him. We walked: it was a long walk, through largely deserted streets, except for a sporadic pedestrian, ambling conspiratorially, or an ominous truck of soldiers, roaring by, under a roof of tree crowns touching one another above the street. We didn't talk much; we heard birds chirruping and ruffling the leaves above our heads; the concrete was warm, and the light was soft, diffused by the humid air and the tree shade; fall was near. We walked by open windows exuding boiled-dough steam; by basement doors giving off damp coal-dust scent; by shuddering lacy curtains, behind which a shadow of an old woman's face was recognizable for a moment. A cat crossed the street with her belly lowered, and her head ducked, and then stopped in the middle to look at us in affronted amazement. The sun twinkled from the tree crowns, for a whir of wind divided the leaves for an instant. But then we turned the corner and there was Khreshchatek: giant ore-brown men looming over austere concrete steps, too big to be human, their gaze directed at the horizon of rooftops, over our heads. There was a large crowd at the bottom of the stairs, with a speaker elevated above it, thundering into the squealing microphone something I could not understand. We saw a line of policemen standing a little below the giants' feet, up on the stairs, solemnly lined up like a choir, their hands on their asses. And then another police line, behind the speaker, in the shadow of the trees. We joined the crowd—I followed Jozef, who moved closer to the speaker—and stood there, unsure what to do, other than applaud when everyone else did. The mustached guy standing next to me, with an unruly dandruffy lock poking his eyebrows, spoke to no one in particular about the police coming down and wiping the demonstrators out. I was taken aback, because he was the King of Midnight himself; even if I was not sure about his face, I recognized Antarctica. I don't know if he recognized me, but he pointed at the trucks behind the backs of the umbrous policemen, deeper in the shadow.

"We go closer. I want to listen that man," Jozef said, and started moving closer to the speaker.

"I don't think that is a good idea," I said, but Jozef was already pushing his way through the throng, so I followed him. We ended up practically in front of the speaker, only a few wide-shouldered security men in front of us, looking up at him. The speaker had tears in his eyes, and he clenched black-and-white photographs in his hand. He kept ranting about genocide and Russians and plague, flipping and showing the photographs: a wasteland recognizable as Chernobyl; crooked and cramped tree branches, with misshapen monster leaves; a two-headed mouse, with only two eyes, the two snouts pointing in different directions.

My mind was brilliantly clear, aware of everything around me: the screeching and buzzing of a transistor radio; the hairy rungs of fat on the neck of the man right in front of me; the lemony smell of Jozef's skin; the policemen's seal-skin batons, doubtless bloodied many a time; the striped shirts of the KGB men who stepped out of their trucks and smoked, staring at us; the rustle among the policemen, the shuffle of their feet; the crowd cringing and contracting, before the policemen stopped; the woman high up in the window of one of the buildings, leaning out and calmly smoking, watching the whole shebang without particular interest.

Jozef gently put his hand on my shoulder and whispered into my ear, his lips touching the lobe: "When police attack, we must run, and if we lost ourselves we must run this way"—he pointed toward a red kvass kiosk—"and meet there."

"Sure," I said, but did not really want to leave, for I knew that nothing could happen to us today, that even if they arrested us we would get away together, that this was our souls' wedding; a wave of euphoric tranquillity went over me. I did not want to move, cherishing Jozef's palm on my shoulder—I can feel its weight now, his breath brushing the side of my neck. There was nowhere to go beyond this moment. I knew I should try to live in it for as long as possible. There was nothing to lose and everything to gain by being as present as possible.

So I turned to him and grabbed his face with both of my hands, and pressed my lips against his, feeling the air coming out of his nostrils on my cheek. To the men around us, it could have seemed a typically Slavic outpouring of brotherly feelings, but Jozef knew what I was doing, for I tried to put my tongue into his mouth. He opened his mouth and let my tongue in, then kept it in. Then he kissed my neck, bit my shoulder gently, and slipped his hand under my shirt. I grabbed his shoulders and pulled him closer to me. We kissed for an eternity, could not separate.

A bird slams into the window of my office and startles me—my heart is galloping in frantic circles. The bird—a comatose sparrow—lies on its back on the windowsill, its little claws grasping nuggets of nothingness. I stored that kiss in the cryogenic chamber of my soul for some future, whose prospects are diminishing daily, and sometimes I take it out and tempt myself with the thought of thawing it. Outside, I can hear the din of the waiting students: a few young women with their feminist paper proposals on *Midsummer Night's Dream;* a winsome young fellow who wants to write about Hamlet and Kurt Cobain. Around me, there are stacks of knowledgeable books, some of which I have flipped through impatiently in the past few years, looking for some kind of wisdom or, at least, references to my published articles. I loved Jozef Pronek because I thought that he was the simple me, the person I would have been had I known how to live a life, how to be accommodated in this world. Today, I garbled through the class, teaching *Lear,* soliciting ideas from my students about the ways in which Lear's power was *discreated,* and what it meant to him as a man. But it was routinely absurd—everyone had something to say, everyone had half-baked opinions based on how they felt about this and that—and I kept wanting to read them the passage when Lear and Cordelia are about to go to prison, and Lear says: "Come, let's away to prison." And he tells Cordelia about all the things they can do together in prison: they will live, and pray, and sing, and tell old tales, and laugh at gilded butterflies, and hear poor rogues talk of court news, and they'll talk with them too—who loses and who wins, who's in, who's out, and take upon themselves the mystery of things, as if they were God's spies. And Cordelia says nothing beyond that point, she does not utter a word, they take them to prison and she's killed, Lear dies. I wanted to read that with them, and then sit in silence, make them imagine all the things that Cordelia might have said, think of all the things I could have said, and let the uncomplicated sorrow settle in and stay with me, like a childhood friend.

We stood there, his hand on my neck, and listened to exhilarated speeches about the greatness of this moment, about the future shining bright behind dark clouds that hid our horizons. People cheered, and applauded, and sang songs about freedom. Police-men did not move, the KGB did not move, the giants did not move, I never kissed Jozef. I pretended to be listening carefully to the speakers, while I was trying to make a decision, one moment after another, and then turn to him, grab his face, and press my lips against his, dizzyingly aware all along how impossible it was. Jozef stood next to me, oblivious to my desire, unsinged by the fires of my hell. My stomach quivered, and iron fists pressed against my temples, until my sinuses were throbbing. He might have said something, I might have responded. He might have touched me a few times, I might have shuddered. But I looked not at him, and I touched him not, and it all lasted for years. Finally, we walked back to the Party dorm. Jozef went to look for Andrea. I went back to my room and fell asleep.

When I woke up, Vivian was resting her face on her palm, curled next to me. I thought for a moment that I had dreamt it all: the putsch, the non-kiss, my life. Vivian stroked my cheek, and told me that Ukraine was independent now. I told her to go away, that I didn't want to see her anymore, that it was not her, it was me. "Why? Why?" she cried. The image of her arched back and her craning neck as she left the room still, often, makes me contemplate my cruelty, producing a sneeze of intense grief. But I take out a handkerchief and wipe my runny moral nose.

I crept out of bed in the days after freedom arrived only to call home. Exhilarated gangs of newly independent Ukrainians still roamed the streets with blue-and-yellow flags. I talked to my father, who vociferated, in an exhausted, coarse voice: "*Shche ne vmrela Ukraina!*" Ukraine hasn't died yet! But he was about to die, my mother outright told me, too fatigued to lie. Everything inside him, she said, had been eaten away by cancer—it was a matter of days.

I found Jozef in Andrea's room playing chess with her. Andrea's things: underwear and shirts and bras and crumpled tissues were strewn around, as if a hand grenade had exploded in her room. I kept it simple and poignant. I told Jozef that I had just found out that my father was dying, from belatedly discovered cancer. He hugged me, his breath sliding down my neck. Andrea hugged me too, kissed my cheek, her lips warm and sincere. I thought then I would look her up in Chicago, but I never did. I never saw her again, and I never saw Jozef. Although there have been passersby and strangers who cruelly wore his lovely face and sometimes I recognize him among the extras in a lame Hollywood movie. Once I saw his face on TV in the crowd of Greenpeace protesters chanting some nonsense in front of a nuclear facility. I am used to those fantasies now, as one gets used to the voices of the dead talking to him.

I packed up, said good-bye to Will—there were actually tears in his eyes when he said: "I know your old man will be okay." I took the night train to Warsaw and flew to Chicago, via Frankfurt, all in dazed numb pain, my only entertainment nightmares full of remorse. The funeral was the day of my arrival—he perished while I was in the Frankfurt Airport duty-free shop, considerately buying a few bottles of Absolut vodka that would be consumed at his wake. Straight from the airport, I sat in the first row at the Muzyka funeral home, with my sobbing, shuddering mother, dressed in deep black, while my father lay in an open coffin, and his war comrades—old men in dun suits that had been growing bigger on them, exuding defunct-prostate stench—held on to Ukrainian flags, and delivered speeches about my father's loyalty and generosity, about his love for Ukraine, about his final moments of sublime joy as he lived to see his homeland free. *Pan* Bek wept as he read a Taras Shevchenko poem that had our wheat fields extending into eternity. Then they all sang *"Shche Ne Vmrela Ukraina"* looking up, as if freedom were hiding its misshapen face behind fire alarms and dim ceiling lights. Finally, my mother and I stood up and walked to kiss my father good-bye, before they closed the casket for good. His face was laminated and hardened, his eyelids stiff as bottlecaps. As I leaned over him, I could see the tips of his trimmed nose hair, peering out of the dark nostril holes, but not moving, no breath coming out to tickle them. I kissed my father gently: his lips were frigid and tight. I know now when one is dead and when one lives.

4

Translated by Jozef Pronek

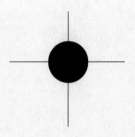

SARAJEVO, DECEMBER 1995

Dear Jozef!

Here I am writing you. Maybe you thought I am dead, but I am not. It is hard here, but we are happy that war is over. How are you? How is America? When are you going to come back?

I am little sad. Yesterday I remembered when I saw horse near Koševo and I think about it all the time. I don't know, I must tell you some things. This horse was walking on street, free, and five minutes ago there was granading, everywhere dust and pieces of glass. I was guarding hospital and horse was standing in front of the big window that didn't break and he was looking himself, like in the mirror. He turned to one side, he turned to another side and he was thinking, Look how beautiful I am. He was turning and he was liking himself. Then the shell rocked and explosion broke the window and horse run away. He was beautiful, big eyes, pretty face, he was white and high, with black tail. He ran away like those horses in American films.

I never used gun in this war. I was working in the hospital help-ing people dying. Sometimes I would go to the line and they give me the gun, but I never used the gun. I was waiting in the dark, and you look in the dark and you know Chetniks are there and maybe they are watching you. One time I was with my friend Jas-min (you don't know him) and we are talking and I see red full stop on his forehead and one secund later his head explodes like pomegrante. That second when I see it but I cannot say nothing, because the death is very fast, that second is the worst second of my life. I was on Žuč, also. I don't know if you know where is Žuč, but many people died there. I saw many bad things. It is hard to sleep. I saw bad things on our side. One time, I talked to one man who was our sniper and his position was on Hotel Bristol. And everyday he watched this soldier meet his woman. She would come from home and he would come from his position and they kiss and hold hands. Then she goes home and he goes back to his unit. This sniper man said that he thinks it is nice, you know, this love, so he watches them everyday. He can kill them, but it is nice, love. The woman was pretty. But one day she comes and stands little far away and he can see the soldier standing at normal place and she tells him with her hand to come to her, and he says no and then she calls him and then he comes to her. And the sniper man kills him. He tells me, if woman can tell him what he must do, he cannot live, so he killed him. And you know what is worst, I thought it is funny, we laughed like crazy. We were little crazy then, Chetniks killed us all the time. You didn't see nothing until you see when grenade hits line for water. People have to wait, because that is only water they can have, and they know Chetniks are watching and then the grenade rocks and you see brains and stomach and spine, children, women, all dead, small pieces of meat.

But I talk too much. See I don't know what about can I talk. War is everything to me. I want to talk about something different, but I didn't see no movies, no music, no books. No, I read one book, from our childhood: Heroes of Pavlo's Street. You know that book, about boys who build the fortress and they fight other boys. When I went on Treskavica I brought the book with me. You don't know Treskavica. We grew up in Sarajevo, we are children of asphalt.

You cannot imagine Treskavica. That mountain is so wild, it is nothing: stones and cliffs and canyons and holes and three million years old. Human foot did not go there for hundred years. Last battle of the war was on Treskavica, I don't know if you know that. Bosses were in Dayton, talking like friends and we had to go and fight for that desert. And you know what I did. I had to carry wounded and dead. Us six, we had to carry one stretcher and change, with one wounded man. Sometimes this wounded man has no legs, just bleeding and they give him morphine. But we have to carry him six hours over the stones and the cliffs and over canyons and if we slip we fall into abyss. After two hours morphine stops to help and his pain is back and he is throwing himself around like little pig and he is hitting us with his hands in the head, like we are gulity for his pain. Sometimes he dies, and we like that, because we don't have to hurry. We sit down and smoke and somebody has some alcohol. But wounded man has his friend or brother following us and he says, If he dies I kill you and he makes us run, we have to run down the hill so steep and so high you get vertigo. We run six hours, we think we will die. Treskavica is very far away from everything. Sometimes we run for six hours to take this man to the hospital and he died after five minutes and we didn't know. It was crazy. I saw a horse kill himself on Treskavica. We carried this man which had to hold his stomach with hand so it doesn't fall out. He was screaming all the time, and we must run. But we ran by one unite, they had camp nearby the edge of one cliff—you look down, and it is just one big deep hole in the earth. This man died finally, so we stop to have little water and we are sitting there, we cannot breath. It is so high there is not air. We see their horse, who carried their munition, very skinny and hungry and sad. The horse goes slowly to the edge, we think he wants some grass there. Some soldiers yell, Come back! But he walks slowly and then he stops on the edge. We watch him three meters away. He turns around, looks at us directly in our eyes, like person, big, wet eyes and then just jumps—hop! He just jumps and we can hear remote echo of his body hitting stones. I never saw anything so much sad.

I am sorry I talk too much. We in Sarajevo have nobody to talk, just each other, nobody wants to listen to these stories. I cannot talk more. You talk now. I am waiting for your letter. You must write me. Send me one book, I can read little English language, maybe one detective novel, maybe something about children. See I'm little crazy. Write me.

Yours.
Mirza

P.S. Happy New Year!

5

The Deep Sleep

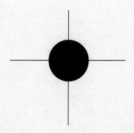

CHICAGO, SEPTEMBER 1/
OCTOBER 15, 1995

The slumbering guard, about to slide off his chair, had his fingers on the holstered revolver. Pronek passed him by, pushed the grill door aside, and stepped into the elevator. The elevator was rife with a woman's fragrant absence: peachy, skinny, dense. Pronek imagined the woman who might have exuded that scent, and she was worth a stare. She was tall and rangy and strong-looking; her hair was black and wiry and parted in the middle; she had black eyes and a sulky droop to her lips. She took a cigarette out of her purse, which was heavier than it needed to be, turned to him and said, expecting a friendly lighter: "I've been searching for someone, and now I know who."

Pronek's eyes narrowed as he looked at the space where the woman would have stood, and he saw himself through her eyes: tall, formerly lanky, so his relaxed movements did not match his fat-padded trunk; his head almost shaved, marred by a few pale patches (he cut his own hair); a gray sweatshirt that read ILLI-NOIS across his chest; worn-out jeans with a few pomegranate-juice splotches; and boots that had an army look, save for the crack in his left sole—September rains had already soaked his left sock. As he stepped out of the elevator, a whiff of the fragrant cloud followed him out. He stood in the empty hall: on the left and on the right, there were rows of doors standing at attention in the walls. Above a door on the right was a lit exit sign. Pronek made an effort to remember the position—in case he was too much in a hurry to wait for an elevator. He was looking for office number 909 and decided to go right. The colorless carpet muffled his careful steps. The elbow-shaped hall reeked of bathroom ammonia and sweet cigars, and the fragrant whiff dissipated in it. Pronek tried to open the bathroom door—green, sturdy, with a silhouette of a man—but it was locked. When he pushed the door with his shoulder, it rattled: he could break it open without too much force. He figured that there would be fire stairs behind a milky bathroom window, and that the alley would lead to Michigan Avenue, where he could safely disappear in the street mass.

All of a sudden, Pronek became aware of a sound that had been in his ears for a while but not quite reaching his brain: it was a smothered, popping sound—first one, then two—with a click at the end. Much like the sound of a gun with a silencer. Pronek's muscles tensed and his heart started thumping like a jungle drum—he was convinced that the hall was echoing his accelerating pulse. He felt his eyebrows dewing, thick loaves of pain forming in his calves. He tiptoed past the doors: 902 (Sternwood Steel Export); 904 (Marlowe Van Buren Software); 906 (Bernard Ohls Legal Services); 908 (empty); 910 (Riordan & Florian Dental Office)—the popping, along with the murky light, came from behind the dim glass of 910. Pronek imagined bodies lined up on the floor facedown, some of them already dead, with their blood and hair on the wall, their brains bubbling on the carpet. They were shivering, waiting for a quiet man with a marble-gray face to pop them in their napes, knowing they would end up in unmarked graves. They reacted to the surprising bullet with a spasm, then death relaxation, then their blood placidly soaking the carpet. There was another pop. There had been at least six of them, and Pronek reckoned that the killer must be running out of bullets. It was risky, it was none of his business, so he twisted the door handle and peeked in.

A large man in a yellow helmet was pressing his orange staple gun against the far wall. He sensed Pronek and turned around slowly. His skin was pale and he needed a shave. He had dirty overalls and a green shirt underneath, with tiny golf balls instead of buttons. He stood firmly facing Pronek, his jaw tense, as if expecting a punch, his staple gun pointing to the floor. "Can I help you with something?" he said, frowning under his helmet. Pronek could see his eyebrows almost encountering each other above his nose. "Sorry," Pronek said. "I look for the office 909."

Office 909 had a sign that read GREAT LAKES EYE and a black-and-white eye with long, upward-curling eyelashes. Pronek hesitated for a moment before knocking at the door—his fingers levitated, angled, in front of the eye. Pronek knocked, using three of his knuckles, the glass shook perilously, then he opened the door and entered an empty waiting room. There was another door, closed, and there were magazines strewn on the few chairs, even on the musty floor, as if someone had searched through them all. The waiting room was lit by a thin-necked lamp in the corner, leaning slightly as if about to snap. There was an under-developed cobweb without a spider in the upper left corner. A picture of an elaborate ocean sunset—as if somebody lit a match under the water—hung on the opposite wall. ACAPULCO, it said in the lower right corner, WHERE YOU WANT TO DREAM. Pronek stood in front of the picture, imagining himself playing the guitar on a beach in Acapulco, tears welling up in his eyes.

The door opened and a man and a woman came out. They

were laughing convivially with someone who remained invisible. The man—tall and black—put on a fedora with a little bluish feather, which went perfectly with his dapper navy blue suit, snug on his wide shoulders, and his alligator boots with little explosions on his toes. The woman was pale and slim, with blond boyish hair and a pointy chin. She had a tight, muscular body, like a long-distance runner, and a beautiful lean neck. She kept the tip of her finger on her chin as she listened to the man inside, who said: "What you wanna do is get some pictures." Pronek imagined touching gently the back of her neck, below the little tail of hair on her nape, and he imagined the tingle that would make her shudder. "You bet," the woman said, stepping out of the waiting room, barely glancing at Pronek. "You got yourself a client, Owen," the dapper man said, following the woman, and a head sprung out of the door, eyes bulging to detect Pronek. "Gee, a client," the head said, and the couple giggled as they closed the door. "Why don't you come in."

Pronek followed the man inside, closing the croaking door behind him. The room was bright, its windows looking at Grant Park and the dun lake beyond it, waves gliding toward the shore. There was a sofa with a disintegrating lily pattern and a coffee table with a chess board on it. Pronek landed in the sofa and the fissures between the cushions widened and gaped at Pronek's thighs.

"My name is Taylor Owen," the man said.

"I am Pronek," Pronek said. "Jozef Pronek."

"Good to meet you, Joe," Owen said.

Owen had sweat shadows under his armpits and a hump on his back, as if there were a pillow under his beige shirt. His tie was watermelon red, tightly knotted under his Adam's apple, which flexed sprightly like a Ping-Pong ball as he spoke. He was bald, with a little island of useless hair above his forehead and a couple of grayish tufts fluffing over his ears. He sat behind a narrow desk piled with papers, the back of his head touching the wall as he leaned in his chair.

"I called. I talked to somebody," Pronek said, "about the job. I thought you need the detective."

"The detective?" Owen chortled. "Lemme guess: you seen a few detective movies, right? The Bogart kind of stuff?"

"No," Pronek said. "Well, yes. But I know it is not like that."

Owen stared at him for a long instant, as if deciding what to do with him, then asked: "Where you from?"

"Bosnia."

"Never heard of it."

"It was in Yugoslavia."

"Ah!" Owen said, relieved. "It's a good place not to be there right now."

"No," Pronek said.

"You a war veteran?"

"No. I came here just before the war."

"You have a blue card?"

"What?"

"You have any security experience?"

"No."

"See, son, we don't have detectives around here no more. Detectives are long gone. We used to be private investigators, but that's over too. We're operatives now. See what I mean?"

"Yeah," Pronek said. There was a black-and-gray pigeon on the windowsill, huddled in the corner, as if freezing.

"No Bogey around here, son. I been in this business for a good long time. Started in the sixties, worked in the seventies. Still work. Know what I mean?"

"Yeah."

"I worked when Papa Daley was running the Machine . . ."

The phone rang behind the parapet of papers, startling Pronek. Owen snatched the receiver out of its bed and said: "Yup." He turned away from Pronek toward the window, but looked over the shivering pigeon, out to the lake. It was a sunny day, cold and blustery still. The wind gasped abruptly, then pushed the windowpane with a thump, overriding the grumbling hum of Michigan Avenue. Above Owen's hump there was a picture of an army of bulls chasing a throng of men with red scarves down a narrow street. Some of the men were being trampled by bulls who didn't seem to notice them.

"You can kiss that sonovabitch good-bye," Owen said, throwing his feet up on the corner of his desk and rocking in his chair. "You're kidding me. Shampoo? You gotta be kidding me."

On the desk, there was a pile of letters ripped open, apparently with little patience, and a couple of thick black files. Owen scratched the hair island, the size of a quarter, with his pinkie, beginning to rock faster. The pigeon barely had its eyes open, but then it turned its head back and looked straight at Pronek, smirking. Pronek crossed his legs and tightened his butt muscles, repressing a flatulence.

"I know what you up against. It sure is tough. Join the rest of the fucking world." He listened for a moment. "Skip the wisecracks, darling, all right?"

The pigeon was bloated, as if there were a little balloon under the feathers. What if the pigeon was a surveillance device, Pronek thought, a dummy pigeon with a tiny camera in its head, pretending to be sick, watching them.

"All right, I'll see you after the fight tonight. Love ya too," Owen said, and hung up. He swung back on his chair toward

Pronek, sighed and said: "My wife is a boxing judge. Can you believe that? A boxing judge. She sits by the rink, watching two guys pummel each other, counting punches. Hell, people think I'm making that up when I tell them."

"It's normal," Pronek said, not knowing what to say.

Owen opened a drawer in his desk, the drawer resisting with a bloodcurdling screech, and produced a bottle of Wild Turkey. He poured a generous gulp in a cup that had CHICAGO BULLS written around it, shaking his head as if already regretting his decision. He slurped from the cup and his face cramped, as if he had swallowed urine, then it settled down, a little redder now. He looked at Pronek, trying to see through him.

"So you wanna be an operative?"

"I would like to be," Pronek said.

"We don't solve big cases here. Rich women don't make passes at us. We don't tell off big bosses, and we don't wake up in a ditch with a cracked head. We just earn our daily bread doing divorces, checking backgrounds, chasing down deadbeat dads, know what I mean? It's all work, no adventure, pays the rent. Got it?"

"Yeah," Pronek said.

"Do you know where the Board of Education is?"

"In the downtown," Pronek said.

"Do you know where Pullman is?"

"No."

"Way south. Do you know where the Six Corners is?"

"No."

"Irving Park and . . . Oh, fuck it! Do you have a car?"

"No. But I want to buy the car." Pronek started fidgeting in his chair. A drop of sweat rolled down from his left armpit.

"Do you have a camera?"

"No."

"Do you know how to tail."

"Tale?" Pronek asked, perplexed. "You mean, tell the tale?"

Owen formed a pyramid with his hands and put its tip under his nose, then pushed his nose up a little, so the bridge of his nose wrinkled. He glared at Pronek, as if affronted by his sheer presence, curling his lips inward, until his mouth was just a straight line. Pronek wanted to tell him that he could learn, that he was really smart, that he used to be a journalist, talked to people—he could make himself over to be an operative. But it was too late: Owen was blinking in slow motion, gathering strength to finish the interview off. He dismantled the pyramid, unfurled his lips and said:

"Listen, son, I like you. I admire people like you, that's what this country is all about: the wretched refuse coming and becoming American. My mother's family was like that, all the way from Poland. But I ain't gonna give you a job just 'cause I like you. Gotta pay my rent too, know what I mean? Tell you what I'll do: give me your phone and I'll call you if something comes up, okay?"

"Okay," Pronek said.

Owen was watching him, probably expecting him to get up, shake hands and leave, but Pronek's body was suddenly heavy and he could not get up from the sofa. Nothing in the room moved or produced a sound. They could hear the ill cooing of the pigeon.

"Okay," Owen repeated, as if to break the spell.

Pronek stood at the corner of Granville and Broadway, watching his breath clouding and dissolving before his eyes, waiting for Owen. The picture-frame shop across the street had nicely framed Halloween paintings in the window—ghosts hovering over disheveled children, ghouls rising out of graves. The shop window was brightening as the sun was moving slowly out of the lake, most of it still underwater. A man with a rotund goiter growing sideways on his neck was entering the diner on Granville. Pronek thought that the man was growing another, smaller head and imagined a relief of a little, wicked face under the taut goiter skin. Across Broadway, they were tearing down a Shoney's: what used to be its parking lot was just a mud field now. The building was windowless; floors ripped out; cables hanging from the ceiling like nerves. Just in front of Pronek, a throbbing car stopped at the street light, inhabited by a teenager who had a shield of gold chains on his chest. He was drumming on the wheel with his index fingers, then looked up, pointed one of his fingers at Pronek, and pretended to shoot him. Pronek smiled, as if getting the joke, but then the teenager turned east and disappeared down Granville. Pronek was cold, Owen was late. A *Chicago Tribune* headline, behind the filthy glass of a newspaper box, read THOUSANDS KILLED IN SREBRENICA. In the distance, Pronek saw a boxy Broadway bus stopping every once in a while on the empty street, sunlight shimmering on its windshield.

Owen pulled up, materializing out of nowhere, brakes screeching, right in front of Pronek. He drove an old Cadillac that looked like a hideous offspring of a tank and a wheel cart. Before Pronek could move toward the car, Owen honked impatiently, and the sound violated the early morning hum. Pronek opened the door, and an eddy of cigarette smoke and coffee smell escaped into the street. Owen said nothing, put the car in gear and drove off—a bus whizzed by, barely missing them. He drove with both of his hands on top of the wheel, alternately looking at the street and frowning at the tip of his cigarette as it was being transformed into its own ashen ghost. Finally, the ash broke off and fell into his lap. Owen said, as if on cue: "Damn, it's early. But what can we do? We gotta get this guy while he's home sleeping."

Pronek was silent, mulling over a question that would not require too many words. They were waiting at the light on Hollywood. The car in front of them had a bumper sticker reading: IF YOU DON'T LIKE MY DRIVING CALL 1–800–EATSHIT.

"Who is this man?" Pronek asked.

"He's a character, lemme tell you. He's Serbian, I believe. Been here for fifteen years or so, married an American girl, had a child, and then split after years of marriage. He's a runaway daddy, is what he is. Couldn't find the sonovabitch, wouldn't show up in court, the lady couldn't get child support. I gotta get him to accept the court summons, so if he doesn't show up in court, we can get cops on his ass. Are you all like that over there, sonovabitches?"

He put out his cigarette in the ashtray already teeming with butts, a few of them falling on the floor. Pronek imagined himself snorting up all those ashes and butts: it would be a good way to exhort a confession under torture. He coughed nauseatedly.

"What are you?" Owen asked. "It's Serbs fighting Muslims over there, right? Are you a Serb or a Muslim?"

"I am complicated," Pronek said, and retched. The car was like a gas chamber, and Pronek felt an impulse to rise and breathe from the pocket of air just under the roof. "You can say I am the Bosnian."

"I don't give a damn myself, as long as you speak the same language. You speak the same language, right? Yugoslavian or something?"

"I guess," Pronek said.

"Good," Owen said. "That's what we need here. That's why I called you. You get the job done, you get sixty bucks, you're a happy man."

Owen lit another cigarette, snapped his Zippo shut, and inhaled solemnly, as if inhaling a thought. The hair island had developed into a vine growing out of his forehead, nearly reaching his eyebrows. He drove past Bryn Mawr, where a crew of crazies was already operating: a man who kept lighting matches over a bunch of cigarettes strewn on the pavement before him, muttering to himself, as if performing a recondite ritual; an old toothless woman in tights with a wet stain spreading between her thighs; a man with thick oversized glasses hollering about Jesus. They drove past the funeral home: a man in a black coat was unlocking the front door and adjusting the welcome mat, yawning all along—there must have been an early death. They stopped at Lawrence, then turned right.

As they were moving westward, Pronek felt the warmth of a sunbeam tickling his neck. The windshield had thick eyebrows of dirt and a few splattered insects under them. As if reading his mind, Owen said:

"Lemme ask you something: what's the last thing that goes through a fly's head as it hits the windshield?"

He glanced sideways at Pronek with a mischievous grin, apparently proud of his cleverness. "What is it?" he asked again, and slammed the brakes, honking madly at the car in front.

"I don't know," Pronek said. "I should have gone the other way."

"Went," Owen said.

"What?"

"Went. You say I should've went the other way." He slammed the brakes again. "But no, that's not what it is. Think again."

"I don't know."

"It's the ass. The last thing that goes through a fly's head as it hits the windshield is its ass." He started laughing, nudging Pronek, until his guffawing turned into coughing, and then nearly choking. They stopped at the Clark light and he thumped his chest like a gorilla, his vine of hair quivering, his throat convulsing.

Pronek realized that there was an entire world of people he knew nothing about—the early morning people. Their faces had different colors in the morning sunlight. They seemed to be comfortable so early in the morning, even if they were already tired going to work: he could tell they had had their breakfast, their eyes were wide open, their faces developed into alertness—in contrast to Pronek's daze: the itching eyes, the tense, tired muscles, the crumpled face, the growling stomach, the pus taste in his mouth, and a general thought shortage. The six A.M. people, the people who existed when Owen and his people were sleeping: old twiggy ladies, with a plastic cover over their meticulously puffed-up hair, like wrapped-up gray lettuce heads; old men in nondescript suits, obviously performing their morning-walk ritual; kids in McDonald's uniforms on their way to the morning shift, already burdened with the midday drowsihead; joggers with white socks stretched to their knees, who seemed to be running in slow motion; sales associates in black stockings, freshly made up, dragging screaming children into a bus; workers unloading crates of pomegranates onto a stuck-up dolly—they all seemed to be involved in something purposeful.

Owen completed his coughing, cleared his throat confidently, and asked:

"You still have family there?"

"Where?" Pronek responded, confused by a sudden change in the communication pace.

"Phnom Penh, that's where! Wherever you're from, you still have folks there?"

"Yeah, my parents are still there. But they are still alive."

"Now, who's trying to kill them? I can never get this right. Are they Muslim?"

"No," Pronek said. "They are in Sarajevo. Some Serbs try to kill the Muslims in Sarajevo and Bosnia, and also the people who don't want to kill the Muslims."

"You probably gonna hate this sonovabitch then."

"I don't know yet," Pronek said. What if, he thought, what if he were dreaming this. What if he were one of those six A.M. people, just about to wake up, slap the snooze button, and linger a few more minutes in bed. Owen hit the brakes again, and Pronek slapped the dashboard, lest he go through the windshield. They were at Western: a Lincoln statue was making a step forward, worried as ever, his head and shoulders dotted with dried pigeon shit. "That sonovabitch lives around here," Owen announced. He crossed Western, almost running over a chunky businessman who was hugging his briefcase as he scurried across the street.

They parked the car on an empty street with two rows of ochre-brick houses facing each other. Owen adjusted his curl, adhering it to his dome. He was looking in the rearview mirror, his hump breathing on his back, his eyes shrunken because of the fuming cigarette in his mouth. The houses all looked the same, as if they were made in the same lousy factory, but the lawns were different: some were trimmed and orderly like soccer pitch; some had strewn litter, little heaps of dog turd, and wet leaves raked together. Owen pointed at the house that had a FOR SALE sign, like a flag, in front of it.

"What I want you to do," he said, handing him a stern envelope, "is to go to that door, ring the bell, and when he asks who it is, you talk to him in your monkey language and give him this. He takes it, you leave, I give you sixty bucks, we all happy and free. How's that?"

"That is fine," Pronek said, and wiped his sweaty palms against his pants. He considered getting out of the car, passing the house, and running away—it would take him forty minutes to walk back to his place.

"You all right?" Owen asked. "Piece of cake, just do it."

"What is his name?" Pronek asked.

"It's Branko something. Here, you can read it." He pointed at the envelope.

Pronek read: "Brdjanin. It means the mountain man."

"Whatever," Owen said, and excavated a gun from under his armpit—two black, perpendicular, steely rectangles, the nozzle eye glancing at Pronek. He looked at it as if he hadn't seen it for a while and offered it to Pronek: "You want it?"

"No, thanks," Pronek said. He wondered what would be the last thing going through his head.

"Nah, you probably don't need it," Owen said. "I'll be right here, caring about you."

Pronek stepped out of the car and walked toward the house. The number on the brass plate next to the door was 2345, and the orderliness of the digits seemed absurd against the scruffy house: blinds with holes, dusty windows, a mountain of soggy coupon sheets at the bottom of the stairs, blisters of paint on the faded-brown door with a red-letter sign reading NO TRESPASSING in its window. There was a squirrel sitting in an empty bird bath padded with damp leaves, watching him, with its little paws together, as if ready to applaud. Pronek walked up the stairs to the door, clenching the envelope, his heart steadily thumping. He pressed the hard bell-nipple, and heard a muffled, deep dingdong. He looked toward Owen in the car, who looked back at him over the folded *Sun-Times*, with an eager pen in his hand. "If this is a detective novel," Pronek thought, "I will hear shooting now." He imagined going around the house, jumping over the wire fence, looking in, and seeing a body in the middle of a carmine puddle spreading all over the floor, a mysterious fragrance still in the air. Then running back to Owen, only to find him with a little powder-black hole in his left temple, his hand petrified under his armpit, too slow to save him. There was no doubt that he would have to find the killer and prove his own innocence. Maybe Mirza could come over and be his partner, they could solve the crime together. He rang the bell again. The squirrel moved to a better position and was sitting on a tree branch, watching him intently. "*Dobro jutro*," Pronek muttered, rehearsing the first contact with Brdjanin. "*Dobro jutro. Evo ovo je za Vas*." He would give him the envelope then, Brdjanin would take it, confused by the familiarity of the language. Piece of cake.

But then he heard keys rattling, the lock snapping, and a bare-chested man, with a beard spreading down his hirsute front and a constellation of brown birthmarks on his pink dome—a man said: "What?" Pronek stared at him paralyzed, his throat clogged with the sounds of *dobro jutro*.

"What you want?" The man had a piece of lint sticking out of his navel and a cicatrice stretching across his stomach.

"This is for you," Pronek garbled, and handed him the envelope. The man snatched it out of Pronek's hand, looked at it, and snorted.

Should've went the other way.

"You no understand nothing," the man said, waving the envelope in front of Pronek's face.

"I don't know," Pronek said. "I must give this to you."

"Where you from?"

"I am," Pronek said reluctantly, "from Ukraine."

"Oh, *pravoslavni* brother!" the man exclaimed. "Come in, we drink coffee, we talk. I explain you."

"No, thank you," Pronek uttered. "I must go."

"Come," the man said growled, and grabbed Pronek's arm and pulled him in. "We drink coffee. We talk."

Pronek felt the disturbed determination of the man's fingers on his forearm. The last thing he saw before he was sucked in the house by the man's will was Owen getting out of the car with an unhappy, worried scowl on his face.

As Pronek was walking in Brdjanin's onionesque wake, he saw a gun handle—gray with two symmetrical dots, like teeny beady eyes—peering out of his pants, which were descending down his butt. Brdjanin led him through a dark hall, through a couple of uncertainly closed doors, into a room that had a table in its center and five chairs summoned around it. On the lacy tablecloth, there was a pear-shaped bottle of reddish liquid with a wooden Orthodox cross in it. There were five shot glasses and a platoon of crushed McDonald's bags surrounding it.

"Sit," Brdjanin said. "Here."

"I must go," Pronek uttered, and sat down, facing a window. A fly was buzzing against the windowpane as if trying to cut through it with a minikin circular saw. There was an icon on the wall: a sad saint with a tall forehead and a triangular beard, his head slightly tilted under the halo weight, his hands touching each other gently.

"Sit," Brdjanin said, and pulled the gun out of his ass, only to slam it on the table. The five glasses rattled peevishly. The window looked out at the garden: there was a shovel sticking out of the ground like a javelin, next to a muddy hole and a mound of dirt overlooking it. Brdjanin sat across the table from Pronek, and pushed the gun aside. "No fear. No problem," he said, then turned toward the kitchen and yelled: *"Rajka, kafu!"* He put the envelope right in front of himself, as if about to dissect it. "We talk with coffee," he said.

A woman with a wrinkled, swollen face and a faint bruise on her cheek, like misapplied makeup, peeked in from the kitchen, pulling the flaps of her striped black-and-white bathrobe together, and then retreated. There was a din of drawers and gas hissing, ending with an airy boom.

"You Ukrainian," Brdjanin said, and leaned toward him, as if to detect Ukrainianness in his eyes. "How is your name?"

"Pronek," Pronek said, and leaned back in his chair.

"Pronek," Brdjanin repeated. "Good *pravoslav* name. *Pravoslavni* brothers help Serbs in war against crazy people."

Pronek looked at Brdjanin, whose beard had a smile crevice in the middle, afraid that a twitch on his face, or a diverted glance would blow his feeble cover. Brdjanin was staring at him enthusiastically, then pushed the envelope aside with contempt, leaned further toward Pronek, and asked fervently:

"You know what is this?"

"No," Pronek said.

"Is nothing," Brdjanin said, and thrust his right hand forward (the gun comfortably on his left-hand side), all his fingers tight together and his thumb erect, as if he were making a wolf hand-shadow. His thumb was a grotesque stump, like a truncated hot dog, but Pronek was cautious not to pay too much attention to it.

"You must understand," Brdjanin said. "I was fool, *budala*. Wife to me was whore, was born here, but was Croat. Fifteen years. Fifteen years! I go see her brothers, they want to kill me." He made the motion of cutting his throat with the thumb stump, twice, as if they couldn't kill him on the first try. "They Ustashe, want to cut my head because I Serb. Is war now, no more wife, no more brothers. My woman is Serb now, you brother to me now. I trust only *pravoslav* people now. Other people, other people . . ." He shook his head, signifying suspicion, and pulled his thumb across his throat again.

Pronek nodded automatically, helpless. He wanted to say that Croats are just like everyone else: good people and bad people, or some reasonable platitude like that, but in this room whatever it was he used to think just an hour ago seemed ludicrous now. He wanted the woman to be in the room with him, as if she could protect him from Brdjanin's madness and his cutthroat thumb stump. The room reeked of coffee and smoke, stale sweat and Vegeta, a coat of torturous, sleepless nights over everything. The woman trudged out of the kitchen and put a tray with a coffee pot and demitasse between the two of them, and then dragged her feet back, as if she were ready to collapse. Pronek looked after her longingly, but Brdjanin didn't notice. "This Serbian coffee. They say Turkish coffee. It's Serbian coffee," Brdjanin said, lit a cigarette and let two smoke-snakes out of his nostrils. Pronek imagined saving the woman from this lair, taking her home (wherever it may be) and taking care of her, until she recovered and regained her beauty, slouching somewhere in her heart now—and he would ask for nothing in return. Brdjanin slurped some coffee from his demitasse, then reached behind his chair and produced a newspaper. The headline said: THOUSANDS KILLED IN SREBRENICA.

"Killed?" Brdjanin cried. "No killed. Is war. They kill, they killed."

He threw the paper across the table and it landed right in front of Pronek, so he had to look at it: a woman clutching her teary face wrapped in a colorless scarf, as if trying to unscrew her head.

"Hmm," Pronek said, only because he thought silence might be conspicuous.

"You know what is this?" Brdjanin asked, and spurted out an excited flock of spit drops. "You know?"

"Nothing," Pronek mumbled.

"No, is not nothing. Is Muslim propaganda."

"Oh," Pronek said. Where was Owen? If Owen broke in now, taking out Brdjanin as he was trying to reach his gun, Pronek would run to the kitchen, grab the woman's hand, and escape with her. "Come with me," he would say. "*Podji sa mnom.*"

"You know when bomb fall on market in Sarajevo?" Brdjanin asked, frowning and refrowning, sweat collecting in the furrows. "They say hundred people die. They all dolls, *lutke.* Muslims throw bomb on market. Propaganda! Then they put dolls for television, it look bad, like many people killed."

Pronek's mother had barely missed the shell. She had just crossed the street when it landed. She wandered back, dazed, and trudged through bloody pulp, torn limbs hanging off the still-standing counters, shell-shocked people slipping on brains. She almost stepped on someone's heart, she said, but it was a tomato—what a strange thing, she thought, a tomato. She hadn't seen a tomato for a couple of years.

"I have the friend," Pronek said, trying to appear disinterested, his heart throttling in his chest, "from Sarajevo. He says the people really died. His parents are in Sarajevo. They saw it."

"What is he?"

"He is the Bosnian."

"No, what is he? He is Muslim? He is Muslim. He lie."

"No, he's not Muslim. He is from Sarajevo."

"He is from Sarajevo, he is Muslim. They want Islamic Republic, many *mudjahedini.*"

Pronek slurped his coffee. The gun lay on the left-hand side, comfortably stretched like a sleeping dog—he wouldn't have been surprised if the gun scratched its snout with its trigger. Pronek could see the woman's shadow moving around the kitchen. Brdjanin sighed, and put both of his hands on the table, pounding it slowly as he spoke:

"How long you been here? I been here twenty years. I don't come from nowhere. I leave my parents, my sister. I come here. Good country, good people. I work in factory, twenty years. But not my country. I die for my country. American die for his country. You die for Ukraine. We all die. Is war."

Pronek looked out and saw Owen getting around the shovel, the paper and pen still in his hands, almost falling into the hole. Owen looked up at the window, saw Pronek and nodded upward, asking if everything was all right. Pronek quickly looked at Brdjanin, who was looking at his hand, gently hacking the table surface, muttering: "I Serb, no nothing."

"I must *go,*" Pronek said. "I must go to work."

"You go." Brdjanin shrugged and stroked his beard. "No problem."

Pronek stood up. Brdjanin put his hand on the gun. Pronek walked toward the door. Brdjanin held the gun casually, no finger near the trigger. Pronek opened the door, Brdjanin behind him. It was the bathroom: a radiator was wheezing, a cat-litter box underneath was full of sandy lumps. As Pronek was turning around, slowly, Brdjanin grasped Pronek's jacket, his left hand still holding the gun, and looked at him: he was shorter than Pronek, with an exhausted yeasty smell, his eyes were moist green. He had a coffee shadow on the beard around his mouth. Pronek nodded meaninglessly, paralyzed with fear. Brdjanin bowed his head, saying nothing. Pronek could see the woman framed by the kitchen door, watching them. He looked at her, hoping she would come and save him from Brdjanin's grasp. She would come and embrace him and say it was all okay. But she was not moving, as if she were used to seeing men in a clinch. She had her hands in her robe pockets, but then took out a cigarette and a lighter. She lit the cigarette and Pronek saw the lighter flame flickering with uncanny clarity. She inhaled with a deep sough and tilted her head slightly backward, keeping the smoke in for the longest time, as if she had died an instant before exhaling. Brdjanin was sobbing: squeally gasps ending with stertorous, shy snorts, his shoulders heaving in short leaps, his hand tightening its grip on Pronek's jacket. Pronek imagined Brdjanin's gun rising to his temple, the index finger pulling the trigger in slow motion—a loud pop and brains all over Pronek, blood and slime, dripping down. The woman looked down, drained, her bosom rising, patiently not looking up, as if waiting for the two men to disappear.

"It is okay," Pronek said, and put his hand on Brdjanin's shoulder. It was sticky and soft, with a few solitary hairs curling randomly. "It will be okay."

"What the hell were you doing in there?" Owen asked curtly, standing at the bottom of the stairs with his hands on his hips. "I almost went in there shooting to save your ass."

Pronek descended the stairs. The sun was creeping up from behind the building across the street, making the black trees gray. The same squirrel stopped, now upside down, midway down a tree and looked at Pronek. It was skinny and its tail fluff was deflated—it was going to be a long winter.

"Did he take the thing?"

"Yeah," Pronek said. "But I don't think he cares."

"Oh, he'll have to care, believe you me, he'll care."

"There is the woman in there," Pronek said, wistfully.

"There always is," Owen said.

Owen patted Pronek on the back, and softly pushed him toward the car. All the weight of Pronek's body was in his feet now, and his neck hurt, as if it were cracking under his head. They walked slowly, Owen offered him a cigarette and Pronek took it. Owen held the lighter in front of Pronek's face, and Pronek saw the yellow flame with a blue root, flickering under his breath—he recognized with wearisome detachment that he was alive. He inhaled and said, exhaling:

"I don't smoke."

"Now you do," Owen said.

They drove up Western, past the cemetery wall, past the used car shops—cars glittering in the morning silence, like a timorous army. Owen turned on the radio: Dan Ryan was congested,

Kennedy moving slowly, the day was to be partly cloudy, gusty winds, high in the fifties. They turned right on Granville. Pronek felt his muscles tense, a cramp in his fingers, as if they were transforming into talons, clutching the dollar bills Owen had given him.

"I used to know a guy like you in Vietnam," Owen said. "Never said a fucking word. Kept to himself. He was a sniper, popped them like bottles on a fence. He would sit in a tree camouflaged, for hours, not moving, not making a sound. Guess you get used to it. He'd watch a village, wait for Charlie to crawl out, and then bam! Once we were——"

"You can leave me here," Pronek said abruptly. "I'm the next block."

"Sure. Thanks again, man," Owen said, and pulled up. "I'll sure call if I have something for you. Okay?"

"Thanks," Pronek said, and got out of the car. The morning was crisp, with just enough snap in the air to make one's life simple and sweet. But he was sleepy, with the feeling that he had just spent time with someone who didn't exist, a feeling that was slowly turning into anger. Way down Broadway, there was a quick shimmer coming off a moving bus windshield. Pronek stood on the corner, letting his eyelids slide down like blinds, gathering strength before walking home. He looked at the Shoney's being razed, and imagined himself destroying it with a huge hammer, slamming the walls, ripping out pipes, until there was just a pile of rubble. And then he would go on, until there was nothing left.

6

The Soldiers Coming

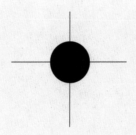

CHICAGO, APRIL 1997–

MARCH 1998

THE DOLPHINS

So I kissed Pronek's forehead for good luck and sent
him up.

Stage fright made his elbows shiver, but he ascended a long,
narrow staircase and stopped at the top. He looked down, visualizing himself tumbling, big head over small heels. He flexed his
back, as if appreciating the unbrokenness of his spine. He
opened the door that had a picture of a pretty green-and-blue
globe—SAVE OUR MOTHER, the poster demanded. He thought of
his mother and recalled her sitting with her feet propped on the
coffee table, tufts of cotton between her toes, the arches of her
feet symmetrical. The office smelled like ocean and pines and
perspiration. He walked to the reception desk and a black
woman with shorn hair told him to sit down and wait. In the
corner there was a wizened palm of an uncertain green color, its
flaccid leaves looking down at the pot. He looked at his hands,
and they appeared bleached.

"My name is John," the man said, "but everybody calls me JFK."
The Handbook of Good English was on someone's desk. "Here is
fine," JFK said, and offered him the only chair, squatting in front
of him, grasping a clipboard. In a whisper, he asked him why he
wanted to work for Greenpeace, and Pronek delivered the mantra

he repeated in many an unsuccessful interview: he had communication skills; he liked working with people; he thought this was the right *invyromint* for him, where he could develop to his full potential. JFK was rocking in his squat, and Pronek imagined pushing him over. A clot of tenebrous panic started forming in his stomach, as he realized he might not get the job, even though he was afraid that he might get the job. "Here is fine," he repeated to himself. "*Here* is fine." It was a demanding job, JFK said, canvassing door to door—he would have to talk to between twenty and forty people per night. Was he sure he could do it? Was he comfortable speaking English?

"I am evil," she said.

"She is Rachel," JFK said. "She will train you tonight."

"E-V-O-L. Love in reverse."

She wore a T-shirt with a tranquil candle below which DAYDREAM NATION was written.

"I am Jozef," Pronek said. "Nothing in reverse."

JFK tightened his lips and opened his eyes wide, arching his eyebrows, then vanished. Pronek did not know what to do with his hands—they overlapped over his genitals for a moment, then he deposited them on his hips and stood akimbo, as if reprimanding Rachel.

"Where are you from?" she asked him.

"Bosnia."

"I am sorry."

"But I live here now, for five years."

"I am still sorry."

"It is not your fault."

She had short spiky hair, with a crest heaving over her forehead, above her sparkling eyes. Her upper lip, dark cherry red, had the shape of a musketeer mustache. She had a dimple in her chin. She had cheek apples Pronek wanted to touch.

"When you're done staring at my face, I can show you my tits too."

"I am sorry," he said, looking toward a remote corner of the ceiling, where, he noticed, there was absolutely nothing.

"That's okay," she said. "I like your face too."

"Can you turn that shit down?" Rachel snarled.

"It. Is. Radiohead," Dallas slowly said, as if nobody could speak his language. "Black Star, man. It is awesome. It is rock 'n' roll."

"It. Is. Stupid," Rachel said.

Pronek sat in the back seat, next to Rachel, their thighs rubbing. He furtively glanced at her—her right earlobe was beautiful: the mazy curves inside it were perfect. He imagined himself curled and snug, pinkie-nail-sized, resting at the mouth of the ear funnel, singing a sweet song.

"Did you have rock 'n' roll in Yugoslavia?" Dallas shouted over Radiohead. The van was the slowest vehicle on the highway, overtaken by coffin-like Cadillacs steered by old ladies sunk in the front seat, passed by garbage trucks with black bags stuck between the rear-end teeth. Monster trucks honked at them furiously.

"Jesus, JFK," Rachel said. "It's like you're pulling us in a Radio Flyer. Step on it."

"Why are they calling you JFK?" Pronek asked. JFK was a large man, his meaty back spilling over the edges of the seat, hair sprouting from his neck.

"He's the size of an airport," Rachel said.

" 'Cause my name is John Francis Kirkpatrick."

"Did you?" Dallas shouted again. His arms were tattooed with dragons licking naked women, some of them singed by flames.

"See, there are many ways to get the money at the door," Rachel said. "You can appeal to the sexual frustration of suburban housewives, flirting like a crass cowboy, as Dallas does. You . . ."

"Fuck you," Dallas said.

"Hey, hey, hey!" JFK said.

". . . can exhaust them with facts and moralistic appeals, until they pay you to go away, as JFK does. Or you can look at them with big, beautiful eyes, dazzle them with a smile, then strike like a cobra, as Vince does."

Vince was sitting in front of Rachel, grasping a small red bag with Chip and Dale pictured on it. Pronek wanted to be nice to Vince, because Vince was black, but didn't quite know what nice things to say, so he only smiled vaguely.

"I like blues," he said, finally, but no one responded to his statement: Vince continued looking out the window; Dallas was using his knees as a snare-drum; JFK was slowing down, because half a mile ahead of him, there was a truck with an American flag spreading across its rear end. Only Rachel glanced at him, perplexed, then put her left foot on her right knee, exhibiting her boot sole to Pronek—there was pink chewing gum on the heel.

"Schaumburg is tough," Rachel said. Pronek looked down a row of houses bending around an empty street. "This town has an ordinance prohibiting straight streets, because they want it to be more interesting, they say, more diversified."

The houses were identical—pale plastic-blue walls; a white porch; a lattice with a nascent crawler; a figure on the lawn: a dwarf; a black jockey; a Virgin Mary.

"This, my friend, is called devo."

"Devo," Pronek repeated. The sky was car-commercial blue, with a lonely plane here and there, like a gnat without a swarm. The air was warm; spring buds on the trees exuded a syrupy smell.

"Just watch what I do first."

Rachel touched his elbow tenderly, as if it were the source of his pain. There was a steel ball grinding Pronek's bowels, and a tingle of paralyzing fear scurrying across his skin to his head, where it stopped to throb. He needed a cigarette. He imagined good Americans opening their doors, hating him for his foreign stupidity, for his silly accent, for his childish grammar errors. He imagined them swinging baseball bats at his elbows and smashing them, bone splinters flying around.

"I hate baseball," he informed Rachel, but she was already pressing the bell button.

"Hi, I'm Rachel, and this is Joseph. We're from Greenpeace." Rachel beamed at the woman, pressing her clipboard against her chest, the Save-the-Whales leaflet facing out. The woman was skinny, her hair wet and hanging in springy curls. She was clasping the collars of her white robe, looking at Rachel, then cautiously glancing at Pronek, as if his presence there were secret.

"How are you today?" Rachel asked her, nodding.

"Who's that?" a man hollered from somewhere inside the house. The house smelled of something familiar to Pronek—it contained paprika, but he couldn't figure out what it was. He could see a carpet with flat panthers gazing upward at him with their yellow eyes. A huge bowl of brownish popcorn stood on a glass-top table. A python was gulping down a mouse on the TV.

"We are not interested," the woman said. There was a cavity at the bottom of her neck and a droplet of water in it, slowly sliding down.

"I'm sure you care about the environment," Rachel said.

"No, thank you."

"Who the heck is it?" the man yelled again. The woman closed the door and locked it, a wooden hand with flowers painted on it and the word "Welcome" swung first left, then right.

"Let me give you some advice," Rachel said very quietly, her gaze grazing Pronek's hip. "Never look inside while you are talking to them and never, never prop yourself on your toes to peek inside. They think you wanna rob them. Look them in the eyes."

"In the eyes," Pronek said. "Good."

The man was in his underwear, with Rudolph-the-Red-Nose-Reindeer slippers—the red nose erected toward them. His shirt was unbuttoned, and Pronek could see the head of an eagle touching the left-nipple circle with its beak. Pronek tried to focus on the man's droopy eyes, but could not help surveying the man's whitish underwear with an intermittent yellow stain.

"I'm a hunter," the man said. "I enjoy killing animals."

"Many hunters support Greenpeace," Rachel said.

"Well, I ain't one of them," the man said. "Now, leave my property."

"I like your slippers," she said.

"Thank you. Now get off my fucking property."

———

"This is hell. I run out of smiles and kindness quickly."

"It's very hard."

"Do you want to try?"

"No, not yet."

"You gotta try it at some point."

"Okay. Not yet."

Pronek regarded Rachel as she was talking to a pimply Motörhead teenager; or a Catholic lady with her index fingers stuck between the pages of the Bible; or a college boy wearing a baseball hat backward who told them he hated Chomsky. ("Who is that?" Pronek asked.) He watched her lips part—she would expose her lower teeth, tightening her chin, the dimple deepening, while making an important point. She would roll her lips into her mouth, after she had asked for money, waiting for an answer. He tried to imitate the smile she was flashing at a community-college professor who listened to her enthralled, with a pen and a checkbook in his hand, scrawny and bending forward, as if cancer were breaking his back as they spoke. The college professor glimpsed Pronek with the corner of his eye: Pronek was raising his eyebrows, stretching his eyelids and pulling his cheeks back, keeping his teeth close, replicating a Rachel smile.

"Are you okay?" he asked Pronek.

"Yes, I am," Pronek said, and tidied up his face into a solemn expression.

They stood at the corner of Washtenaw and Hiawatha. Pronek was smoking, self-conscious, the cigarette tasteless. Rachel watched him, her head tilted.

"The important thing is to listen to them. They'll tell you things, and they'll give you money for listening."

"Why do you call yourself evil?"

"E-V-O-L. Love in reverse. It's a Sonic Youth album, my favorite."

"I never listened them."

"Listened *to* them."

"Listened to them."

"It's kind of noisy, a lot of guitars."

"I used to play the guitar."

"Well, this is different."

"What do you do in you life?"

"In my life? What is this? Do you Balkan boys always ask questions like that?"

"I am sorry."

"I do photography in my life."

"Oh, I like photography."

"Let's work now. We gotta make some money."

They avoided the dark houses, going only to the ones that had lit porches and windows, shadows gliding along the inside walls. She moved from door to door quickly, employing always the same serious, deep voice. Pronek marveled at her resolute moves, at the tautness of her muscles, at the determination in her stride as she hurried between houses, although she once tripped on a hose snaking on the lightless pavement, her clipboard spinning up, then falling and skidding along the pavement.

"Fuck," she said, sitting on the ground. Pronek offered her his hand, and she snorted furiously, but then accepted it. "I just learned to walk last week."

"I love Greenpeace," the man said. "Greenpeace is the greatest."

"Well, then you can give us a lot of money," Rachel said.

The man laughed. He had a dark wart resembling a blackberry on his cheek.

"Go get your checkbook. You know we need your support."

"I'd love to," the man said, "but I spend all my money on the wolves."

"On the what?"

The man was smoking. Pronek wanted to ask him for a cigarette, but instead surreptitiously inhaled the smoke coming out of the man's nostrils and wafting toward him.

"You know, they want to shoot them in Wyoming, wipe them out."

"Wolves are beautiful animals," Rachel said. Pronek was grinning and nodding, joining in the wolf appreciation. He remembered the story his father had told him about their Ukrainian ancestor so bent on killing the wolf that had slaughtered all his sheep that he tied his wife to a tree in the middle of winter to lure the beast. But the poor woman wailed and wailed, her toes freezing, and the wolf stayed away.

The man was describing a dying wolf, running wounded from those choppers packed with armed assholes in cowboy hats, running until all his blood was drained and then just dropping down.

"Wow," Rachel said, and lowered her clipboard to her stomach, crossing her hands over it. Pronek noticed that the man checked out her breasts, and it was the first time that Pronek looked directly at them—they were bulging, stretching her Daydream Nation T-shirt.

"Do you want to see my wolf? I got him in the garage. I'm driving out to the UP tomorrow, we're going hunting together."

The wolf's fur was gray and linty and he looked lachrymose. When he saw the man, he started pacing frantically back and forth in a humongous cage in the space next to a pickup truck. The man put his hand inside the cage and the wolf stepped rapidly toward it. Pronek had an instant vision of the man's hand being snapped off, blood spurting from the wrist veins. He imagined explaining the situation to paramedics who wouldn't understand him because of his accent. But the wolf put his snout into the man's hand and the man scratched it. "Look," he said to Rachel, paying no attention to Pronek. She shook her head, her mouth agape in admiration.

"You can do it too."

Rachel slowly put her clipboard on a lawnmower and offered her hand to the wolf's nostrils—he sniffed and looked up at the man. Pronek was paralyzed—now he could envision both of Rachel's hands torn off, and he noticed a full moon in the sky hovering over the thick darkness of the street. Rachel held the wolf's snout, sticking out between the bars with one hand and stroked it with the other. She leaned over and kissed the wolf on the lips. She extended her lips symmetrically, like a flower opening, and the wolf showed his dagger teeth to Pronek. Pronek whimpered, and the man turned toward him and grinned, as if some sinister plan were being fulfilled.

As they were walking away from the house, Pronek decided he needed to busy Rachel with himself in order to make her forget the wolf.

"I like dogs," he said.

"That wolf was so sad, the guy should just let him go."

"I had a dog. His name was Lucky."

"That wolf had some meat rotting inside him," Rachel said.

Back in Chicago, they walked down Jackson, neon and street lights comfortingly glaring, Pronek half a step behind Rachel, as if trying to catch up. She had her hands in the back pockets of her jeans, so her elbows stuck out, like pool-ladder handlebars.

"Where are you living?" Pronek asked.

"Where do I live? No woman in this lovely city would tell a complete stranger where she lives. Don't ask a single woman that question."

"I am sorry," Pronek said, looked down and fell another half step behind.

"But you're a stranger no longer. I live in Uptown. Where do you live?"

"Rogers Park."

They crossed Halsted. A policewoman, her chest encrusted with Kevlar, was frisking a man facing the wall, his left hand up, his right one gripping a walking stick. In the window of Zorba's they saw a gyros chunk like a misshaped planet, slowly revolving.

"When did you come here?" Rachel asked.

"Nineteen ninety-two, just before the war."

"Is your family there?"

"Yes."

"Are they all right?"

"They are old."

"You watch it on TV and feel nothing but numb helplessness. It just makes me angry."

"I know."

"It must have been hard for you."

Pronek nodded, but he didn't want her to pity him, yet he liked that she paid attention to him. She talked to him over her shoulder, her head twisted, and Pronek imagined her turning into a pillar of salt.

———

They took the same train. It sped underground, producing apoc-
alyptic, isolating noise, as if everything above ground had just
collapsed. Rachel was in the seat in front of him, next to a black
woman grasping a tiny Bible in her hand, breathing heavily and
mumbling between the breaths. The only words he could make
out were "weeping for her children." Rachel scratched her neck,
her index finger coming down from her right ear toward the collar, leaving ruddy curves.

Pronek lay supine in the darkness, pressing his eyelids tight together, determined to force himself to sleep, feeling tension in his
facial muscles, as if his face were ossifying. The man was screaming: "You ain't gonna get me, motherfuckers!" A train rattled by,
and Pronek felt anger rising in him—he wanted silence, no crazies bellowing, no trains screeching, no sirens warbling mania-
cally. His kneecaps were sweaty and sticky—he turned sideways
and put the blanket between them. He imagined walking Rachel
home—strolling down her linden-tree-lined street, rich scents in
the air, then sitting on her stairs and talking, then going upstairs
and making love.
     "You ain't gonna get me, motherfuckers!"
     Pronek jumped from bed, his hands curling into painful fists,
and looked out: a preppy-white businessman in an orderly dark
suit, holding a briefcase close to his chest, was stomping his feet,
pointing his finger toward the sky every now and then. Pronek's
tension transformed into a clean, simple hatred of the man. He
opened the window and glared at the man as if his hateful fury
could be carried through the ether of the city.
     "You ain't gonna get me! Fuck no! I don't fucking think so!"
     Pronek wanted to think up a killer sentence, something that

would make the man shut up instantly and think about his behavior. He juggled the words in his head, stressing them differently, inserting and re-inserting necessary curses, ascertaining the voice-power necessary to crush the man's demented will. He huffed and puffed and finally, with the anger stuck in his throat, he opened his mouth and hesitantly shouted:

"That is not polite!"

The man stopped hollering, shook his head as if he had received a punch, and stood petrified for a moment. Then he slowly looked up at Pronek, pointed his finger at him, and thundered:

"And you ain't never going to get me, because the Lord is with me, in all his might!"

Pronek retracted inside and stood near the window, afraid to move or look outside, the darkness throbbing around him, his knees giving way.

"Just be relaxed and look them in the eye," Rachel said.

Pronek knocked on the door, once, then twice, although there was a buzzer in clear sight. A gaggle of croquet mallets was leaning on the fence and a family of wooden raccoons huddled on the porch. Pronek closed his eyes, because when he closed his eyes, there was an instant of hope that he was dreaming all this and that it would all vanish when he looked out again. The door opened and Pronek opened his eyes and there was a woman wearing sunglasses, her dark hair coiled up, wearing an oversized Hawaiian shirt, her face pallid, as if she were a vampire.

"Hello," Pronek said. "I am Joseph and I am from Greenpeace. We like to talk to you."

The woman said nothing.

"And this is Rachel. From Greenpeace too."

It was unnerving not to know where the woman was looking. Perhaps she was blind.

"How are you?"

"I'm just dandy peachy," the woman said, her voice coarse. "What can I do for you?"

Pronek wanted to look at Rachel to get a signal of approval, he didn't know whether he was doing it right. But he didn't dare take his eyes off the woman's face, as if she should disappear if he did.

"We like to talk to you about envir—*enviro*—environment. Maybe you can help us."

"Where are you from?"

She opened the door wider. Pronek could see the TV—a pair of hands was building something in silence.

"From Greenpeace."

"No, what country are you from?"

Above a gas fireplace with flimsy flames flickering, there was a portrait of an Indian in profile with a huge feather, sunset orange the dominant color.

"I am from Bosnia."

"Bosnia is far away," the woman said, slurring the words. "But I like your accent."

"Thank you."

"So what can I do for you?"

"We like to talk to you?"

She pointed at Rachel: "Is this your girlfriend?"

"No. I don't know. No."

"Ma'am, we come out here to talk to you," Rachel said, "and ask for your support."

"You got my support."

"Financial support."

"Hey, I can give you a drink or a massage, but dough—no! I am a single woman."

"Thank you, ma'am. Sorry to bother you."

"Thank you. Sorry," Pronek echoed.

"Come back any time," the woman said, and stepped out on the porch, as they were walking down the driveway. "Any time."

"One day," Rachel said, "I am going to bring my camera and take pictures of these people. They are unbelievable."

"I like them," Pronek said.

"Okay, advice: don't let them suck you into babbling. There are a lot of lonely people out here, you know, housewives, senior citizens, perverts, unemployed fratboys. They got nothing to do all day long."

"It is hard. My English is bad."

"Just be relaxed. If you speak English with an accent, you speak at least two languages and that is twice as many as the people in this godforsaken place. People who like you will give you money, and people who don't won't."

It started raining again, reactivating the puddles on the street, raindrops shattering their surface.

"You know," Pronek said wistfully, "I think that everywhere there is the home, you have the puddle where you see when it rains."

"What do you mean?"

"I mean you look through the window when you don't know if is it raining and you have your puddle where you can see the rain."

"Yeah, I see. That's nice."

"I had one in Sarajevo, in front of my home."

"I like that," Rachel said.

"Hello," Pronek said, "my name is Jozef and I am from Green-peace. Do you care about the dolphins?"

The old man was sitting on the porch wrapped in a check-ered blanket, with earmuffs pressing on his temples and wool-mittened hands gently deposited in his lap.

"Nope," he said. "I couldn't care less."

His face was splattered with dun dead-skin blotches.

"Okay. Do you care about the rain forests?"

"Nah."

Pronek noticed a little oxygen tank lying next to the chair, like a steel pet.

"Do you care about the clean air?"

"Where are you from?"

"Bosnia."

"Bosnia? It's hell there."

"Not now. The war finished."

"I see. So why are you here in America?"

Pronek looked for Rachel down the street. The street was lit-tered with stray, soaked brown leaves stuck to the asphalt. The man took off his mittens.

"Because it is better here."

"It sure is. Land of the free, home of the brave."

"Anyway, sir, we come here to talk to you . . ."

"So what was that war all about?"

"I don't know. Many things."

"Wasn't it religion? Muslims fighting Christians?"

"I don't know. I don't think so."

"Are you Muslim?"

Pronek didn't want to answer this question, he hated this ques-tion.

"No. But I know many Muslims."

"I killed a Muslim once." The old man took off his earmuffs and pressed his thumb between his eyebrows. "But it was a car accident."

"I am sorry," Pronek said.

The old man banged the wall behind him with his knuckles, startling Pronek.

"Have you ever killed a Muslim?"

"No. I never killed nobody."

"But you were fighting in that war, weren't you?"

"No."

"I fought in a war. I was a sharpshooter. Forty-six successful terminations."

He banged the wall again, until a young woman came out, with a towel turban on her head and crescent pads under her eyes.

"What?" she asked peevishly through the screen door. She wore a black bra and panties; a rose was tattooed around her navel.

"Give this young man ten bucks. For the dolphins."

"What dolphins?" She snarled and looked at Pronek.

"Just shut up and get the money."

The young woman went back in. Pronek grinned stupidly, glancing around: a wizened juniper tree leaned against the porch; a dog chain was coiled in the corner; a flag pole with a wet black flag fluttering in the wind stood in the center of the lawn.

"Dolphins, no dolphins," the old man said, "one day we will all tumble down into the pits of hell."

To a young couple in Evanston who sat on their sofa holding hands, Pronek introduced himself as Mirza from Bosnia. To a college girl in La Grange with DE PAW stretching across her bosom he introduced himself as Sergei Katastrofenko from Ukraine. To a man in Oak Park with chintzy hair falling down on his shoulders, the top of his dome twinkling with sweat, he introduced himself as Jukka Smrdiprdiuskas from Estonia. To an old couple from Romania in Homewood, who could speak no English and sat with their hands gently touching their knees, he was John from Liverpool. To a tired construction worker in Forest Park who opened the door angrily and asked, "Who the fuck are you?" he was Nobody. To a Catholic priest in Blue Island, with eczema and a handsome, blue-eyed boyfriend, he was Phillip from Luxembourg. To a bunch of pot-bellied Christian bikers barbecuing on a Walgreen's parking lot in Elk Grove Village, he was Joseph from Snitzlland (the homeland of the *snitzl*). To a woman in Hyde Park who opened the door with a gorgeous grin, which then transmogrified into a suspicious smirk as she said, "I thought you were someone else," he was Someone Else.

THE SECRET CITY

Black-tar rain glittered on the highway, soaked cars plowing through puddles. They passed forlorn warehouses brandishing billboards announcing happy sitcoms and talkless radio. They passed desolate stripped lots with herds of bulldozers and diggers, and cranes roosting on the edges. They saw impenetrable business buildings, encased in glass, reflecting nothing. They passed devo houses hiding behind tall fences, then strip-mall neon lights blinking irksomely under a sky crisscrossed with endless wires. They a saw lonely car disappearing into a lightless tree-lined street, then exposing the middle-class waste like lightning: mowers and rakes and footballs and plastic ghouls and solitary papers sitting on the stairs and swings hanging from a tall tree shuddering under the wind slaps. The car slowly penetrated the garage, the embers of its brake lights inhaling for the last time, fading out under the ashes of the night.

They left Chicago while it was still dark. Their van stopped at the Skyway toll booth, no other cars were around, then it ascended across the bridge. Casino billboards announced the loosest slots, fortune waiting in Indiana. Nobody said anything, except for an excited radio broadcaster blurting out nonsense about depressed porn stars. When they reached Indiana, the sky was clear, the last few morning stars barely twinkling.

"You know," Pronek said to no one in particular, "some of those stars maybe don't exist."

Rachel looked at him askance.

"You know," she said, "it is too early in the morning for ontological doubts."

"Sorry," Pronek said.

They passed steel mills looming against the dawn, their squareness ominous, their smokestacks spewing tongues of fire and plumes of smoke. Vince coughed when the stench of liquid steel reached them. On the steel-mill parking lots there was an occasional, solitary pickup truck coated with dew, waiting for its master.

"Not to mention the stars you cannot see anymore and that don't exist," Rachel said.

"Yeah," Pronek said.

"How can you see stars," Dallas grumbled, "if they don't exist."

"Don't know," Rachel said, "ask our foreign resident philosopher."

"They send the light, and then they die, and then the light comes to the earth."

"Still don't get it," Dallas said.

"It could be another billion years before the light reaches the dark recesses of your fucking brain," Rachel said.

Vincent chuckled, still looking out. They passed large white cisterns huddled by the road, ladders on their sides like scars.

"When I was a kid," Rachel said, "my mother told me that these cisterns were full of orange juice, and that those steel mills produced cookies."

"Maybe they are," Pronek said.

"Don't think so," Dallas said.

"Yeah, mothers tell you things like that," JFK said. "When I was a kid I fell off a pickup truck and was in the hospital for a month and my mom told me that it was because I didn't pray enough."

"Jesus," Rachel said.

"Exactly."

They drove through a wooded stretch where the cobwebby fog still clung to the feet of the trees. There were a couple of does grazing calmly in a ravine.

"Look!" Rachel exclaimed. Pronek leaned toward her window and their shoulders rubbed. His left hand was on the seat behind her, nearly touching her neck. He imagined his fingers gliding down the tip of her spine, then between her shoulder blades.

"I used to be very smart," JFK said, "before I fell off the truck."

It was cold in Ohio. The van pushed against the wind, smashing snowflakes on its windshield. Snow whorls fidgeted on the fringes of the road. A silhouette of a person followed by a silhouette of a dog walked across a prairie patch, a cloud of snow twirling around them. A silvery train glided across the horizon. In a car passing them, there was a boy asleep in the back seat, strapped and peaceful. Then a monumental truck cast its shadow over them, the word MOVING appearing in Pronek's window, letter by letter.

"Let me tell you about Oak Ridge," JFK said, one hand on the wheel, the other on his pate. "Although you probably know everything already."

"Oh, enlighten us, our kind leader," Rachel said.

"Let's hear this song out first," Dallas said. The voice was whining: "Mom and dad have let me down . . ." JFK turned off the radio.

"It's a great song."

"Sorry, cowboy." JFK cleared his throat. "Oak Ridge was built under a cloak of great secrecy during World War Two. It was part of the Manhattan Project. The plutonium they dropped on Hiroshima and Nagasaki came from Oak Ridge. A hell of a lot of plutonium they put in warheads after the war came from Oak Ridge."

"Can we stop to piss?" Dallas said.

"Now they produce who knows what. So there'll be an action there, we'll do a little demo, some might get arrested, the usual stuff."

"I can't get arrested," Pronek said.

"Can we stop to piss?"

"Perhaps you can be quiet?" Vince said, with a deep tranquil voice.

They stopped.

It was still cold—cloudlets of steam escaped their mouths. Pronek smoked, trotting in place, his left hand in his pocket. A man in a fedora was sleeping in a decrepit Cadillac in the parking lot, his hat pulled over his eyes. Vince and JFK were in front of a vending machine in the rest-stop building. Rachel embraced herself, lifting her gaze toward the sky, as if expecting something to come down. Pronek looked up, and there was nothing but endless grayness.

"My grandfather worked at Oak Ridge," Rachel said.

Pronek shook his head, disbelieving her to make her tell more. He stuck the cigarette in his mouth and put the other hand in his pocket.

Her grandfather, she said, survived Auschwitz. His entire family perished, except for an uncle who had moved to Chicago after World War I. Her grandfather was in his late twenties, but he looked older. He came to Chicago and stayed with his uncle, sharing a room with his two teenage cousins, boys who only cared about girls. They despised Rachel's grandfather—he was skinny and rugged and exuded the scent of European death and sickness, the fetid refugee smell. They pegged their noses with their fingers when he walked in the room. He slept on their couch, and sometimes he would open his eyes and they would be leaning over him, sniggering. He left after a month—he had a biology degree and found a job in a butter factory. She imagined him walking between the vats of butter, Rachel said, his hands greasy, his heart soaked with sorrow.

"Let's go," JFK said.

He didn't want to work in a butter factory. He wrote a letter to the University of Chicago. It was in broken English, but he managed to convey that he was a biologist and that he had studied with a famous scientist in Prague. He didn't mention that he was an Auschwitz alumni, because he thought that they wouldn't want to hire him.

"Where's Dallas?" JFK asked them.

"He's urinating," Vince said.

"Right now," Rachel said, "he's holding in his hand what he likes most."

They could see him at the far end of the parking lot, standing in the dry, frozen grass up to his knees. He shook it off, zipped up, and ran toward them, flapping his arms as if flying.

"Why couldn't you use the facilities like everybody else?" JFK grumbled.

"I'm Mother Nature's son," Dallas said.

"Well, Father Society might get you arrested and have your ass whupped," Rachel said.

They filed into the van.

"I reject society," Dallas said, "and its stupid rules."

"Buckle up!" JFK ordered.

He got a letter from the University of Chicago and they offered him a job in the lab, studying the effects of radiation on living organisms. The person who offered him a job sent him back his letter with little grammar lessons in the margins. It was at the University of Chicago that he met her grandmother: she was an astronomy student, but worked part time as a secretary for the nuclear people. He asked her out and they went to the Aragon Ballroom, where he could not jitterbug or swing or whatever they danced, all he knew were waltzes and polkas. They fell head over heels in love. Rachel's grandfather lived in a basement in Humboldt Park, and Grandmother lived with her parents, moral Hyde Park Jews, so all they could do was dance. Anyway, he would go down to Oak Ridge. They would expose plants and mice to radiation, plutonium and isotopes and shit, and watch what would happen.

"Yeah," JFK said, "there is an African-American community called Scarboro there, and they lived downstream from the lab, you know, kids swimming in a radioactive stream. Sometimes they'd let the steam out too. And they watched what would happen."

"What happened?" Pronek asked.

"Oh, you know, the usual stuff, kids born without a spine, cancer, tumors."

"Shit!" Dallas said.

"Proud to be American," Vince said.

Rachel's grandfather went down to Tennessee every once in a while with a driver, because he didn't want to drive. He sat in the back seat writing letters to Grandma, describing the landscape and all his thoughts and all his love. They would stop some-where and he would mail the letter, and start a new one imme-diately. It took them two or three days to get down there and she would get ten, fifteen letters. He would stain the letter with grease and write "Kentucky grease" below. He would send her flowers and dry tree leaves pressed in the envelope. When he saved up money, he bought a camera and had the boys at Oak Ridge develop the film and make photos and he'd send them to her—he wanted to be with her all the time, all the time.

Rachel had seen the letters: his English was bad, no articles, no tenses, scrambled sentences, but they were beautiful, she said, brimming with old-fashioned, old-worldly schmaltzy love.

———

They passed houses tiny on the horizon, and clouds above them, a shadowy curtain of rain hanging down. They passed furrowed fields and mall clusters with gas stations and McDonald's and Subways, then the van would sink between hills and go up and down into valleys with vapid ponds. Pronek imagined writing letters to Rachel, describing these hills and how they reminded him of places in Bosnia.

He would do his experiments thinking of Grandma. In those days, they didn't care much about radioactivity—in fact, until the day he died, his bones rotten, he claimed that radioactivity was harmless. Anyway, he would stir uranium in a pot, as if cooking, no masks or gloves, nothing, and he would be thinking of Grandma, her alabaster thighs and her gentle hands, whatever, and a drop of uranium would leap out of the pot and land on his lip, and he would just wipe it off.

Rachel moved her thumb across her lips, slowly, then licked them, while Pronek watched, mesmerized.

"Where did you get that corny shit?" Dallas said.

"Shut up!" Vince said.

The spot where the uranium drop fell burned and he wrote to Grandmother that his lips were burning to kiss her.

They drove through Kentucky, over high bridges spanning lumpy red and ochre hills. They drove through towns consisting of boarded-up houses and a Jiffy Lube shop. They drove past tranquil grazing horses, tall and lean, raising their heads to look into the distance, then moving, trot by trot, until they were galloping in circles enclosed by a white fence. Pronek imagined them rising and jumping over the fence, but then was afraid that they might break their legs landing.

"I have the friend," Pronek said, "who likes horses very much. My best friend in Sarajevo."

"Does he have a horse?" Rachel asked.

"I had a horse," Dallas said. "My grandfather in Texas—"

"That's nice," Rachel said. "Except nobody asked you."

"Oh, no, he doesn't," Pronek said. "But he always dreamed about the horses. I will show you his letter that he wrote me. It is very sad."

"The letter he wrote you," Rachel said.

"Right," Pronek said.

"Not his letter that he wrote you."

"Okay."

"I noticed," Dallas said, "that you use a lot of the's."

"The what?"

"The none-of-his-goddamn-business the!" Rachel hissed.

"What the fuck is wrong with you?" Dallas slammed his hand against the dashboard—a puff of dust rose under the Kentucky-hill light.

"Nothing the fuck is wrong with me. I just can't stand you."

"Hey, hey, hey!" JFK said.

"I will read you the letter," Pronek said. "I have it at the home."

"At home," Dallas said. "*At home.*"

They slept in the same tent, Pronek squeezed between Dallas and Rachel, JFK on the far end with Vince. They felt the chilly night pasting the frost on the tent, the moon scintillating through the walls. Pronek lay on his back, feeling the warmth of Rachel's body through the sleeping bags. He heard her breathing, peaceful and deep. He inhaled the smell of her hair, her sweat, and her fatigue. Dallas was snoring, JFK was tossing and turning. Pronek turned toward Rachel and watched her face under the feeble, diffuse moonlight seeping through. Her forehead unwrinkled and her eyelids curved beautifully, her eyelashes still. Her lips were motionless, no word forming in her mouth. The sleeping-bag hood framed her face, as if holding it up for Pronek to see, a stray lock resting on her temple.

Then she opened her eyes.

Pronek was petrified. She gazed at him from her depths, she clearly knew he had been watching her. She blinked without fuss, comfortable with Pronek's look stroking her face. She moved her head toward him, closed her eyes, and planted a kiss on his lips. Pronek was so frozen, the unreality of the moment stiffening the muscles in his back and neck, that he couldn't respond, until he felt her tongue parting his lips and he let it in.

"If you press your dick against me one more time," JFK said, "you're going to have to sleep outside. How's that?"

"What the fuck are you talking about?" Dallas said, and turned toward Pronek. Pronek felt the heat of Dallas's body on his back, but Rachel's hand was moving across his face, and he closed his eyes, his lips burning.

They had a couple of hours before the protest, and JFK dropped them off at the American Museum of Science and Energy. Rachel made Pronek stand under an American flag, got down on her knees at his feet, and took a picture of his face, headed by his chin, the flag limp over him. Pronek had woken up that morning thinking that he might have dreamt it all. Rachel gave him no reassurance: she busied herself with excavating a toothbrush from her backpack. She'd look up at Pronek smilelessly, wearing the CONFUSION IS SEX shirt, which he could not help finding ominous. On their way to the museum, she sat in the front seat, and he was convinced that whatever peaks of love they had reached last night, whispering and softly kissing, they tumbled down to the bottom this morning. JFK drove them through the fields of forlorn malls, parking lots, and fast-food joints, like forts, on their edges. They went by a pond on which a couple of swans floated with their heads bowed, but Pronek could not tell whether they were plastic or real. The possibility that the world could never respond to his desires tortured him.

The museum was full of elderly women in floral jackets, their wrinkles made-up, their glasses magnifying their eyes. One of them said: "Well, if you want a chain reaction, you gotta have graphite," with a thick Southern accent, and Pronek was afraid that they might address him in their general enthusiasm—his accent would sound even more foreign and conspicuous. He anchored himself to Rachel and followed her like a shadow, hoping all along that she would give him a signal that would make last night real. She paced slowly through The Secret City room, her hands in her back pockets.

There was a prophet, a panel on the wall said, whose name was John Hendricks. In the 1890s, the prophet had put his ear to the ground and heard a terrible voice saying that this valley would be flooded with strangers seeking salvation, arriving here to unleash the soul of the stars. Rachel frowned at the panel and walked on toward a poster of a red-haired forties beauty pouting her thick, gorgeous lips—WANTED! FOR MURDER! HER CARELESS TALK COSTS LIVES! the poster read. But Pronek wondered about the prophet, what had happened to him. Had they hung him? Had they rolled him in tar and feathers? Had he become their leader? Could he have known what would happen in the end? Rachel was standing in front of black-and-white pictures of mud fields and "Negro Hutments" in their middles. There were pictures of a herd of smiling white-clad nurses; of women happily smoking in a prefabricated house; of uniformed, unsmiling guards searching through Santa's bag, his hands up. Pronek wanted to ask her about last night and kept rehearsing the question, but could not get it right. The question-forming addled his brain and he stood in front of the pictures uncomprehending. There were boys playing marbles and a theater marquee reading IS EVERYBODY HAPPY? There were Geiger counters and nylon hoses in glass cases. There were army officers standing next to a uranium cache. Pronek could smell Rachel: the wet-autumn-leaves scent of unchanged clothes and slumber sweat, the scent that had entered his nostrils last night and would not leave. There were two young women, with their legs prudently together, sitting in front of a wall of containers populated with lab mice. In the Big Boy room, there were nuclear mushrooms swelling in leaps in the desert. Rachel stopped in front of the mushroom pictures and rolled her eyes and shook her head, and Pronek feared that the old Southern ladies might see her, think it unpatriotic, and start admonishing her for her behavior, just as he was about to ask her about last night. He caught up and stepped in front of her. "The last night . . ." he murmured. She rose on her toes and kissed the Y between his eyebrows, her hands still in her pockets, as the old ladies ambled and swerved around them, scoffing.

Pronek watched a couple of Greenpeace people chain themselves to the gate of the Laboratory, while bodies lay strewn on the driveway, eager to passively resist, Rachel's body in the center, her arms at her sides, her palms pressing the concrete. He stood across the road with the sign saying WE WANT THE FUTURE! and feared for Rachel. He saw security climbing over the gates, moving swiftly and angrily, yelling at the chained people. A couple of guards started cutting the chains, the rest started picking up the bodies and telling them their rights as a Black Maria came from around the curve as if it had been hiding there all along. "One two three four we don't want no nukes no more!" Pronek chanted, standing next to a midgety guy with pork-chop sideburns and heavy boots. He occasionally corrected the chant: "One two three four we don't want *any* nukes *any*more!" and the midgety guy looked at him askance as if suspecting him to be an FBI spy. Two tough-looking security guards picked up Rachel, one grabbing her ankles (Pronek imagined them delicate and fragile), the other grabbing her armpits (Pronek knew the smell), and she slumped between them, her butt almost touching the ground. He closed his eyes, and mumbled to himself: "Bring her to me," as if sending a telepathic message. But the men in uniform did not receive it and packed Rachel away into the Black Maria. Pronek envisioned himself in jail with Rachel, then getting away with her. They would drive across America together, and then sail across the Pacific.

The South Side factories still spewed fire and smoke. Pronek saw the Chicago skyline on the horizon, the boxy shapes alight against the navy-blue sky, cold and splendid.

"This is pretty," he said, to no one in particular, as everybody except JFK was asleep: Vince put his Chip-and-Dale bag under his cheek and leaned against the window. Dallas drooled in the front seat. Rachel had her head on Pronek's shoulder, her hand touching his thigh. Warm air was coming out of her nostrils down his arm, her hair tickling his cheek. His back was tight and it hurt, but he didn't want to move.

"Yeah, it's pretty," JFK said.

Rachel slept on the El, still pressing her temple against the tip of Pronek's shoulder, despite the hellacious noise and a posse of kids rapping over it about their life in the Robert Taylor homes. Two young women sat close in front of them, their long dark hair falling over the handlebars. Pronek saw the left one leaning toward her friend, touching her ear with her lips ever so slightly and saying: "I love you." The train surfaced from the underground and the lights of the city glared through the grimy windows. The women got off at Belmont, holding hands.

Rachel got off at Lawrence, drowsy and barely conscious. She said she would see him tomorrow, and tomorrow seemed so distant to Pronek that he wanted to weep. He watched her descending the stairs and vanishing—he was already pining for her, the argon-neon lights making his face red.

When he unlocked the door of his studio, everything was in its place: the coffee mug that said KISS ME, I'M IRISH he had whimsically bought in a thrift shop still on the verge of the table; the map of the world still taped to the wall; the clock shaped like a pumpkin, which someone had left in the laundry room, still ticking; a pair of brown shoes turning away from each other in disgust; the washed plate in the rack leaning over the sink, as if wanting to see its own reflection—everything was precisely as he had left it. The amazing thing was, he thought, that when he wasn't there, nobody was there—the space he occupied was empty when he was elsewhere. But the smell was different—he could sense a pungent, plastic scent, wholly unfamiliar to him. He moved, sniffing, stepping carefully on the tips of his toes, not turning on the light, ready for an attack, like a wolf returning to his violated den, his body tense and cocked, his eyes scorched with fatigue. He pussyfooted into his bedroom—his shirt stretched on the mattress as if playing dead. He went back to the kitchen, touched the bottom of the empty sink (a cockroach slipping into the hole), headlights flickering on the walls. He dropped to his knees and smelled the carpet in the middle of the room and under the radiator, but he couldn't locate the source. He imagined someone sneaking into his place and browsing crassly and impatiently through everything in this little museum of his life: a green toy chopper he had stolen from someone's porch; a tin windup frog; a frame with a picture of his parents, raising glasses, drunk; a puny wooden bowl full of marbles; a piece of wooden board with nails in it resembling the outline of the Great Bear. He imagined the intruder trying on his clothes, buttoning up his shirts. What would the intruder think of him, Pronek wondered, of his life? He moved on to the bathroom, where there was a new shower curtain the landlord had put in, exuding a sharp, chemical odor, shimmering in the dark.

DEATH IN VENICE

Pronek woke up with a vague, flabby erection and an itchy feeling that his life was happening to someone else. He sat at the table drinking coffee from the Irish mug, watching the people at the El stop waiting: a woman reading a book on a bench; a teenage boy twitching his head, following an obscure rhythm; a man with a straw hat and a sallow face, bending forward as if the morning were a sack of cement; a teenage girl with a palm of hair on top of her head and concentric gold chains on her chest. They stood far apart, not looking at one another. The sun glittered on the rails. This moment, Pronek thought, would not be remembered by anybody but him, and one day it would vanish from his memory too.

William stood at Pronek's door in his dancing-teddy-bears underwear, his head huge, his face armored with acne. His phone was disconnected, and he needed to use the phone, he said, to respond to a singles ad.

William was from Portland and had come to Chicago to break into the improv comedy business, but was currently delivering pizzas and working in a moving company, his hands bruised every time Pronek saw him. After a small-talk session in the elevator, whereby William detected foreignness in Pronek's curt responses, he had knocked at Pronek's door and wanted to pick up Pronek's accent for his improv routine. He had asked Pronek the standard questions (When and whence he came to the US?), then tried to imitate him, improvising a situation in which he was a foreign taxi driver. Pronek had listened to him and his morbidly unfunny performance that included idiotic grimaces and an accent that to Pronek sounded Irish. He felt his chest hollowing with fear and sorrow, while William kept laughing at his own lamentable jokes.

Pronek let him in and stood leaning against the kitchen counter, while William called the dating service. Pronek could see the sink cockroach emerging from the hole, then cautiously scurrying toward the stove, but he didn't move.

"Hi, my name is William. Uhmm, I like *Pulp Fiction* and Asian cuisine and David Sedaris."

He stuck his head into the bathroom, stretching the phone cord to the end, slowly pulling the phone off the table.

"There is nothing I want more than to give you a foot massage by the fireplace, sipping a foreign beer, singing my favorite song, which is, uhmm, 'Yesterday.' It would go like this . . . Yesterday, all my troubles seemed so far away . . ."

William sang in a feeble, flat voice, occasionally reaching the hoarse pitch of a tubercular baritone. The bathroom echoed the awful sounds and Pronek imagined the person listening to this hapless message, cringing. He remembered when he used to sing this song and was suddenly retroactively ashamed—he recalled himself with a guitar, strumming, trying to express the deep emotions contained in the song, and his skin crawled at the horror of his own stupidity, at the times when he thought that "Yesterday" was anything but a sappy song, at the times when he was someone else.

"Suddenly, I'm not half the man I used to be, there's a shadow hanging over me . . ." sang William, pulling up the edge of his boxers to scratch his thigh and revealing a pimple clearly evolving toward a boil. The phone slid off the table and crashed on the floor.

Rachel canvassed on the other side of the street. He could see her going up to the porch and ringing the bell, then looking around at the mailbox stuffed with magazines, at the lawns with wooden ducks and marble frogs and plastic angels and sprinkles, aluminum spiders with long green tails. He watched her head moving left and right as she spoke to the people who opened the door. Occasionally, she smiled and waved at him, walking between houses, the light diffused by yellow leaves softening the pallor of her face.

Pronek stood in front of a closed door, procrastinating, and when he rang the bell he prayed to the gods of corporate employment that nobody be home. He tried to talk about the dolphins to the people who opened the door, but they stared at him with dim contempt and no interest whatever. Door after door was slammed in his face and anger accumulated in his stomach. He kicked a neon-green plastic bucket and it banged against the picket fence.

"Come on in," the woman said. "I've been waiting for you."

She was short and frail, a humongous scarf coiled around her neck. Pronek stepped into the house, reluctantly, particles of something crackling under his shoes. The screen door banged him in the back, as if hurrying him inside.

"Are you hungry?" she asked Pronek. The house had a humid noodly smell. A fat little Buddha sat on a bookshelf, grinning, next to a hedgehog of incense sticks. There was a mirror above the mantelpiece and Pronek stared at himself for a moment.

"No, thank you," Pronek said.

"But I made the won-ton soup you like," she said, "and some fried chicken too."

Won-ton soup was Pronek's favorite, and fried chicken too.

"Thank you," he said, his stomach suddenly empty.

"Johnny and Grace might join us," the woman said. "I might need you to go and get some sprouts."

Let me suggest that if Pronek were a building with an elevator sliding up and down the chute between his brain and his stomach, at that particular moment the elevator would have dropped a hundred floors, pulled down by horrendous gravity, and it would have slammed into the ground, collapsing whoever was in that elevator into a painful, mushy pile.

"And you could have called me to say you would be late," the woman said. She put her hands on her hips and shook her head admonishingly.

"I am not," Pronek said, his throat tight, "who you think I am."

"Oh, I know you better than anyone," the woman said, waved her hand toward him and frowned benevolently.

A jungle of lush plants was arrayed on the windowsills. A calendar with a picture of a street in Saigon and things written in an impenetrable alphabet hung on the wall, smiley faces in some date boxes. The woman's skin was dark and she had a wide, cheeky face, framed by thick black hair. She might be Vietnamese, Pronek thought, but who am I?

"I am with Greenpeace," he said to the woman, and exhibited as evidence his clipboard with a green-and-blue-planet leaflet. The year on the calendar was 1975, Pronek realized.

She laughed heartily, clapping her hands, applauding his performance.

"You always make me laugh," she said, and touched her stomach, as if laughing hurt her.

"Ma'am," Pronek tried again, but had no will to push it further, as he could not remember how he got here, how he had become what he was. He sat down into an embracing armchair facing an extinguished TV. There was a pair of man's slippers, blue and soft, carefully aligned next to the armchair, within his reach. He closed his eyes, hoping that the woman would vanish when he opened them. But she was still there. What would happen, Pronek thought, if he simply took off his shoes and put the slippers on his feet, swollen from walking? If he had some of that won-ton soup? Who would get hurt? Pronek saw himself trudging to the kitchen in his slippers, taking his seat and eating his soup, the woman gently rubbing his back. Why couldn't he be more than one person? Why was he stuck in the middle of himself, hungry and tired?

"Ma'am," he said, still hesitant, whispering, his words teetering on the edge of silence. "I am very sorry, but I am not somebody you know."

"Don't worry about it so much," the woman said, softly, moving closer to him, a touch away. "The soup is getting cold."

Rachel unlocked the door, and a large cat tried to push its way through, only to be pushed back by her foot.

"This is the cat," she said.

"What is her name?" Pronek asked.

"I call him the cat. He's Maxwell's cat. He calls him Zora."

"Who is Maxwell?"

"My roommate."

"Oh."

Rachel turned on the light and locked the door behind her. The Cat sniffed Pronek's shoes, then looked up at him. "*Zora*," he said, "means very early morning in my language."

The walls were painted turquoise with a thick red line going wall to wall along the middle. The Cat leapt on the sofa and crawled under a cushion.

"Well, he's no early morning. Maxwell spoils him beyond words."

"Is he your boyfriend?"

"Maxwell is beautiful," she said. "Unfortunately, he's gay."

"Oh."

Rachel then dimmed the lights. Pronek slumped onto the sofa and felt fatigue dropping to his pelvis and his thighs.

"Maxwell's a musician, plays the trumpet. Has a jazz band with his boyfriend Aaron. He thinks he's the hip-hop Miles."

"Who is the hip-hop Miles?"

"You know, Miles Davis, the hip-hop version."

"Oh."

There was a black-and-white photo of a man crossing the street, slouched, one of his feet about to land on the ground, as if he were stepping on a spider. Rachel sat next to Pronek, put her hand on his thigh, and said:

"Would you like something? To drink?"

Her eyebrows were converging toward each other, the gossamer glistened on the convex slope above her nose, her eyeballs glossy—he imagined touching them with the tip of his tongue and thought: *Blago*.

"No."

"Well, I would. A man can use some whiskey after a hard day's work."

"Okay, give me one whiskey."

It was while Rachel was in the kitchen—glasses clinking, water running, indeterminate noises ebbing—that he imagined himself imagining himself in this room, dimly lit, waiting for a woman who could only know what he told her in his sloppy English and distorting accent. He saw clearly that who he thought he was and who she thought he was were two different persons. He imagined himself doubled, the two of them sitting next to each other on the damn sofa. The Cat was suddenly across the table, nestling in the armchair, panning from Pronek to his twin and back. Rachel appeared out of the dark hall with two glasses and said: "Let's go to my room." Pronek slowly got up, pushing himself with his fists off the sofa.

I wait for a moment, then lurch forward, scaring the Cat. I follow him to Rachel's bedroom, and slip in before they shut the door.

They sit on the bed, Rachel backlit with the bedside lamp, Pronek's back to me, as I soundlessly deposit myself at her desk in a dark corner, breathing in through my mouth and out through my nose, barely, inaudibly.

They sip the whiskey, in desirous silence, probably looking into each other's eyes. Rachel kisses his mouth, then pulls back, waiting for his move. Pronek gulps his whiskey then leans toward her and grabs her pate, pushing her face toward him. In his other hand, the glass is slowly leaning on his knee, until the diluted whiskey starts dripping on the floor.

They slowly stretch on the bed, their feet still on the floor. Oh, I've seen it many times before, the foreplay. I know the disbelief, the doubt as he's peeling off layer upon layer of her clothes, as she unbuttons his shirt. I look at the things on her desk: a message from one Daren, a Ciccione Youth CD; an application for an ESL teaching position. There are contact copies with small photos of an empty picture frame; of a light post broken in half, like a pencil; of an anonymous suburban porch; of Pronek looking out of the picture, the American flag limp above his head. There is a thick stack of papers with notes scribbled on them in handwriting leaning down, like wheat in the wind. I read them:

They swallowed cheeseburgers like pills. Yet they were sad.

My violence is a dream.

Rachel is taking off her shoes, having some trouble untying them, giggling.

Jozef had a blues band back home. He is a good man, but there are bubbles coming up from the creature at his bottom.

Fall arrived August 28, around noon. Suddenly the light was soft, the sun rays were coming at you with their heads bowed, chaffing their cheeks against your sides like a purring cat.

Rachel has unbuttoned Pronek's shirt, her legs are bare, I can see her crotch and her panties. Pronek is looking down at her hands. She slides the shirt down his shoulders, then pulls up his undershirt, laughing and shaking her head. "I was cold," Pronek says. She kisses his chest and tickles his left nipple with her tongue. Pronek gasps.

Dog eyes crusted with dog tears.

Pronek works on unfastening her bra, as she rakes his hair with her fingers. "It is dirty," Pronek says. "Not yet," Rachel says, and laughs again, leaning back just as Pronek solves the bra riddle——her breasts lunge forward.

Outside I can hear squirrels cackling. How can I know they are not talking to me if I don't know their language?

Slowly and carefully, as if an unsoft touch would break everything, Pronek pulls Rachel's panties down her thighs, over her knees, until she wiggles her feet through the loops. She is naked now, a beautiful body to look at, the light scintillating on her skin. "Let's put a condom on," she says.

Everything in the supermarket has a non-negotiable name. Love will tear us apart.

Pronek is ripping the condom wrapper, like an excited puppy, his back arched, his spine saw-toothed. "I hate condoms," he says, and bites into the wrapper again. Rachel chortles: "If we start dating seriously you can get the washable kind and never take it off." Pronek produces a grim laugh, the condom still unconquered. "Oh, give it to me," Rachel says, and the condom is offered on her palm in no time. "And let me put it on."

Oh, what is that sound which so thrills the ear
Down in the valley, drumming, drumming?
Only the scarlet soldiers, dear,
The soldiers coming.

"Can I turn off light?" Pronek says.

"The light."

"What?"

"Can I turn off *the* light?"

"Turn off the light."

Rachel turns off the light.

I sit in the darkness, only an occasional headlight mirage appearing on the walls and perishing fast. I listen to their sobs and pants, the tossing and turning and wrestling, the collision of flesh with flesh, a wheeze, a word: yes, *blago*, no, slowly. I cannot help being aroused, hearing their bodies wrangling in the darkness. I have to breathe timing the intake to coincide with the noises of their passion, the hand of lust gripping my throat, my loins burning. I move and the chair screeches.

"What is that?" Pronek says.

"Nothing. It's okay. Come here."

"I heard something."

"It's nothing. Let's fuck."

She starts producing a submerged squeal, which then turns into a fitful roar, while Pronek produces a sibilant, teeth-clenched sound as if someone were punching him in the chest. Then, to my relief, it is over—they come in duet.

Silence.

"Did you enjoy it?" Pronek says.

"Quiet."

The room smells of their sweat and clothes. I can feel Pronek's untense body and the tension slowly rebuilding itself—he is flexing his fingers, crushing an imaginary object.

"Can I smoke?" he pleads.

"Not here. On the deck."

Then there is a short knock on the door and someone bursts into the room. Pronek lurches out of bed and falls on the floor and stays down.

"Rachel," the man said.

"For God's sake, Maxwell. I am not alone. What the hell is wrong with you?"

"Shit," Maxwell said, and stepped out of the room, closing the door behind him.

"Sorry," he said behind the closed door. "Rachel, I need a condom, I'm out."

"Oh, God," Rachel said, and got out of bed.

Pronek lay facedown on the floor, his heart beating so hard he imagined it trying to dig its way out with its little paws.

Rachel would not hold hands—it made her feel like a little girl, she said. But they walked all around Uptown: they looked at the old houses on Beacon, imagining crazy old ladies sheltering hundreds of cats; they sneaked into the Uptown National Bank, admiring its marble counters and high-domed ceilings, fantasizing about robbing it like Bonnie and Clyde; they strolled through the park, past a homeless camp, Rachel taking pictures, past the squash-shaped Russian ladies gibbering up soft consonants. They went to Montrose Harbor and watched the waves slamming into the embankment. She liked to take photos of the back of his neck, Pronek facing the lake, the cresting waves and a few displaced clouds lingering over the thin horizon, moving toward the skyscrapers, Rachel's camera clicking behind him, like a hiccuping clock. At dusk, they gazed at the downtown skyline twinkling in the moist mist and were hypnotized by the dotted-light snake slithering up Lake Shore Drive, cars on their way home.

"I love you."

"Don't say that."

"But I love you. I never felt the love like this."

"Don't say that."

"Why?"

"Don't ruin it."

"Ruin what?"

"This."

"What is this?"

"Just hold me and kiss me."

Kiss.

"What is that?"

"What?"

"That sound."

"What sound?"

"That sound like somebody digs."

"Somebody is digging."

"Who is digging?"

"Somebody is digging, not somebody digs."

"What is the difference?"

"Well, one is right, the other is wrong."

"Okay, who is digging?"

"Well, it sounds more like scratching and moving. It's probably a mouse."

"Can I smoke?"

"Not here."

The floor was cold, and Pronek regretted being barefoot—he
couldn't afford to get sick. He saw himself lying alone in bed,
sweating and sneezing, his head throbbing, waiting for Rachel to
come back from work. The thought of being separated from her
had become unbearable. He trudged into the kitchen, tiptoeing
like an elephant ballerina to protect his soles from the cold.

Maxwell was washing a throng of wineglasses, naked, his springy dreadlocks falling on his shoulders.

"Good morning, Maxwell," Pronek said, but was not sure that he heard him.

"Hey, good morning," Maxwell said, glancing at Pronek, but not turning toward him. Pronek wanted orange juice, but all the glasses were being washed by the naked Maxwell, so he sat at the kitchen table, trying not to look at him. But his shoulders were wide, the blades resembling armor plates; his biceps shapely and round, twisting toward his elbows, the morning light absorbed by their brownness; his spine curving into a shallow valley above the half-moons of his butt. He turned toward Pronek.

"You've never seen a black man's body, have you?"

Pronek was terrified—he didn't want Maxwell to think he was gay.

"No."

"It's beautiful, isn't it."

Pronek felt an urge to run out of the kitchen, toward the safety of the bedroom, but was paralyzed. Maxwell's body was beautiful. The only move he could make was a slight turn toward the neutral zone of the blank opposite wall. The chair shrieked, stressing the ominous silence. Maxwell's nipples were pierced, the two rings akin to door knockers. He looked straight into Pronek's eyes and said:

"Would you like to touch it?"

He made a step toward Pronek, who leaned back, glancing around, pretending that he didn't see and didn't care. Maxwell's thighs were thin, curls strewn over their curves.

Aaron walked in, naked, his penis dangling, long and thick, his skin pink. Pronek looked away, at the friendly blank wall.

"Hey, what's going on here?" Aaron said. Maxwell raised his hands, turned toward Pronek, and shrugged.

"Are you trying to seduce my boyfriend?"

Pronek licked his lips, spotted a strawberry-shaped fridge magnet, and affixed his gaze to it. "No," he whimpered.

"You foreigners think you can just walk in and take our men," Aaron said. "But I understand—he is beautiful."

Pronek blinked rapidly, as if blinking itself were to produce a witty retort. But all he could say was:

"I am sorry."

Maxwell bent forward and burst out laughing. Aaron threw his head back and gave out a cough-like chortle. They high-fived, then hugged and kissed, their lips pressed hard—it all seemed like a well-rehearsed dance. Pronek was trying half-heartedly to laugh, still determinedly staring at the strawberry magnet, his back in rigid pain. He wanted to cross his legs, but it would have been conspicuous—they might think he was having an erection—whereupon the thought overwhelmed him that he might in fact get an erection. He heard Rachel coming out of the bathroom and she walked in, wearing a blue silk bathrobe, her hair wet, her face bright and beautiful.

"Jesus," she said, "this is like a fucking beach. All you need is a volleyball net."

"You'll never understand male bonding," Maxwell said.

Aaron filched a pomegranate seed from Maxwell's cereal bowl. Pronek claimed he wasn't hungry, even though he was starving, because he didn't want them to watch him while he was eating.

"Jozef used to have a band too," Rachel said. "Didn't you, Jozef?"

"No kidding!" Aaron said. "What kind of band?"

"Blues," Pronek said.

"A blues band?" Maxwell shook his head. "Wait a minute, did you come from a family of slaves?"

"No," Pronek said, "but the Bosnian music is like the blues."

"Bosnian music is like blues," Rachel said.

"Oh, leave him alone," Aaron said. "It is frightfully cute."

"So did you, like, have a blues name? Like, Blind Joseph Jefferson or something?"

"Well," Pronek said, and sighed, "it was Blind Jozef Pronek. That's me, Jozef Pronek."

Aaron and Maxwell high-fived each other and guffawed. Pronek tried to laugh too, but his throat was hoarse and Rachel wasn't laughing. It seemed that he had been stuck in the kitchen all day long.

"Oh, boy," Aaron said, and wiped his eyes. Maxwell examined Pronek's face, then Rachel's: "Blind Joseph Jefferson and Evol, love in reverse. You breeders crack me up."

Aaron was drumming on the steering wheel with his fingers, and Maxwell was slapping his thighs along with the music.

"Do you know what this is, Jefferson?" Maxwell said.

"No," Pronek said.

"It's Bitches Brew, the bitchin' Miles," Aaron said. It sounded hysterical to Jozef, but he said nothing.

"Stop calling him Jefferson," Rachel said.

"Hey, Blind Joseph Jefferson, the Czech blues singer, it's no joke," Aaron said, and cackled.

"I also was in the band that played the Beatles music."

"Man, how old are you—sixty-seven?"

They drove through a maze of bending suburban streets—

ghouls and pumpkins and plastic tombstones still strewn on dun lawns. The sky was gray, the drizzle sparkled under headlights. They could see porch lights going on and empty living rooms flickering around the TV, a silhouette moving across the window frame.

"Hundreds of serial killers are breeding in these basements as we speak," Maxwell said.

"You grew up in the suburbs," Rachel said.

"He just hasn't been caught yet," Aaron said.

"Hey, it was different, it was a loving family."

"Sure it was. You had a green lawn and a garage, unlike anybody else," Aaron said, and turned up the music.

There was a single plastic skeleton hanging on the lightless porch. Pronek had a vision of a body hanging, its flesh rotting and falling off in chunks, and he coming up to the door to canvass.

"I canvassed this house," he said, to no one in particular.

"That wasn't you," Rachel said.

The door opened and a flood of light fell on them. A shorn-haired woman with wide hips and narrow shoulders stood in the middle of it, like an apparition. The steel ball in Pronek's stomach started grinding his intestines.

"Hello, Mom," Rachel said, and kissed her on the cheek.

"Howdy, Rebecca," Aaron and Maxwell said in unison.

"Good evening," Pronek said.

"This is Blind Joseph Jefferson," Aaron said.

"Yes, ma'am," Maxwell said. "Every night he gets naked with your daughter and does naughty, naughty things. Naughty."

Rachel's mom looked at Pronek stone-faced, her lips straight and tight—Pronek could see the sinews on her neck tensing.

"Is that true?"

Pronek gulped and glanced at Rachel, who was looking at Maxwell and shaking her head.

"Yes," Pronek said, "but . . ."

"Oh, stop it!" Rachel said.

"I'm just kidding," Rachel's mom said. "Come in."

"I was in Sarajevo once," Rebecca said. "Long time ago, in the sixties. I was on my way to Dubrovnik."

"Dubrovnik is very beautiful," Pronek said, although he had been there only once, for half a day.

"I liked the old town in Sarajevo, those old Turkish shops and beautiful mosques. People were very nice."

"He's nice too," Rachel said. "Too nice."

"Did they have, like, little curtains over their faces?" Aaron asked.

"Oh, no," Pronek said. "That was long time ago."

"I met a Bosnian man there. He took me to these coffee shops and we drank strong, oh, my God, strong coffee from little cups and there was this sad music coming from the radio. He told me—very good English—he told me I must enjoy life because life is short."

"He just wanted to get into your pants," Aaron said.

"Jesus," Rachel said.

"Well, he did," Rebecca said, and threw her head back, releasing a fluttering laughter-bird toward the ceiling.

"What kind of music was that?" Maxwell asked.

"I don't know." Rebecca shrugged and pointed at Pronek. "Ask the native. It was very sad is all I remember."

"It was probably the *sevdalinka*. It is sad, but it is so sad that it makes you free. It is like the Bosnian blues."

"Do you know any of those songs?" Maxwell asked.

"Yeah."

"Sing."

"No."

"Why don't you sing us a song?" Rebecca said.

"No, thank you." Pronek's palms were sweating.

"If you do," Aaron said, "Rebecca will let you get naked with her daughter and do naughty things."

"Fuckin' naughty," Maxwell said.

"Please!" Rachel said and blushed, smiling.

Pronek cleared his throat.

> *Snijeg pade na behar na voće;*
> *Snijeg pade na behar na voće;*
> *Neka ljubi ko kod koga hoće;*
> *Neka ljubi ko god koga hoće...*
>
> *Ako neće nek' se ne nameće*
> *Ako neće nek' se ne nameće*
> *Od nameta nema selameta*
> *Od nameta nema selameta...*

He finished in a soft sussurous voice, allowing the last breaths to leave his lungs before he closed his mouth.

"That was beautiful," Rebecca said, and clapped.

"That's a beautiful song," Maxwell said. "What is it about?"

"I don't know how to translate," Pronek said.

"Try," Rachel said. "Please."

"The snow falls on the flowers in the spring and the fruit, and it is strange time."

"That is strange," Aaron said.

"And one dog wants to become the wolf. He goes to the forest and is free, but some men want to kill him."

"Why?" Rebecca asked.

"I don't know," Pronek said. "Because they have guns. And then it later says like this: If the dog is lucky as he is unhappy, he would go back home and be free."

"That reminds me of a Chinese proverb," Rebecca said, "that says: It's better to be rich and happy for a hundred years than to be poor and miserable for one day."

Rebecca kissed Pronek on the cheek and he could smell her perfume and alcohol breath. He wanted to kiss her too, but instead just said: "Thank you." It was cold outside, snow flurries flying out of the darkness into the light, like moths, some of them sticking to their clothes and then melting away with a sparkle.

"I loved that song."

"Thank you."

"I never knew you could sing like that."

"Thank you."

"My mom liked you."

"I liked her."

"You know, Maxwell and Aaron are moving in together. They found a place in Evanston."

"Good."

"I'll have to find a roommate."

"I see."

"My dad moved in with my mom the day they met."

"The same day?"

"Yeah. She met him in a bus station. He had no place to stay so she took him home."

"How long he stayed?"

"Twelve years."

They heard Maxwell and Aaron playing their trumpets, the plaintive wails coming from the kitchen. Pronek was a little drunk and when he closed his eyes he could see flashing spirals, and he could smell Rachel's hair, her elbow touching his ribs.

"I'm happy we are together," she said.

Some of his cracked chairs and the shabby table he left by the Dumpster, along with cracked dishes, permanently smudged glasses, and a rotten mattress, which Pronek suspected was home to a fresh brood of cockroaches. The rest fit into five boxes, which he carried upstairs one at a time. He put the towels in the dresser, next to his underwear. He hung up his clothes in his half of the closet. He put the box of Mirza's letters under the bed. He positioned a couple of picture frames on the TV: Pronek on stage with Dead Souls; his drunk parents holding hands awkwardly. He deployed the toy chopper on the bookshelf and the marble bowl on the coffee table. He hung up the map of the world in the kitchen and scattered other things that belonged to him around the apartment, marking his territory, like a dog pissing on trees—wherever he looked there was a trace of him. And when he was brushing his teeth while Rachel waited in bed, it exhilarated him that he was in the bathroom while she was in the bedroom.

Rachel said: "I'll wait here." Pronek went through a maze of walls, then through low, arched gates, and he realized he was inside a castle. He found his way to a locker room and was waiting in front of a locker for it to open, but then decided to tinker with the lock. He was sticking a graphite pen into it, when someone walked in. He quickly collected himself and with a perfect American accent, so perfect it seemed someone else was speaking, as if he were a soul-infested ventriloquist's dummy, he said: "Do not trespass on my domain!" The trespasser was Sila the Drummer, wearing a green beret, a snare drum hanging from his neck. "This place stinks with foreigners," Pronek said. "Damn right!" Sila said. Then Pronek was rummaging through the locker, which had a bedroom and a bathroom and a garden with an ear-shaped bird bath. He took a silver cell phone from the garden and a roll of film from the bedroom, and a condom from the bathroom and put them in his pocket. Then he was crawling along the inside walls of the castle and was out in no time. He saw people going down the craggy hill backward, everybody holding on to their own rope. It was some kind of pilgrimage in reverse—somehow he knew that at the bottom of the hill there was a bleeding saint who had tumbled down. Everybody was carrying their possessions in their hands, still managing to hold on to the rope—he saw Maxwell carrying a kite; he saw Dallas carrying a shoe box with a nuclear reactor and a banjo. He saw his father dragging a dead, rotten Rottweiler on a leash. There was a herd of three-year-old boys with hairy chests, each of them holding a swarm of flies forming different shapes in their hands: a banana, a revolver, the shape of Yugoslavia. He saw strangers carrying downhill things he recognized as his own: the guitar he had sold before coming to America; the blue UNHCR letters he had received from Mirza; a jar full of marbles in different colors. He saw a couple of Siamese twins, joined at the hip, a box in their four hands containing a soulless football; a broken-boned umbrella; some sacred scrolls; a bundle of shoes with crescent soles. One of the twins shot a vicious glance at Pronek and Pronek understood that he had broken into their locker. He got terribly afraid, he sped up running backward down the hill, faster and faster, the rope burning his palms, and he couldn't see where he was going—all he could see was the huge rock on the top of the hill the saint had pushed up and left there.

Pronek listened to Rachel's even breathing, trying to calm down, but his heart was pounding, the balls of his feet sore, the arches tense, as if he had just stopped running.

"Rachel, what is that sound?"

He leaned over her. Her face was calm, her eyelids relaxed, she murmured something he could not understand and for a moment he hated her because she could sleep so peacefully, so far away from him, dreaming different dreams.

"Rachel, what is it?"

He touched her shoulder and she shuddered, yelped, and snapped her eyes open. She looked at Pronek with frightened surprise as if she couldn't recognize him.

"Rachel, it's me."

She pushed him away and sat up in bed, suddenly snorting and breathing heavily.

"Rachel, what is that sound?"

"What are you talking about?"

"Listen!"

There was nothing to hear. They were motionless, silent, in the darkness.

"Go to sleep, Jozef."

"No. Listen."

There was scraping and scuffling, barely audible, somewhere in the hall. Pronek leapt out of bed and tiptoed out of the bedroom, then turned the hall light on abruptly.

"What the hell is wrong with you?"

Rachel put on her robe and followed him out. Pronek was advancing toward the kitchen, his body taut and ready in his flannel pajamas.

"It's three in the morning, for God's sake."

Pronek turned on the light in the kitchen, then determinedly got on all fours and crept along the floor. Rachel stood at the door, barefoot and cold.

"Listen."

"Oh, Jesus."

Pronek went under the table in the corner, she could see only the soles of his feet. "Mouse!" he shouted, and banged his head against the table. Something darted past Rachel's cold feet and she trotted for an instant as if dancing. It ran along the walls of the living room and went behind the sofa. Pronek got out from under the table holding his pate and got up.

"It's the mouse," he said.

"It's behind the sofa."

Pronek strode toward the sofa, then pushed it away from the wall. The mouse was in the corner shivering, huddled, a light-tentacle reaching its tail.

"Give me something," Pronek said. The mouse was fat, a short evolutional step from a rat, its cheeks bulging as if it had been caught eating and still was chewing the food.

"What do you want?"

"Something."

Rachel grabbed a book off the shelf: "Here."

Pronek took the book, looked at the title page, and flipped through it—it was *The Idiot*.

"Not this one."

"You gotta be kidding me! What difference does it make?"

"Not this."

She put the book back on the shelf and stood, with her hands pressing against her back, choosing another one:

"Do you want fiction or biography?" she asked, irked.

The mouse dared to move, its back against the wall, but Pronek stomped his foot.

"Here is *Death in Venice*," she said.

Pronek grasped the book—it was a small paperback, thick and reeking of library must. He slammed the mouse—once, twice. The mouse squealed and squeaked and writhed as Pronek kept hitting it until it stopped moving and producing sounds.

"God!" Rachel said.

"I think it's dead."

"What are we going to do now?"

"I don't know."

He was still holding *Death in Venice*, his eyes fiery—he had just killed a living creature and felt nauseated, as if he had swallowed blood. Rachel came back with a broom and a dustpan and offered them to Pronek.

"Why me?"

"All right, step back."

She pushed the mouse onto the bin with the broom and it rolled over, but then it shook its head and flexed its legs, as if waking up from a long sleep.

"Jesus, it's alive," she grunted.

"Fuck," Pronek said, and realized that if someone were listening he'd think Pronek was saying it like a real American. "Motherfucker," he said.

"Get a bucket and fill it up with water," Rachel said.

Pronek found a tin bucket in the bathroom, emptied it of rags and sponges, and filled it up halfway with water—he watched the deluge coming out of the faucet and imagined himself at the bottom of the bucket, the water coming down crashing on him.

Rachel was pressing the mouse down on the pan with the broom. She dropped it into the bucket. For a moment the mouse floated on its back, a grin of horror on its little pointy face, but then it turned over and started swimming. The water was clear, they could see the bottom. The mouse was scratching the walls with its claws, trying to climb up, but it was clearly hopeless.

"Drown it," Rachel said.

"I can't."

"Drown it!" She pressed the mouse's head with her index finger, the mouse sank but then resurfaced. She pressed it again, but then recoiled when it tried to grab her finger. The mouse flapped around with its tiny paws, its tail snaking behind. When it reached the bucket wall, it scratched it frantically.

"Maybe we can leave it there," Pronek said.

"I don't think so. I don't want to listen to its death throes all night long."

"Maybe we can throw it outside."

"No, it has to die."

"I have never seen the mouse like this."

"A mouse like this."

"What?"

"A mouse like this. Not the mouse like this."

"Why you have to correct me all the time?" He stood up and turned away in anger from Rachel and the bucket.

"Why do you have to correct me all the time?"

"What's difference? You understand me."

"What's the difference."

"Stop it!" he yelled.

"Don't you yell at me!" Rachel screamed back.

The mouse was swimming in circles. Pronek felt rage leavening in his stomach, something pushing the inside of his temples, the heat swarming in his eyeballs. He stood facing Rachel, who looked at him with belligerent disgust. It became clear to him at that moment that he didn't want to be there—the thought spread out before him like a ski slope—and there was nowhere he wanted to be. He heard the mouse scraping the bucket, the horrible din. And then, with a motion of his foot that seemed incredibly slow to him, but startled Rachel, he kicked the bucket and it flew toward the wall, the water splashing and sloshing around, stray droplets sparkling. He felt the release inside—the fury deluge broke the dam in his stomach and flooded his body as the bucket smashed into the wall.

"What the fuck are you doing?" Rachel grabbed her hair and pulled it.

"Correct this!" he screamed, and flung *The Idiot* across the room. He grabbed the marble bowl and emptied it on the floor—the marbles cackling hysterically and rolling away in myriad directions. He smashed a flowerless vase against the wall. He swept the picture frames off the TV and they crashed on the floor, the shards scattering around. He kicked the pumpkin-shaped clock like a soccer ball and it landed on the sofa. He walked over the shards toward the Kiss-Me-I'm-Irish mug and pitched it at the floor. He flung the tin frog toward the kitchen, stomping over the shards, cutting his soles. In the kitchen, he ripped the map of the world off the floor and stamped on it, leaving bloody smudges.

"What are you doing? I'll call the police!"

He grabbed a pomegranate and smashed it against the wall, the pomegranate exploding like a head, the crimson brains everywhere.

"Call the goddamn police. Let them throw me out of this fucking country!"

He snatched Rachel's photos off the wall and smashed them. He pulled books off the shelves, tore them apart, and launched the pages toward the ceiling. And all along there was a tranquil nook inside him, from which someone else was calmly observing him wreaking havoc.

"What got into you?" Rachel cried. "I love you! What did I do to you?"

He pulled the phone cord and the receiver split from the phone and fell on top of the book pile. He pushed the TV off the stall and it came down with a thud. Rachel ran toward the bedroom, and Pronek followed her, ready to do the bedroom too. He punched the bedroom door, bloodying his knuckles.

She emerged from the room with the camera. She started pressing the camera button frantically, saying: "What did I do to you?" and Pronek saw the aperture blinking.

"You want to take a picture of me? You want to take a picture of me?"

He started ripping his pajamas apart, the buttons flying like ricocheted bullets. He ripped off his undershirt, then his underwear, and stood naked, the sweat glistening on his skin. He tottered toward the camera, with his hands extended toward it.

"You want to see me? You want to see the real me?"

He banged his chest with his fists, as if trying to break it open.

"Here! Here!" he screamed, until he lost his voice.

And here we are: he is down on his knees, bleeding; he is surrounded by the debris. Dizzy with the violent adrenaline, he closes his eyes, and waits for Rachel to stop taking pictures and touch his cheek, redeeming him. A hand touches his face, tenderly, delicately, sliding its tips across the hollow of his cheek. He gasps and slowly, one sob at a time, he starts to cry.

But he doesn't know that the hand stroking his cheek is mine. He cannot hear me saying to him: "*Ne plači. Sve će biti u redu.*" Calm down, I'm telling him, everything will fall into place. Let us just sort through this destruction. Let us just remember how we got here. Let us just remember.

7

Nowhere Man

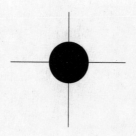

KIEV, SEPTEMBER 1900–

SHANGHAI, AUGUST 2000

On the horizon you could see black, bloated, heinous clouds leading a storm charge. And the sea kept licking the rusty ship—the *Pamyat*—loaded with destitute men, officers and soldiers alike, left with nothing but their honor, still wearing impeccable uniforms, exuding a faint scent of the Trans-Siberian railway. The officers' wives, the finest ladies all, choked with swallowed tears, waving at their loyal servants on the shore, lined up like a choir in a great tragedy, hating the Bolsheviks even more than their mistresses. There was a young captain going around, politely imploring the ladies to get rid of excess baggage, and they obeyed—what difference did it make now? You could see millions of rubles in fur, bobbing in filthy water, like rat corpses. Amid the sinking fur and suitcases, there was a little lap dog barking shrilly, paddling feebly with its tiny paws, slowly losing its strength, until it drowned. Our hearts sank with it.

And the *Pamyat* sailed off, and no one on it could take their eyes off the beautiful shoreline, the lush forests and the curved mountains under the clouds: our Russian land, our mother's breasts. We all wept, women and men, waves slamming the ship, as if they were waves of tears. And I stood at the prow, the Pacific wind ripping the skin off my face [he touches his scar], Vladivostok devoured by the mist behind me. You must believe me, I was deliberating whether to shoot myself, to empty my head and my heart, the devil take it all, for what is life, little sister, what is life without Russia. But then I heard my men singing with deep sonorous voices, coming straight from their Russian hearts, singing as no men had sung before: "Do not close your eyes, Mother Russia, for it is not time to sleep." And it gave me strength. I did not kill myself, and here I am in Shanghai now, alive and swimming, although there are days, and this is one of them, when I regret that I did not blow my brains out, on the *Pamyat*, with my final gaze locked on Russia.

This is the story that Evgenij Pick—*Captain* Pick—told to Russian ex-princesses and ex-baronesses and ex-nobodies earning their paltry living in Shanghai as prostitutes and taxi dancers, even dressmakers. They would listen to him, swooning, warm tears in their Russian eyes, stroking their new, local lap dog until they hurt it with their hands shriveled from the work they had never done before, the dog slipping off their lap. They would not even notice Captain Pick's nimble hand crawling up their thighs, then deeper, much deeper, and he never paid them for anything.

To drunken Russian ex-officers, surviving in Shanghai as bodyguards and extortionists (or not surviving at all), prone to scorching their nostalgia with poisonously cheap vodka, he would tell about the saber given to him by his father, a Cossack colonel, on his deathbed. His father made him swear on the saber that he would defend Mother Russia's honor until his last breath. It was with that very saber (resting now in a pawnshop, he said, waiting for better days) that he decapitated a Jewish Bolshevik, in Smolensk, in 1919. Sometimes he would use a watermelon to demonstrate how the head flew in a perfect arc ("rainbow-like") and fell on the ground with a thud that im-

plied hollowness. His audience would always enjoy the joke, ordering more vodka for Captain Pick. He would cut open the watermelon with his rosewood-handle knife, and they would gorge
on the crimson insides, using their fingers, kissing each other after every downed glass of vodka. And he would keep them en-
raptured, dizzy with common memories and alcohol, telling
them how the Germans caught him in 1914, and how he escaped—he just walked out of the prison, ordering the guards in
a thunderous voice to open the gate and they had to open it,
saluting him, because even in large numbers and heavily armed
they were afraid of a real Russian. The Germans caught him ten
more times, and he escaped ten more times—he would slam his
hand against his chest and holler: "They thought I was the devil
himself!" and the crowd would proudly guffaw, delighted that
the devil is Russian, one of our own. Pick would then start
singing, "Do not close your eyes, Mother Russia, for it is not time
to sleep," and they would weep, as they wept leaving Vladivostok. Not infrequently, a mob of wobbling Russian patriots would
carry Pick on their shoulders to their favorite brothel or an
opium den, where they would pool money to treat him with a
cure, admittedly temporary, for his wounded Russian heart.

At the beginning, a few of them would have trouble remembering his being on the *Pamyat*. Nor could the officers from the
units he claimed to have served in remember him serving with
them. Some of them even recalled a man with the same face, albeit scarless, working for the Soviets in Harbin and Shanghai under a different name. But after a while his stories, told in minute,
plausible detail, absorbed along with a China Sea of vodka, displaced their memories, and they started generating their own, new
memories featuring trench brotherhood with Captain Pick, his
doughty feats, and legendary drinking binges, from which some of

them never recovered. Eventually, Pick—*Captain* Pick—became the dearest brother of every true Russian in Shanghai.

The likely story, we have to say, is somewhat different. Evgenij Pick is born as Evgenij Mihailovich Kojevnikoff, in Kiev, in September 1900, son of a Cossack army colonel and a raped Jewish mother, who dies giving him birth. His father takes some care of him, paying an unmarried, crazy aunt to bring him up, until Papa gambles away all his money and kills himself, leaving Pick nothing but embarrassing debts and the unpaid aunt's fury, conveyed through a beating with a broom handle. There is no record of the saber whatsoever. Apart from the broom-induced anguish following his father's demise, little is remembered about Pick's childhood, boyhood, or youth. After a few blank years, we find him serving in the Russian army in 1917, until he is captured by the Germans, but only once. We do not know when and indeed if he did escape, but in the fall of 1917, he is in Sankt Petersburg, caught up in the Revolution. It seems that the revolutionary fervor, not to mention numerous opportunities for pilfering and plundering, excited him enough to become a revolutionary. His duty becomes the duty of a political commissar, his job is to deliver speeches on a rich selection of injustices, and when he raises his arm and points in the general direction of bloodthirsty capitalist bloodsuckers, his audiences are always eager to go there, however distant and dangerous *there* may be.

His good revolutionary work allows him to study in Moscow, from 1919 to 1922, at the Military Academy and, simultaneously, at the Academy for Music and Drama. After graduation he is said to have worked as an assistant military attaché in the Soviet embassies in Afghanistan and Turkey—jobs whose uneventfulness would be unbearable, were it not for the abundant availability of first-class opium.

In 1925, he arrives in Shanghai, via the Trans-Siberian railway, Vladivostok, and Harbin. His official duty is as an assistant to the Soviet military mission there—that is, a spy—working undercover as a businessman, selling advertising space in Russian papers. He really serves the Comintern, building networks, acquiring acquaintances who can provide fruitful information, some of which he fails to share with his comrades, but rather hoards it for the day he might need it.

And the day arrives in 1927, when, according to Wasserstein, he turns coat and furnishes the British intelligence in Shanghai with a carefully assembled collection of pertinent information, embellished with fantastic sub-narratives of ubiquitous Comintern conspiracies in China and—why stop there?—the world at large. All of it is delivered in a reasonable, measured, yet mesmerizing tone—all the accents are in the right places, and the ephemera (useless characters, pointless details, frequent digressions regarding his own unremarkable, woeful self) is effectively scattered throughout Pick's narrative, providing the inevitable randomness of common existence, the sloppiness necessary for the illusion of a real, uncontrollable life. His briefers, all from good families and universally educated at elite British universities—evidently intellectually superior to an effusive Russian vagrant—cannot have enough of his stories. They promptly and passionately send Pick's confession to the Foreign Office, followed by a note from the British ambassador, Sir William Senson, saying that "while [the accuracy of Pick's information] cannot be guaranteed, it has the ring of truth."

The ring of truth is a golden one, it seems, for with the generous British reward and the profits from small but lucrative deals with his acquaintances Captain Pick is able to open his own theater in Shanghai. The theater has the ambitious name of the Far Eastern Grand Opera, and he is the impresario, stage manager, opera singer, ballet dancer, and its star actor. Let it be noted that his stage name, ever present on the glamorous marquee of his theater, is Eugene Hovans.

It is on the Grand Opera stage that Pick/Hovans performs his greatest role—the role of Chichikoff in Gogol's *Dead Souls*. In Hovans's rendition, Chichikoff becomes a Moses, leading the spiritless, soul-dead people of Russia to the promised land. The culmination of the performance was Chichikoff's troika speech, inevitably resulting in women pulling their nicely combed and coiled hair off their heads in tufts, and men pulling out their guns and threatening to shoot themselves, right there, the devil take it all, enough of this misery. "Ah, you horses, horses—what horses!" vociferated Hovans, thumping his chest with his fist, as if intent on breaking it open and taking his heart out to exhibit its purity to the audience. "Your manes are whirlwinds! And are your veins not tingling like a quick ear? Descending from above you have caught the note of the familiar song; and at once, in unison, you strain your chests of bronze [chest thumping] and, with your hooves barely skimming the earth, you are transformed into arrows, into straight lines winging through the air, and on you rush under divine inspiration ... Russia, where are you flying? Answer me! [sobs, hair-pulling, revolvers cocked, etc.] There is no answer."

Apart from being a Chichikoff, Hovans is a swan—as a matter of fact, the swan in *Swan Lake;* he is a man driven to suicidal madness in a single night, by a tenacious mouse pitter-pattering across the floor of the man's mind; he is Raskolnikov, whose murder of the old lady is not justified philosophically, but by the fact that she is Jewish—an interpretation that goes over much better with his audience; and, finally, he is the Russian Hamlet. The

Hamlet performances are crowned—as Fortinbras looms over Hamlet's body—with the audience (whose wounds from the slings and arrows of outrageous fortune have not healed, and never will) sonorously singing: "Do not close your eyes, Mother Russia, for it is not time to sleep."

But when he isn't bringing his audiences to an orgasm of nostalgia, Captain Pick supplements his fame with the lucre reaped in the rich, filthy fields of Shanghai's lawlessness. He blackmails an American judge who, he has discovered, is a homosexual. One day, the judge's body washes off the shores of the Whangpoo, with his rectum cut out. In 1929, Captain Pick is sentenced to nine months in jail for having sold, under the name of Joseph Pronek, bonds of nonexistent foreign countries to a few seducible French mademoiselles and greedy English ladies. Then, Wasserstein says, he hawks worthless pamphlets and books stolen for him by the coolies from the Soviet consulate, wrapped nicely in the preposterous embroidery of Pick's tales of their conspiratorial significance. He writes a column for a Shanghai-published Russian paper, in which he exposes the weaknesses in the pillars of the community, unless the pillars provide a recompense that would make him look at the frailties of other pillars instead. In 1931, under the name of Dr. Montaigne, he represents himself as a military adviser to the Chinese government and takes millions of dollars for arms that do not exist, which is what will ultimately prevent him from supplying them. His clients spend months imagining their future power, waiting for the arms to arrive and retelling Pick's stories, until he is arrested and sentenced to a year in prison. In prison, he acquires a few Chinese friends, some of them loyal members of the Green Gang, hiding from the law in their comfortable prison cells (the Gang kindly providing everything from opium and girls to heroin and boys) until the memory of their crimes is erased by the newer crimes of their colleagues and acquaintances. Once out of jail, Pick shacks up with a Georgian woman who owns a brothel just behind the Astor House Hotel, and starts a modest white-slavery ring of his own. Both his fallen Russian lady friends and his Green Gang comrades come in handy in his new venture—which a sanctimonious Russian paper in Harbin unwisely makes public.

But no one cares about those self-righteous accusations (although a little nick is left on Pick's heart)—Shanghai is a far different place from the priggish Harbin, people do what they have to and what they can to make a decent living. Furthermore, Captain Pick is a well-liked man, "the soul of every party he attends"—and he, God help him, attends many. He is the heart of the Russian community, always able to express the deep, true feelings of the Russian people. An acquaintance describes him as "a highly emotional individual," someone who is "very trusting." But, on the other hand, the acquaintance asserts, "he could be very suspicious . . . He met many people, but quickly tired of them. Therefore, he had many enemies and no intimate friends . . . He used to say: 'Drama and music are my best friends and the stage my entire life.' " Another acquaintance describes him as having "a Mongolian cast of countenance . . . no hair at all, wears a black skull cap, has burn scars on his head . . . a heavy vodka drinker . . . usually goes around with a rosewood-handle knife . . . a friendly, decent fellow."

The scars on his head are not the result of burning oil, as he claims, poured on him during a Bolshevik torture session, let alone the result of a Pacific wind strong enough to rip the skin off his face. Rather, it is a result of his opium stupor, in which he rolled off his opium-den divan and into a hearth.

Even a typically earnest American intelligence report has a hard time resisting Captain Pick's charms, describing him as "well-educated, a good linguist, accomplished actor, fascinating story teller, but a facile writer. He is also a smuggler of arms, pimp, intelligence agent, and a competent murderer."

Ever sensitive to the changing winds of history, Captain Pick has groomed his Japanese contacts with particular care from the beginning of his life in Shanghai, but in 1937, after the Japanese invasion of China, he begins working for the Japanese Naval intelligence Bureau in Shanghai. He assembles a ring of some forty European agents (not counting the gaggle of drugged-up Russian ladies), who are supposed to spy on other Europeans in Shanghai, believing themselves to be protected from the Japanese might in the International Settlement and the French Concession. His ring is the elite of Shanghai's underworld: Baron N. N. Tipolt, a blackmailer, swindler, and informer for the Gestapo; Count Victor Plavchuk, handy with the blade, who would often entertain brothel staff by throwing knives at a terrified novice prostitute, occasionally pinning down her ears, just for a laugh; Admiral Marcus Templar, purportedly a member of the Greek Royal House, whose specialty is taking surreptitious photographs, used for blackmailing; Bernie and Ernie McDunn, Siamese Chicago twins, conjoined at the hip, who would do anything for a dose of heroin; Alex Hemmon, a former member of the Purple Gang in Detroit, a hit man who has to kill somebody every time he gets drunk (which he does habitually), and who moonlights as a professional trombonist in an orchestra regularly performing at the Far Eastern Grand Opera.

In the late thirties, under Japanese protection, Captain Pick's is a cozy living. He's providing plausible information to his employees, running his criminal (which in Shanghai is a term of endearment) enterprises and lovingly managing his Far Eastern Grand Opera. In 1940, Pick goes to Japan for a holiday, where he meets Commander Otani Inaho, the Japanese officer who will later head Naval Intelligence in Shanghai and become Pick's chief Japanese patron. Commander Otani and Captain Pick become the closest friends, often publicly pronouncing their utmost respect and admiration for each other's honor and manhood. Indeed, malicious rumor has it that besides sharing a deeply seated belief in the value of discipline and patriotism, they occasionally shared a messy bed. In 1941, a week or so after the Pearl Harbor attack, the Japanese troops march leisurely into the International Settlement, encountering no resistance, and practically besiege the French Concession, run by a herd of confused, dim-witted Vichy loyalists. Pick becomes Commander Otani's left hand and, thanks to his kind assiduousness, moves into room 741 at the luxurious Cathay Hotel.

The years spent in room 741 at the Cathay Hotel, dozing in the lap of the great power, are the best years of Pick's life: comfortable, pleasant, not requiring a lot of work. A postwar American intelligence report, quoted by Wasserstein (prepared by one Captain Owen), describes Pick's typical day: he gets up before dawn, watches the sun rise through the humid haze over the Whangpoo River, where robust Japanese ships are anchored in the harbor, junks sheepishly squeezing between them; he listens to the radio news from Moscow, London, Honolulu (enjoying the Glen Miller Band, humming along with Glen's trombone); from six to seven A.M. he is on the phone, receiving and dispatching Shanghai intelligence, conveyed often as plain, candid gossip. He reads Russian newspapers and eats breakfast (two eggs, a mountain of bacon, a river of coffee), sometimes spurting a fleet of yolky spit all over the papers, infuriated by their dishonorable lies. Then he goes to the office at the Naval Intelligence, where he organizes files or masturbates in anticipation of lunch with his newest young-lady acquisition. Unless, that is, he goes to the Japanese Thought Police Headquarters to supervise the interrogation of a foreigner, occasionally adding a Russian touch: whipping the prisoner with a knotted whip, until chunks of flesh fall off. At one o'clock he eats lunch with a young lady whom he plans to bed after it. After dessert, he takes her to room 741, makes passionate love to her, and then has a comprehensive nap. The hotel staff risks being shot if they enter the room during his nap, which ends at exactly three o'clock. Between three and four he telephones his Japanese superiors, demanding benevolence toward one of his acquaintances and, sometimes, an iron-fist treatment of the Shanghai Jews. He then sets off for meetings regarding his theatrical, musical, or charity interests. Every Sunday he performs an important role in a play or a concert, aiming to uplift the Russian spirit in these daunting times, always ending the event with "Do Not Close Your Eyes, Mother Russia." After the show he dines with friends and admirers, regaling them with tales of his peregrinations, loves, and suffering, never failing to bring his audience to cramps of laughter or a deluge of tears, sometimes both within moments. After that he goes for a lazy pipe or two of opium in a brothel, where he may or may not join in an elaborate orgy, frequently featuring midgets, animals, and children.

In the spring of 1944, Pick is awakened from his nap by the stirring of a mouse and emerges from his nightmare with a claustrophobic uneasiness and a tingling in his heart, which he recognizes as foreshadowing evil times. He screams at the cowering Cathay Hotel staff, storms down Nanking Road in his black pajamas, like a devil apparition, and charges into Commander Otani's office, requesting, before even sitting down, to be sent off to another place, far from this stinking pit of hell. Commander Otani puts his hand on Pick's shoulder, then strokes his cheek, until Pick calms down.

In the summer of 1944, Captain Pick goes to the Philippines. He arrives under the name of Koji, followed by his usual entourage, reinforced by the playboy boxer Mihalka; a Portuguese black marketeer Francisco Carneiro (Mihalka's manager); and an Italian lawyer and chemist, Dr. Vincente, capable of concocting all kinds of joys. Pick's orchestra does little, almost nothing, in Manila. They help catch and kill a Danish gunrunner. They set a trap for Father Kirkpatrick, an Irish priest, suspected of smuggling food and medicine to American internees—one source claims that it is Pick himself who oversees Father Kirkpatrick's crucifixion. They intercept U.S. naval intelligence talking about imminent attacks all around the Pacific. The information is rejected by the Japanese as "dangerous thoughts," whereupon Pick's men use the equipment solely to record the American hit parade. American music is played at their parties, which instantly become all the rage among the idle Manila elite and prostitutes bored with the never-changing clientele.

But other than those few little jobs and parties, Captain Pick and his crew spend time racketeering, setting up a little, classy, and expensive prostitution ring, and hanging out in nightclubs. Pick's favorite haunt is the Gastronome, because the jukebox there has a record of him singing "Tea for Two" in English, though in the manner of a poignant Russian ballad, a rendition made all the more convincing by his atrocious Russian accent. The B-side of the record contains "Do Not Close Your Eyes, Mother Russia," sung, as it well should be, heartbreakingly.

At the end of the summer, Pick gets uneasy again and returns to Shanghai, complaining of ill health, and taking the entire budget of the Manila operation with him. It was on the ship to Shanghai, with the Pacific winds in his face, that the uneasiness crystallizes into a sense of something coming to an end, into a painful, tormenting anticipation of a future loss.

Indeed, everybody can smell the end, and it has the smell of burning flesh—Tokyo has been leveled, Hiroshima annihilated. On August 9, between the bombs, Evgenij Pick has his last supper with Commander Otani at his home, room 741 at the Cathay. They eat a magnificently prepared yellow croaker, washed down by superbly aged sake, saved by Otani for a special occasion. Having kissed Otani on both cheeks, Pick goes to join the farewell orgy at the Yar restaurant, arranged by a posse of girls known as Mihalka's Harem (Mihalka is still stuck in Manila). Pick complains to the girls, who could not care less in their opiatic daze, that he has reason to believe that the Japanese plan to kill him. Thus no one, apart from Otani, notices when he disappears from Shanghai the next day.

In the fall of 1945, Wasserstein notes, the American authorities in China fruitlessly search for Pick. He is seen in a barbershop in Shanghai; he is seen on a train to Beijing, telling the interested co-passengers how he cut off the head of a Japanese officer trying to rape a Chinese girl, and then had to spend a year behind the double wall of a magician's trunk; he is seen praying in a Russian Orthodox Church in Beijing; he is seen performing a Hamlet monologue, delivering "To be or not to be . . ." with a strange, untraceable accent, in front of an audience of American missionaries, who do not recognize the song he sings at the end.

Pick, in fact, takes a boat to Japan, which then hits a mine. Everyone on the boat dies, except Pick, who is miraculously found floating unconscious but alive, surrounded by a school of corpses and body parts. Pick goes to Tokyo, straight to the navy ministry, on crutches—his leg mauled—and finds Commander Otani, who transfers one million yen to Pick under the name of Koji, beseeching him to open a Russian theater in Tokyo and not to neglect his considerable thespian talents. Pick waits for the right moment to start the theater (for which he already has the name: the New World Theatre), but spends all his money waiting. And with the astute instinct of a veteran survivor he can sense that the American hounds are on his scent.

Hence in February 1946, he walks, limping dramatically, into an American intelligence headquarters and offers to tell them the truth. He consequently delivers to his involved listeners (a Captain Aaron and a Major Maxwell) a cycle of interlocking stories, from the beginning of his life to this day: he tells them about escaping the Germans; about giving information to the British; about subverting Japanese intelligence operations in Shanghai; about his mother, who was an American, and who could be living in America today with her new husband. He tells them that he was the one who tipped off the Japanese about the Sorge spy ring, having remembered him as the Comintern colleague. He slaps his crippled leg, exhibiting it as a result of Japanese torture, and rolls a couple of nacreous tears down his sunken cheeks. He tells the Americans that his motive for going to Japan was to share with them all he knew, and to see the Japanese beasts suffering in defeat. He tells them everything he knows about every Japanese officer he ever met. He tells them everything he knows about Otani, the disgusting, opium-addicted sodomite, and about Otani's liking for torturing prisoners.

The American intelligence officers are very happy with the quality of information coming from Pick. Everything makes a lot of sense, unverifiable though it may be, and they forgive and release Pick, in return for future cooperation. He goes back to

Shanghai and attempts to restore his network to serve the Americans, but to no avail—Shanghai is not the same, and it never will be. Captain Pick swallows his loss with glass after glass of vodka; he eschews looking into the dark future by looking only as far as the next opium dose. Before the People's Liberation Army enters Shanghai in 1949, he flees it. In the spring of 1950, he is in possession of an entry visa to Siam. In the summer of 1950, he is in a prison in Taiwan, where he entertains his fellow prisoners with stories told in broken Shanghai dialect about the wild thirties, singing the songs popular once upon a time, all in return for sexual favors and cigarettes. Then he disappears.

There are few photos of Pick. One of them is a police photo: a balding man, crowned by the remnants of his gray hair; a square, violent jaw; a triangular nose; a pointed Adam's apple; glaring, manic eyes. Another one is a publicity photograph from the Far Eastern Grand Opera days: he wears a top hat and a black cape, like a magician; there is an elegant white scarf casually thrown over his shoulder; in his gloved left hand he holds the other glove; in his right hand he holds a cigarette, with the ashes about to fall off. His face is heavily made up: thick, penciled eyebrows; glittering pomade; rouged lips. He glances at you sideways, as if about to turn to you full face and begin mesmerizing you. And you have to turn your gaze away, but you simply cannot.

In the summer of 2000, my wife and I went to Shanghai for our honeymoon, because that was where her grandparents met (her parents unromantically met in a Chicago bar called Jimmy's). We'd saved enough money from our teaching and took a leave from Ort Institute. We'd promised all our students we would send them postcards and we'd let Marcus teach us a few phrases in the Shanghai dialect. We were in love and spent the flight holding hands and reading—she read *The Idiot*, and I read Wasserstein's *Secret War in Shanghai*, occasionally kissing her lean neck. We stayed at the Peace Hotel, which used to be the Cathay, and we liked it—they changed our towels regularly, the staff who could speak English always asked us how we were, and we would tell them, for they seemed to care. Pretty soon, we started referring to our hotel room, room 741, as our home. We loved Shanghai, went walking everywhere, despite the incredible heat, wiping sweat off each other's bodies upon returning to our room, and then making love. We bought cheap silk, authentic souvenirs, and Mao posters we knew our lefty, ironical friends would like. We walked the Bund and went to museums. We roamed the Old Chinese Town, fueled by the belief that we were getting the real China for very few dollars. In Sun Yat-sen's former residence in the former French Concession, we looked at a saber on the wall, the map of China, and a silk painting of a cat (the guide said: "Please, look at the cat's eyes—they follow you everywhere in the room"). We ate at restaurants in old Western buildings, including a French restaurant in an old Russian Orthodox church, the dome pressing down on us with all the might of an unfriendly Slavic God. We went to Suzhou for a day to look at the magnificent gardens. We rented jalopy bikes, and rode from garden to garden, taking a break only to succumb to a craving for Kentucky Fried Chicken.

And it was in Suzhou, in the Humble Administrator's garden—reading Wasserstein in the shade of one of the pavilions, carps splashing the placid surface, lotus leaves spreading as far as the eye could see, gentle trees leaning over water, as if over a looking-glass—it was there that I found out that we had been staying in and were going back to Pick's room, room 741 at the former Cathay Hotel. Need I say I was overwhelmed, with delight and unraveling fear at the same time? The coincidence—or better, the convergence—implied, glaringly, the existence of an omniscient, omnipotent, but not necessarily benevolent being. When I told my wife about my discovery, she hugged me gently, as if it were all my fault and she were forgiving me. I remembered the first time she hugged me, after I had stumbled down the stairs. "Are you good?" she had asked me, in Russian, for some reason.

And she told me something I had not known. She told me that her grandfather, a Jewish Shanghailander, had been detained after the Japanese took over the International Settlement, and she told me that it may have been Pick who tortured him. My wife's grandfather never talked much about it, but they all knew what it had been like: he had tied him tightly in wet sheets, until his blood vessels were bursting into blotchy bruises (I saw them once, on his chest, shaped like unknown continents, when we went to visit him in Florida). Then the sheets slowly dried, almost squeezing him to death, until the body was so senseless that the only thing left was the part of your mind that could feel the pain. We immediately left the Humble Administrator's tranquillity behind us, and boarded the train to Shanghai, where a devastating fever was awaiting us—we kept wiping the sweat off our bodies, but the perspiration would not stop.

That night someone tried to break into our room—I leapt out of my feverish dream, and charged to the door, yelling, "Who is it? Who is it?" but there was no response. As my heart was slamming against my chest walls, my wife's screams fading, as our nightmares were merging, I imagined Pick's painted face on the other side of the door. When I looked outside through the fisheye peephole, there was, of course, no one outside, just the vacuously buzzing hall. I did not share my vision with my wife, but she must have known what I was thinking. In her eyes, I could see the somnolent terror twinkling as the ludicrous reflection of the exit sign.

But we, of course, knew that it must have been a drunken hotel guest trying to open our door, the wrong door, for that happens in every hotel, anywhere in the world.

The night of August 9—the anniversary of Pick's last supper—I was woken up by my wife squeezing my hand (we held hands sleeping). I heard a body falling on the floor with a feeble thump, and then moving through the room: noises ebbing and flowing rhythmically, purposefully. We listened and received sounds coming from different corners, sometimes simultaneously. We sensed every whiff of air, vibrations of the space around us, frozen with fear, interrupting our breathing to hear better. We could not say anything, but we expected Pick to appear before us, in his magician's cape, and begin to sing in his bass voice, replete with blood-curdling nostalgia: "Do not close your eyes, Mother Russia, for it is not time to sleep." We heard Pick's song in the rustle and bustle of the creature in the darkness, in the pitter-patter of little paws, in the pallid, oval field of the weak firelight, in the center of which there was a mouse, stopped to look at us, waiting for us to make an uncertain move before vanishing. I lay in the darkness, awake, paralyzed, biting the knuckle of my index finger, waiting for the evil to hatch out of the furry lump pulsating with life, and come right at me, and it did. It is right inside me now, clawing at the walls of my chest, trying to get out, and I can do nothing to stop it. So I get up.

THE QUESTION OF BRUNO

Stories

In this stylistically adventurous, brilliantly funny tour de force, Aleksandar Hemon writes of love and war, Sarajevo and America, with a skill and imagination that are breathtaking.

A love affair is experienced in the blink of an eye as the Archduke Ferdinand watches his wife succumb to an assassin's bullet. An exiled writer, working in a sandwich shop in Chicago, adjusts to the absurdities of his life. Love letters from war-torn Sarajevo navigate the art of getting from point A to point B without being shot. With a sure-footed sense of detail and life-saving humor, Aleksandar Hemon examines the overwhelming events of history and the effects they have on individual lives. These heartrending stories bear the unmistakable mark of an important new international author.

"An extraordinary writer: one who seems not simply gifted but necessary." —*The New York Times Book Review*

Fiction/Short Stories/0-375-72700-0